T0380689

the
Judith
Files

Judge Bill Swann

BALBOA.PRESS
A DIVISION OF HAY HOUSE

Copyright © 2021 Judge Bill Swann.

All rights reserved. No part of this book may be used or reproduced by any means, graphic, electronic, or mechanical, including photocopying, recording, taping or by any information storage retrieval system without the written permission of the author except in the case of brief quotations embodied in critical articles and reviews.

This is a work of fiction. All of the characters, names, incidents, organizations, and dialogue in this novel are either the products of the author's imagination or are used fictitiously.

Balboa Press books may be ordered through booksellers or by contacting:

Balboa Press
A Division of Hay House
1663 Liberty Drive
Bloomington, IN 47403
www.balboapress.com
844-682-1282

Because of the dynamic nature of the Internet, any web addresses or links contained in this book may have changed since publication and may no longer be valid. The views expressed in this work are solely those of the author and do not necessarily reflect the views of the publisher, and the publisher hereby disclaims any responsibility for them.

The author of this book does not dispense medical advice or prescribe the use of any technique as a form of treatment for physical, emotional, or medical problems without the advice of a physician, either directly or indirectly. The intent of the author is only to offer information of a general nature to help you in your quest for emotional and spiritual well-being. In the event you use any of the information in this book for yourself, which is your constitutional right, the author and the publisher assume no responsibility for your actions.

Any people depicted in stock imagery provided by Getty Images are models, and such images are being used for illustrative purposes only. Certain stock imagery © Getty Images.

Print information available on the last page.

ISBN: 978-1-9822-7794-9 (sc)
ISBN: 978-1-9822-7796-3 (hc)
ISBN: 978-1-9822-7795-6 (e)

Library of Congress Control Number: 2021924852

Balboa Press rev. date: 12/23/2021

CONTENTS

NAMES OF CHARACTERS

Circuit Court Judge Judith Merchant
Judith's grandmother and grandfather Merchant
Presiding Circuit Judge "Magic Beans" Norton
    Bill, his superannuated bailiff, whom Norton offers to Judith
Tommy, Judith's competent bailiff ("careful and alert")
Metro Medical Examiner Jane Crenshaw
Annette Bundry, attorney, raped in parking garage of courthouse
Jake Pridden, builder of Judith's new house
William and Dora Hensley, on Judith's domestic violence docket
Dr. Orloff, court's own witness
Law Clerk Toby Malone, Judith's half-time law clerk

Connor Graham
    Dana Graham, Connor's first wife, deceased
John R. Morris Jr., MD, responsible for death of Dana
Martin Graham, Connor's son, at Montana State University
Davey Barton (Davey Barton's Flying Service in Kenora)
Nan Hodgkins, co-owner of art gallery with Connor
John Harcourt, Connor's fishing buddy

Harry Mather
Susan Mather, an artist, Harry's ex-wife
Megan Mather, their daughter
Rabbi Shulman, Harry's rabbi

Professor Richard T. Smith of CTSU (Central Tennessee State University)
Gloria Jean Smith, his wife
    Patty Palermo, Gloria's lawyer
    Jess Carey, attorney, Palermo's associate
"The Jellyfish," Richard's first lawyer, fired by Richard
William Terance Bailey, Richard's excellent second lawyer
"David Branstone," false name Richard uses at Mektu Lake Lodge
Ray Martinson, unethical attorney, chosen by Richard for
    Branstetter's defense
Thomas Benjamin Levitt, ethical attorney, not hired by Richard
Kozloski, Chicago passport counterfeiter, used by Richard

David T. Branstetter, of Omega Computing
    His ex-wife, Jeanie
        Joey, their son
        Treece, homosexual predator upon Joey
        Rebecca, employed at arcade where Treece works

Metro Police Chief Larry Bolden

Detective Jay Blake, and his partner, Detective John Carden

WEBSITES

cnr12345@hotmail.com, Connor's email

hmatherpi@yahoo.com, Harry Mather's website

www.branstettersays.com, Branstetter's beginning website.

dbranstetter@aol.com, Branstetter's daily website

everyman666@hotmail.com, religious zealot

cgillespie@esper.com, Charlie Gillespie, Hitler enthusiast.

iowadad@hotmail.com, computer wizard, helps Richard

mountkatahdin12345@hotmail.com, Judith's second website after problems severe

rtsmith@ctsu.edu, Richard's professorial on-line address on campus

rsmith@aol.com, Richard's home on-line address on College Street. Both of these lines are given out, published, by Richard.

freeoxen@earthlink.com, Richard's hidden email, which he uses with iowadad, above

CHAPTER ONE

The first bullet from the .222 broke Judith's front window. Glass flew against the drapes and fell to the pine floor, breaking like skim ice. The next shots came together, through the bathroom window, breaking the mirror and the only light Judith had left on. Shots continued in two-second intervals, ripping up the ceiling of her bedroom.

Judith rolled out of bed, taking her iphone with her. More glass fell. She lit up the keypad and dialed 911. Vorsten answered on the second ring, "You have reached the Davidson County Emergency . . ."

"Vorsten! I know! I know!" Wait, she thought, and started over, calmer, "This is Judge Merchant. I'm sorry to yell. Someone is shooting into my house."

"Right now?"

"Right now."

"I'll have a car there in three minutes, Judge. Two cars if I can." She could hear him sending out the call, "Ten sixty-four. 10412 Brayman Pike. Let's get there, people." He came back. "Judge, stay on the line."

"I can't, Vorsten. Don't worry. I'm going to call a friend. Personal back-up."

"Get back to me."

"I will."

Judith punched in Connor's number, listened to the ring cycle. Three, four, five. He had to hear it! Come on, Connor, answer! His answering machine came on, "This is Connor Graham, please leave a message."

"Connor, if you're there, talk to me now! It's Judith!" Then she remembered. Connor and Harry were fishing in Canada.

The shots had stopped. She couldn't hear anybody outside. She rolled left beneath the bed rail and pulled the nightstand to her. She could just reach the drawer. She pulled it out, got her .357 revolver, a Smith & Wesson. The gun Harry had given her, a gun like his. "Just in case," he had said, when Norton had assigned her the domestic relations docket.

Why are guns always cold? she wondered, pulling it under the bed with her, rolling onto her back, getting the Velcro loose. She flipped out the chamber and saw six cartridges in the phone's light.

Still no more shots. She heard a cruiser's siren as the car came over the top of Brayman Hill and accelerated hard down toward her drive. Then she could hear it bouncing up the two hundred feet of gravel to her farmhouse. Red and blue lights against the bedroom wall. A radio. Pounding on the door.

CHAPTER
TWO

Professor Richard T. Smith was a linguist, a philologist. He was, as he said, a tenured card-carrying intellectual.

Richard was dreaming again. Once more Gloria, the goat woman, was climbing his trunk. Sometimes the trunk was his phallus, sometimes not. Tonight he was an entire tree with a trunk. The goat woman was climbing to Richard's nest up in the top of the tree. Cloven hooves spiked into Richard's bark. He cried out. Gloria's white flanks quivered as she climbed, feet missing purchase, scraping off bark, making his cambium layer gleam. Wisps of goaty hair caught on twigs, hair he knew he would later build into his nest walls. She climbed until she was there in the nest, his nest, squatting, extruding her labia, her moist pink bulging ovipositor, laying the goaty eggs of sickness into his mind.

CHAPTER
THREE

"I'm going up to the little island," Connor said, "see if I'm lucky. I had some muskie rolls there last night. When you wouldn't go out with me."

"Muskie rolls," said Harry. "I'd rather have egg rolls."

Last night the sky had been luminescent long after the sun had set into Manitoba. Maybe even, Connor thought, even into Saskatchewan, the sunset had gone on so long. The light had gotten paler, nacreous, while a muskie did lazy follow-ups, looking at his plug, rolling beneath it, curious.

"I know you'd rather have egg rolls. Or spring rolls. Or cloverleaf rolls. Or Tootsie Rolls," said Connor. Harry was not sensitive about his weight. He had told Connor he figured everyone had a natural shape, and his shape was pear.

"I had to chop wood," Harry said. "I couldn't go fishing last night."

"Harry, we have two cords of wood. In a hard winter a family of four might burn four cords a winter."

"You're making that up."

"I am not. Judith told me," Connor said. "She comes from Maine. She said the Murphys burned eight cords one winter."

5

"There you are," said Harry. "Eight cords. And we'll need some for next winter, too."

"No. The Murphys weren't burning it. They were selling it, selling the town's social-assistance wood. Stuff they got for free."

"Really?"

"Judith said the town's selectmen raised hell, told the Murphys they wouldn't get any wood next winter. Old man Murphy claimed the trailer was airy, and took a lot of wood. But everybody knew."

"Well, I don't care," Harry said. "We need wood. Cutting wood is good for guys like me. I get consistent results. It's not like your hit-and-miss fishing."

This was Harry's fourth trip to Ontario with Connor. Connor had been trying to interest Harry in fishing. Too slow, Harry said. Too boring, he said. No pay off, he said.

But he did like being at the cabin. Harry liked planning food for a place with no re-supply, a place completely cut-off from civilization until the float plane came back for you. No cell phones, not even a satellite phone. Very Thoreau, he said. Clean, simple. Harry was happy to be in Ontario with Connor, look at the eagles, chop wood, clean windows. Tuesday he had fixed the roof on the outhouse. Wednesday he had repaired the old water pump, the one they weren't using. Just in case, he said, you never knew. The new one might go out, then they'd need the Honda again.

"Anyway," Harry said, "I bet Judith made that up about the Murphys. Probably aren't any Murphys. Is that a Down East name? Murphy? I don't think so."

"Judith doesn't lie. You told me so. You said you and she were straightforward, honest, non-devious lawyers."

"Yes, but we always qualify. It's how we earn the fees. And we use phrases like 'including but not limited to,' phrases like that. Magic words. Expensive words." Harry stopped. He looked out over the lake. He was silent for a while. Then he said, "I hate the fucking law."

"Oh, come on. You're still an attorney. You've still got your license."

"Right, but just because you never know. But I do not intend to practice ever again."

A juvenile whiskey-jack landed on the railing to the outhouse, fluffed himself, slipped, and slid down the rail. Harry laughed. "He's having fun. Look at him. I bet he does it again." Harry thought for a minute and then said, "Private investigators like me have fun. I get to carry a gun."

"Right, but you carried a gun when you were a lawyer."

"Yeah, but now I'm really legal. I've got a real carry permit."

"OK, I understand that, but is private investigator money any good?"

"Not yet, but I don't need any more money. Not right now, anyway. Thanks to you. I mean, thanks to Dana." He stopped. He knew he shouldn't have said that.

Dana was Connor's wife. She had died three years earlier. Medical malpractice. Harry and Judith had represented Connor against the doctor and the hospital..

Harry went on, "and thanks to the *Ostrosky* case, and *Smith versus Whalen*, and *Abbott,* and the wreck on the interstate, and the kid Pettengill was diddling. Well, I made a pile. Judith and I made a pile. But I have to say the field of personal injury is terrible, and med mal is too slow."

"You and Judith weren't slow on Dana's case."

"No, but they had to settle. I told you they would, once I got the E.R. notes." Another whiskey-jack slid down the railing. I wonder if they do that on purpose, Connor thought.

Harry said, "Goddamn that bozo, that Dr. Morris. I wish they had the death penalty for docs who screw up like that." They were quiet for several minutes. He looked out over the lake. Then he said, "God, I'm sorry, Connor." Harry had never said that before.

"Thanks. I know you're sorry."

"Do you? She was a great woman. She must have been . . ." Harry was getting upset. He snorted, "Asshole like you, eighteen years. Ah, hell," and walked off to the woodlot, looking down. Connor went to his boat and sat. Soon he heard Harry splitting wood.

Harry and Judith had met while at Vanderbilt law school. Harry told Connor Judith was family. He said they had decided early on they were better friends than lovers.

Harry came from Atlanta, Judith from a little town in Maine. "Hybrid vigor," Harry called it, great study partners. After law school, Judith had clerked one year for the Tennessee Court of Appeals, and then she had gone with a big Nashville firm. Harry had his first job with the state Attorney General.

Connor disconnected the fuel line for the outboard and lifted out the red Duratank. The trolling motor was fine. He had topped up the battery last night after the little island, running the generator while he and Harry played gin.

Eventually Harry and Judith had gone into practice together as law partners. That had lasted for ten years. And then Judith became a judge.

CHAPTER
FOUR

"Cunt," said Professor Richard T. Smith. "Cunt, cunt, cunt. In Middle Low German, 'kunte.' In Old Norse, 'kunta.' He looked across his office to the Oxford English Dictionary, but didn't get up. "A rose by any other name," he thought.

But a very nice cunt, he thought, in the narrow sense—the narrow, tight sense—the only sense she deserved, her only point of excellence. No, her cavity of excellence, he corrected himself, not a point of excellence. Gloria's nethers, the sweet pink rose petals winking, her arms holding the washing machine, skirt hiked up across her back. In and out, the Kenmore connection. Glorious. Gloria. Wet. Now gone.

Gloria was suing him for divorce in the other cunt's court. "She'll understand me because she's a woman, Dickey-boy, you'll see. I'll get alimony. It will be permanent alimony. You're going to pay for what you've done."

This is what I get, Richard thought, for following my tool. E.E. Cummings has a line about that, I think, about following his tool. But I've got the right name, Dickey. Dick needs a home, lots of homes, likes this home, likes this home a lot. See Dick take Jane home. See Dick take Jane all the way home, over and over. All day, twice a day, every day, all night.

And then the milk went sour, sour milk, sauerkraut, cold kraut, wet kraut, hanging in strips, flanking the rose petals.

Richard had been a graduate teaching assistant in an evening course. Gloria had been in the front row the first night. Red hair. Gentle, soft flowing waves. Tight blue jeans. She had smiled at him, had seemed interested. He hadn't seen any goat hair.

By their second date she was on her back and spread wide. Legs up, then drawn back like a crab, knees to armpits, vulva proffered to the sea, the last point of land between curving promontories, waves pounding the littoral, she calling the waves to sluice the shoreline cave.

It had been a defining moment. Richard still saw her red hair fanned out, her eyes tight-closed, intent on the building orgasm. All had been well, no dangers yet. Two months later Gloria's pending divorce in Oregon was final. He didn't ask why that guy in Oregon wanted a divorce. Instead, he thought the man must be a fool to leave this. Richard had cruised the headland twice a day, one Saturday four times up the coast.

He thought about their final journey, standing, she over the washer, breasts flat on the lid, skirt up on her back, his pants at his ankles, he holding the tips of her pelvis. The state university employee sending home the tenured ship of state, again and again one last time, she moaning, loving it with the same devotion that last year as she had loved it the first night.

CHAPTER FIVE

The police had taken four undamaged bullets from the plasterboard in Judith's ceiling. There was still glass on the pine floor and the braided rugs. Judith said to herself, I'll have to take the rugs out and beat them on the clothesline, beat them with a broom, the way Grandmother Merchant did. She made the dust blow across fields of lupine in the summer, fields of snow in winter.

Then Judith thought, I wish I were in Maine and not dealing with this. She looked at the rugs, glass winking up at her. She shouted, "I'm going to beat the hell out of the son-of-a-bitch who shot up my house!" Then she kicked her wastebasket against the wall.

Judith sat down at her desk to cool off. She took Harry's memo from the drawer. She needed to read it again now, because she wanted Connor. I need some comfort, she thought.

She had kept very little paperwork from her law practice with Harry. A couple of files, a few briefs and memos she had written, and this one thing by Harry. Where was *Graham v. Morris, Tri-County Medical, et al.*? There it was, in the back of the drawer.

> *Judith, don't show this memo to anyone. This isn't the Harry Mather I want out there.*

Connor saved my life. I think he did. I don't know. I hate drama, emotional gushing, and all that. You know how I am.

The bad times: let me just say I was in a phase. Serious woe is me stuff. Part of it was the divorce from Susan, thinking how I had screwed up the marriage, how I could have been a better father to Megan, how I should be a better father to her now. Part of it was the ever-present, all-consuming, ongoing, shitty environment of the law.

But having guns around, as I always have, that day I put two and two together. Problem and solution. Problem: unhappiness. Solution: gun. I had never made such a connection before. It came out of the blue: Harry you could do this, you could do this thing. "Quaff, oh quaff this kind nepenthe." Put the gun in your mouth.

So, I'm sitting there in the office, about nine at night, and the phone rings. I let it ring and ring and ring, and it won't quit, so I say, well maybe it's important, so I pick it up, and it's Connor. He says, Harry, I've been thinking about you and about the case, and I want to come over there now. Now? I say. Yes, he says, it's important. Please, he says.

I try to talk him out of it, but he isn't having any, so I say OK. I think, if I'm going to do the deed, I can't leave here owing someone. Someone who needs to see me now, someone who thinks he has an important problem.

It takes him about twenty minutes to get to the office. I put the gun away, get out his file, spread out some papers, turn on the PC. Connor comes in, sees the case spread out, the photos of Dana, and he sits down, looks hard at me, figuring. That way he has. Connor

*looks at the pictures, looks hard at me again, and says,
Harry, there's been too much death. That's all he says.
He gets up, walks to the window, looks out at the night,
the rain, the traffic on Second Avenue, puts his hands
in his pockets, and sits down on the window sill. He
says it again, there's been too much death.*

    *I don't know what to say, I don't know what's
going on. I'm scared, he's scaring me. I say nothing.
Then he starts in, and he just talks, I don't know how
long, just talks, telling me about his life, his theories of
what matters in life. He says, Harry, you and I are in
the improvement business. We help others. You and I
make a difference to others. He tells me it is important
what we do.*

    *He tells me making things work better is good.
Making someone's business system work better, like
he does, he says is important. He tells me making the
justice system work for people is important. That it
validates people, that it integrates them into the social
body. He says good lawyers are important.*

    *He says knowing when other people are in trouble
is something you have so you can help, so you can reach
out. Then he reaches out and grabs my shoulders, hard,
with both hands, squeezes them so hard they hurt. I
can't look at him.*

    *He says, I know things I don't know how I know
them. I know Dana is happy, where she is, that she
doesn't hurt any more. I know she sees us now. She likes
you, Harry. It's not your time to join her, Harry, you
have work to do, people to help. He picks up the picture
of Megan off my desk, says, beautiful child.*

    *Then he tells me how fine a father I am. Things I
didn't know he knew, stuff you told him maybe, stuff
maybe Susan told him at the gallery, stuff I don't see*

how he could know it. He says I'm doing fine, that Megan is going to be a fine young woman, that she has fine parents. That I need to teach her to fish. Hell, I say, I don't know how to fish. I'll teach you, he says.

Then he invited me to go up to the cabin, said he was going in the morning, wanted to teach me to fish, wanted me to see that part of his life, wanted me to come, could I make it. And I don't know what happened: I said yes. You would have laughed at me, uptight Harry. I said yes, I'll dictate some stuff, move some appointments, I'll do it, hell yes, I'll be at the airport at six A.M. He didn't ask any questions, didn't say anything about suicide, didn't ask me what was bothering me. He didn't need to.

But you know the rest, the fishing trip. I had so much fun. Loons, beavers. I saw a moose wading one day, bald eagles in the tree next to the cabin. Ravens, a mink. Mostly, we talked. In the boat or in the cabin, by the fire at night, about lots of things, what makes us mad, what we love, about making time count. We did it day after day.

I have a friend now, a man I can trust, this exceptional man. You take care of Connor.

Judith put the pages back in the file. They were handwritten, Harry's rapid, messy hand, lots of cross-outs. Typical Harry. But not typical. Admitting weakness, her kick-ass partner.

CHAPTER
SIX

Early on, on their second trip to the cabin, Harry told Connor he worried that Connor had no protection in the wilderness.

"Well," Connor said, "I do have a gun here. It is here somewhere. A gallery customer gave it to me because it was pretty, said it would look good hanging on the wall at my place in Canada. But I never got around to hanging it."

Harry beamed. "Let's get it," Harry said. Connor could tell Harry was getting into his useful mode.

www.branstettersays.com

JEWS IN JUDGESHIPS: A THINKING MAN'S ANALYSIS

This website is for you, if you think, and you are male. I emphasize the maleness. (If you are a woman, you will not like what you read here. Read on, if you want. It's a free country.)

Free country. Now there's an idea!! Let us say, rather, it is STILL a free country. America will not be free much longer, *es sei denn* (that means "unless," in case you don't speak German), unless, I say, thinking men unite to throw Jews out of all the judgeships. Especially FJJs, female Jew judges, who some benighted (female) governors in some states I won't name are putting on the bench, desecrating the public trust. These governors should be impeached. They will be impeached. This has happened in some places.

Thinking men are not Jews. The thinking men you and I admire and esteem. The real Americans. (Of course I know Jews can "think," if you want to call it that. They have higher mental function, oh yes. For corrupt maunderings. They have corrupt thoughts, unclean thoughts.)

I will not take a position on the Arabs versus the Jews. You won't find me wasting any time on that soap opera. If you are interested in that soap opera, go to a different website.

A thinking American man is not pro-Arab. He is not anti-Arab. He is ANTI-JEW. If Arabs want to kill Jews, that's their business, in their countries.

This country is what matters. America. The country that still is free. Barely. If all the Jew judges in America left and went to Israel, it would solve a lot of our problems. I would pay for the plane tickets, if I had enough money. Especially for one particular FJJ, I know, a particular Female Jew Judge.

If you have children and get a divorce, Jew judges will fornicate on your children. They will send them to Jew psychologists for Jew opinions about how good a father you are!

Jew opinions about your American children! These Jew psychologists then tell the FJJ, for money (Oh, yes, they get paid, by American parents!) how much time an American father should have with his American son!!!

If this is happening to you, let me know! Write me at my other website, dbranstetter@aol.com. There is awesome power when thinking men unite and plan. You can make a difference, you can take positive actions.

Don't let anybody tell you there's a Jew seat on the Supreme Court. It is a toilet seat.

Harry had given Judith the memo about Connor on the day she was sworn in. It was late in the afternoon in her new chambers, after all the well-wishers had left. *Graham v. Morris, Tri-County Medical, et. al.*, was over. All the defendants had paid up four months earlier. Judith was a judge of two hours' standing, No reason to see Connor Graham again, and Harry knew it.

"Jude, Mather & Merchant is gone, but the two M's aren't. You and I still have choices to make. This is going to be hard to say. But I want you to know that I am here today, I am alive today," here Judith raised her eyebrows, "No, I mean it, Jude, I'm alive today because of Connor."

Here he had patted the top of her desk, palm down, with each word: "I'm alive today because of Connor." He was silent for a few moments. "I want you to know that. I don't want to talk about it, not on your coronation day. But I have something I want you to read."

He had handed her the memo. "Don't read it now. Read it as soon as I leave. I wrote it for you eighteen months ago. Some of it is out of date now, because there's nothing left to do in Connor's case. But there's stuff in it you need to know. You are starting a new phase of your life now. You're not in private practice now. If you do this next stage the way you did private practice, the way you did law school, you will lose yourself in work. It is time for you to make a choice. It is time for you to choose joy. It's time for you to stop thinking about what you have lost."

And he had gotten up and left her sitting there, alone in her new chambers.

When she finished reading Harry's memo, she reread it, and folded it away to take home with her. The vestibule of the courthouse had been empty as she walked to the elevator, her heels echoing off the clerks' counters and locked courtroom doors.

The public space soared overhead, a modern cathedral built to house courtrooms and clerks' offices. It was a security nightmare with twelve entrances, and a parking garage underneath for car bombs. But it was a glorious, uplifting public space. Connor had stood and stared when she and Harry had brought him here, to see the place they would go to trial, to make it real for him. "Gothic majesty without columns and buttresses," he had said. "Isn't it great what steel makes possible?" and he had laughed out loud, turning in all directions, staring up into the arch.

On the way down in the elevator, she had gotten her cell phone out. There had been a rape in the garage the previous week, Annette Bundry, an attorney, going to her car, still no arrests. When she was safely in her Volvo, she locked the doors and called Connor's home number. He had been at her swearing in, had shaken her hand, wished her well.

"Connor, it's Judith. Thank you for coming to the ceremony today."

"I was glad to."

"Connor, will you take me out to dinner tonight? Help me celebrate my new career?"

That had been two years ago. The intervening two years had been good years.

CHAPTER
SEVEN

Connor found the canvas-wrapped package in the back of the storage shed. He had put it there when Martin was a child, so Martin wouldn't find it. He had thought maybe he would hang it on a wall someday, or maybe he wouldn't.

"Oh, this is really nice," said Harry. "Do you know what this is?"

"Well, I think so," said Connor, carefully. "Some kind of reproduction model, isn't it?"

"It's more than just 'some kind'," said Harry. "This is Winchester's 1966 Centennial re-issue of the thirty-thirty. One hundred years of Winchester firearms. That's why they gold-plated it, to make it beautiful."

Harry was in his element. "See how the tines feed the cartridge into the chamber? Listen to that action!" He worked the lever. "That's the sound of progress, the sound of civilization marching west." He put the gun to his shoulder. "Short stock," he said, "for the saddle scabbard." Harry held the gun out in front of him with two hands, grinning. "Let's sight it in," he said, and headed for the door.

Outside Harry set up a rest on the picnic table, using books and a tackle box. He put two sheets of legal paper on a tree in the woods, drew a cross hair on each, and said, "Fire away. Use the top target."

Connor shot three times. "I think it's going high right," he said.

Harry had binoculars. "It is. Let me try, before we make any changes." Harry shot once at the top target, said, "Yes, high right," and adjusted the sights. Connor shot again. Still to the right, but the elevation was dead on. There were five holes in the top target now.

"One more change," Harry said, and adjusted the sight one click left. "Now, top target one more time." Connor fired. "Looks good," Harry said. "Now try the bottom target. It has your name on it."

Connor had forgotten the complex beauties of long guns, had put that chapter on a shelf in the back of his mind, and now here it was again. The quiet, focused task, the light oil smell, the sharp smell of powder, the sights held just so, letting your breath out slowly, feeling your heartbeat, the slow gentle squeeze on the trigger. He put four rounds through the intersecting lines in the lower target, each of the last three exactly through the first hole.

Harry walked up to the target, brought it back to Connor, held it out, looking at him. "Holy shit, where'd you learn to shoot like that?"

"Well," said Connor, "it's a long story."

> To: dbranstetter@aol.com
> From: jajohnson11770@mindspring.com
> April 18, 5:21 AM
> Dear Mr. Branstetter, saw your website, think it is 5 stars. Judge Merchant took my boys from me last Dec. wont let me see them. I pay child support and all. I am very upset. What can I do. I need your help. --James A. Johnson

> To: dbranstetter@aol.com
> From: everyman666@hotmail.com
> April 18, 2:02 PM
> The enemy is no fool. He has a strategically designed game plan, a diabolical method he employs time and time again.

When he wants to destroy a family, he focuses on the man. For if he can neutralize the man, he has neutralized the family. And the damage that takes place when a man's family leadership is neutralized is beyond calculation.

To: dbranstetter@aol.com
From: robertjames4715@aol.com
April 19, 3:18 AM
Mr. B—You need to be careful in court. Do not let happen to you what happened to me.

"Hearsay" can be used against a father who is trying to do the right things by his children.

Simple statements taken out of context, which bloodsucking lawyers know how to do.

CHAPTER EIGHT

When Connor had met his wife in Europe, he had never seen an opera. Dana had taken him to see *The Magic Flute* in Vienna. After the opera they went to the famous Sacher's, where she ordered the tourist thing, Sachertorte with Schlag. It was so good they came back again the next night and had it once more, the rich dark chocolate cake with whipped cream. Small black coffees. The waiters in tuxes.

They traveled to Paris. She showed him all the places she knew. Museums, restaurants, Hemingway's oysters in Les Halles. They had stayed in a cheap hotel on the left bank, Ballantine's Scotch from thick-bottomed hotel glasses, sitting on a swaybacked bed. A bidet in the room.

With the first big slug of money Connor made, he and Dana had gone back to Europe to visit all the paintings he had written about in his dissertation: the pieces by Pieter Bruegel the Elder in Vienna and Naples, and the Franz Hals oils in Berlin, Haarlem, and Amsterdam.

They had gone back to Paris too, but this time to a good hotel. And with the second big slug of money, Connor had bought the cabin at Mantakagis.

Dana had loved the lake, had loved sitting on the dock reading. She had liked fishing, but not as much as Connor.

And now she was gone. Three years dead now. And the two years before that, she had been beyond reach, in a coma, before drifting off, finally.

His girl had left him in her own boat, alone, not talking, drifting downlake among the loons, growing smaller, smaller, no joy now, no bubbling laugh. He thought of her whenever he heard the loons. He thought of her every day in town. He thought of her when he was with Judith.

Judith said she understood, said she had lost someone too, long ago, she knew how it was. That is why she had never married, she said; she couldn't take the loss again.

CHAPTER
NINE

As he always did whenever he had been out of cell range at the lake, Connor called Judith from the airport at Kenora.

"Don't worry," she said, "I'm OK, but I've got to talk to you and Harry as soon as you get in."

"What is it?"

"I'll tell you when you get here."

"Judith, are you sick? Are you hurt?"

"No, no, I'm fine. I'm not going to die on you." She paused. "Sorry. That came out wrong. I love you, Connor."

"I love you, too, Jude. Tell me what's going on."

"No. You and Harry get back here."

Connor and Harry had changed to the big plane in Minneapolis before Connor said anything. "Something's going on with Judith. She wouldn't tell me what. Said she was fine, not sick, not hurt."

"Maybe she wrecked the Volvo."

"I don't think so. It feels like more than that. She said she had to see us as soon as we got in."

Harry was quiet. The flight attendant brought him pretzels and a beer. "I'll bet it's her domestic relations docket. That thing is a powder keg looking for a fuse."

"What do you mean?"

"I mean, there are so many sick people out there, and most of them get a divorce at some point. It only takes one bad case for a judge to get killed. And Judith has three or four going right now I know about."

CHAPTER
TEN

To: <u>dbranstetter@aol.com</u>
From: <u>cgillespie@esper.com</u>
April 20, 5:53 PM
    Dear Mr. Branstetter, I am a thinking man.
You are a thinking man. Please visit my website,
<u>www.alienation-mysondanny.com</u> and tell me what
you think.
    −cg

David Branstetter clicked on the hyperlink and sat back. It was a big site, bigger than his. There were photos, documents, legal correspondence. It was all in Judge Judith Merchant's court.

<u>www.alienation-mysondanny.com</u>

THIS WEBSITE IS DEDICATED TO MY SON DANNY WHO IS NOT OLD ENOUGH TO READ IT

But someday he will be, and he will know all I have done to fight for him and against crooked lawyers and judges. I have spent thousands of dollars just to try to see my son and these crooked shyster lawyers and their crooked shyster social worker pals talk all day long about "best interest".

Let me tell you when someone starts talking to you about the "best interest" of your child, you had better start counting the fucking silverware, cause your house is about to be robbed.

That is their stinking prettyfied code word for screwing you if you are still a man and dont lay down. If you dont play there game and go along, they will "best interest" you right out of town. On a fucking rail.

Please click on the photo links to see Danny and me. Those are pictures my ex-wife took. She cant deny them. They are in the chain of evidence, they cant hearsay them away, no they cant.

That is a happy little boy you see there, and a happy dad. That is when we were out at Percy Priest Park, to feed the ducks. Also there are pictures of us in Centennial Park here in Nashville. That is me with the Titans hat on, and Danny with the little Titans warm-up suit that I bought for him.

If you want the details of how lawyers screwed a good man, see the documents I have scanned in. Let me ask you something. Does your ex-wife throw away the mail you send your son or daughter? Mine does. Does she say your child can't come to the phone to talk with you cause he's to busy, and other lame-ass shit like that. Mine does. Does your ex-wife say the clothes you buy for your child are ugly and throw them away. Mine does.

I did not get to have a trial. The judge and the social worker clinical psychitrist-shrink rigged it all in advance. The so called expert talked about "best interest." His name was Orloff but I call him Jack-Off. He's some big doctor of something clinical.

What the fuck is clinical I would like to know. I have heard of clinical depression, well that fits cause thats what they did to me, Dr. Jack-Off and Judge Judith "Best Interest" Merchant, Judge of the Circus Court of Davidson County.

My ex wife now accuses me of "sexual misconduct" with my son. I mean that is sick. I almost cant believe she is doing it, but she is so desparate she will try anything I guess even character assignation, and my minister will testify on my character any time any place. My minster is not the only witnesses I have. I have many many many who want to help me. But did they get to testify??? No!!! On my trial day, they did not get to testify.

The circus judge would not give me a postponement to get them there, so there I was naked as a little lamb, like the one in the parents prayer poem that is on all the websites.

All l wanted was to raise my son to be a man and love God. I was going to teach him to hunt and he and I would go out in deer season together on the plateau and to Chuck Swan Reserve and maybe get us a buck but no that's not in his "best interest" and he cant do that cause thats all violent and nasty, thats killing animals.

I would like to know where my fucking ex thinks the fucking hamburger comes from at Burger King.

I will update this website as soon as anything changes. Thank you for reading it. If you want to talk to me, or if I can help you, write me at cgillespie@esper.com. My name is Charlie Gillespie and I have been screwed. I hope it doesnt happen to you.

David Branstetter went to his laptop computer and wrote in his diary:

> *This poor man, this Gillespie. So inarticulate, so clumsy. Yet I feel for him. I feel his pain. He has been grossly misused by this Merchant, this Kaufmann person. And by that despicable Jew Orloff. Poor Gillespie. All he wants is to cherish his son. I will write to him. I will write to him tonight after I have finished dinner.*
>
> *If his divorce was in Davidson County, perhaps he still lives here. Perhaps he can be trusted.*

CHAPTER
ELEVEN

Connor and Harry picked Judith up at the airport.

At Judith's place they sat in the kitchen. Harry said to Judith, "It's one of your cases, I know it. What's going on in *Anderson v. Anderson?*"

"Oh, Harry, don't be so paranoid. It's probably just some random crazy."

"Judith, random crazies don't use .222s. Enemies do. That's a very serious rifle. For accurate high-powered killing at a distance."

"Judith," said Connor, "be honest now. What kind of cases have you had lately? What kind of people?"

"The usual stuff, divorces, custody, alimony, nothing special."

"That's a grim diet. People get upset."

"Sometimes it is grim, you're right. But I can really make a difference. I can help people. And I also get to do adoptions," she added. "There everybody is happy."

Harry looked at her. "Judith, you know Judge Norton gave you domestic because you are the new kid."

He turned to Connor, "She's being a good sport. But where she is on the courthouse pecking order, well, it's like being a new cop. You get two years of jail detail before they let you ride in a squad."

Connor knew Norton was the assignment judge who decided who got which dockets. Harry said he was incompetent and lazy.

Harry stood up and started walking around. "Norton is the original magic beans judge. Completely gullible. He'd trade his cow to a stranger for a handful of beans, if the guy said, 'Judge, these are magic.' The voters love him. He goes to both Kiwanis and Rotary every week."

"The jack and the beanstalk thing worked out okay for Jack," said Connor.

"Yeah, in the fairy tale," Harry said. "But I tell you, you don't want a bench trial before Magic Beans Norton. It's a crap shoot. You remember, Connor, that we worked hard in Dana's case to make sure it didn't fall into Norton's division."

"I guess I wasn't paying much attention," said Connor. They were quiet. Connor got up and looked out the window. It was dark. He could hear the creek at the bottom of Judith's pasture.

"He's not incompetent," Judith said. "He's just erratic. He's very intelligent." She looked at Connor and smiled. "Besides, in a judge a certain amount of gullibility is appropriate."

Connor said, "You're not gullible."

"Oh, yeah?" Harry said, "She's dating you."

CHAPTER TWELVE

Richard was a child once more, looking out the upstairs window of his bedroom. He could see his father in the driveway sitting in a white-winged Buick, airfoil rear fenders sweeping up, away, taking flight. It was a convertible. He must have bought it just that day, Richard thought, and he's brought it home from the dealership.

His father had the convertible top down. He wants me to come see it, Richard thought, be excited.

His father pressed the gas pedal down and held it there. The engine roared. Ten seconds of roaring, then no pedal. It was sick, it was embarrassing. In the silence, his father honked the horn, blaring. Then ten seconds of roaring engine again. Then ten seconds of horn. Possessed, crazy.

I won't go out, Richard thought, I'll stay in here with Mother.

The two local papers got Judith's story and played it front page. "Shots Fired At Circuit Judge's Home," was *The Tennessean's* headline. The ever-helpful *Davidson Tribune asked,* "Governor's Appointment Unpopular?"

At the courthouse everyone was sympathetic. It was horrible. Could they help? How did she feel? They certainly would be nervous, oh, yes. Did she have a dog? A single woman living alone needed a dog.

After a while, it all got to Judith. She decided to leave town, drive to Monticello, and buy a new revolving bookcase. Her own had been ruined by the shooter.

"Couldn't you buy it online?" Connor asked.

"Yes, but that bookcase is so personal to me, so special, Connor, I want to pick it out myself. And also . . ." she paused, "I really need some time to think things out. It's tiring, being an object of concern."

"You'll call me?"

"Yes," she said, "I promise. Every night. This whole thing has gotten to me more than I've admitted. I need to think. I'm going to go over my list of cases."

Richard was in the stable. He had hip boots on. That was good. The shit was up to his knees. It was the mythological task again. Impossible for him. He wasn't Hercules. The oxen had fouled the barn too long. All those years with Gloria. The offal was in piles.

He had tried in the early years, had plied his manure fork day after day, month after month, year after year, but it had not sufficed. He had failed. The flies were riot. Swallows swooped in and out, scolding him for the choice he had made.

Guano was mounded high on the edges of the stable, beneath the swallows' nests. The walls of their nests had goat hair worked into the mud.

The oxen stood about, red-eyed, lowing in the muck. This whole kingdom of shit was his fault.

Once a week Connor looked in at his gallery. He still had a half interest in the business and he liked going there. Nan Hodgkins, a friend from Yale graduate school, had the other half. She opened and closed every day, but Connor still ordered the stock, talked with the art profs, kept his hand in. Two of the professors who had taught him at Yale were now on the Vanderbilt faculty. Connor got on well with all of the art faculty at Vandy, and at Fisk, and Central Tennessee State. He made it a point to attend all the Vanderbilt student shows when he was in town.

But his real job now was with Connor Organizations, making systems work better. He was good at it. "Horizontal and vertical efficiencies," he told Harry. "All I do is find them, tease them out, make them grow. Soon there's a nice little flow of money, and then it gets bigger. I don't advertise for clients. It's all word-of-mouth. I figure out what to do, and I tell others to do it."

"Soft work," said Harry.

"Yeah," said Connor, "just like lawyering. But you know, there are really only two kinds of work in this world. The first is changing the position or condition of objects at or near the earth's surface. That sort of work is difficult and poorly paid. The second is supervising others who do so. That work is enjoyable and highly compensated."

"You do the second," said Harry.

"So do you," said Connor.

"Did you make that up, that definition?"

"No, Marshall Peterson did."

"Who's Marshall Peterson?" Harry asked.

"A lawyer."

"I thought so," Harry said.

Before Connor had become a consultant, he had been able to tease out little efficiencies in the gallery: improving his marketing of shows, hanging new shows every three to four weeks, never a longer gap. He kept strong base holdings in addition to the shows, to underline the new shows, giving them a context. A carefully and regularly manicured mailing list. New lines of art supplies. All small things, but they soon added up to a thriving little business.

It had worked that way again, only better, with the medical lab, a quirky business he had fallen into. A customer from the gallery, Robert Boyle, had brought him in, initially just for management issues, but one thing had led to another: setting up profit-sharing for the six laboratory employees (now fifteen), reorganizing the workflow through the benches, marketing the lab's services to small hospitals in the region. And then they found a real cash cow, double udders and eight teats.

He and Boyle, now partners, had looked for a better and cheaper way to work with blood products. The two of them had built a shop, then a small factory, in the back of the space at Connor Organizations. They had used a sponge-type filter, long hours, and, Connor knew, luck, to arrive at a filter that attracted and contained hepatitis viruses. It had proved a godsend for blood banks. By attracting viruses, the filter allowed the blood to be cleaned. The filter also attracted money, as it turned out, about nine hundred thousand a year for each of them, paid quarterly by Pfizer, God love them.

He had been thirty-two when the cow started giving cream. Suddenly he was comfortably well off. His son Martin had been ten. Dana cut back to part-time at the museum where she worked. Connor finished his thesis in art history. Then they went to Europe. Six happy years passed. And ended when Dana got a headache one night, and Connor took her to Davidson Central Hospital's emergency room.

CHAPTER
THIRTEEN

"No, doctor," Connor had told Dr. John R. Morris Jr., "she does not have a migraine. She has never had a migraine in her life. She has no family history of migraine. She is athletic, she is in excellent shape. You can see that." Morris said nothing.

"She can't open her eyes," Connor said. "She's been vomiting."

"Photophobic," Morris said.

"Look," Connor said, "I know vomiting can be a symptom of migraines. But this is not a migraine. It's something else."

"Now, Mr. Graham, migraines can be strange. Adult onset is possible. It's in the literature. We've done a CT scan. I see no evidence of bleeding or tumor in her brain. What would you have us do now?"

"She has blood in the spinal fluid."

"Yes, but the spinal tap itself can cause that. It was a traumatic stick. I'm sure of it." He wrote on Judith's chart. "I'm sending her home, with two prescriptions. Imitrex for the pain, and Phenergan suppositories for nausea."

"Doctor, this is not a migraine."

"Mr. Graham, it is. I am the doctor. You need to be Dana's husband and take her home."

Twenty hours later, thirty-three hours after first arriving at the

E.R., Dana was back. This time Connor by-passed the emergency room, got Dana admitted directly to the hospital by a friend. A neurologist.

Dana was blind, crying, and vomiting her stomach walls. Her electrolytes could barely be measured. She entered a coma. Two years later and forty pounds lighter, she was dead.

It had been a pituitary tumor. It had ruptured that night, causing the acute symptoms. Simple. A completely benign tumor. No cancer. A physical presence. Nothing more.

No problem if diagnosed and removed promptly. The CT Morris had ordered had actually suggested its presence: the blood in the spinal fluid was caused by the tumor. An MRI found it immediately upon the hospital admission. If Morris had ordered blood work in the ER to check Dana's electrolytes, the diagnosis would have been made even then, even without an MRI.

At the hospital, Connor's neurologist friend called a neurosurgeon, who operated at once. But physical pressure had damaged the optic chiasm. Judith's sustained imbalance of electrolytes had done the rest. She was adrift, his girl, going down the lake, and she could not be called back.

"Diagnostic failure," the neurosurgeon said to Connor, softly, in the hospital cafeteria. "It can happen to anyone. I'm so sorry it happened to your wife."

"Doctor Sendler, if you had been in the E.R. that first night, would you have ordered an MRI?"

"Of course. I mean, if I had made the initial mistake of not requesting the pituitary sella in the CT. If you don't ask for that, you don't get it. If you do ask for it, you don't need the MRI. The tumor will be obvious."

Mather & Merchant had filed suit for Connor. They made him a lot of money, even after they took their third off the top before expenses. Money he didn't want or need. But it was money that came along with the lesson he was determined to teach.

The emergency room group had been the first to settle. Tri-County Medical, some forty doctors who covered the E.R. as subcontractors of the hospital. The rest of the dominoes had followed, one by one, just as Harry had said they would. Davidson Central Hospital had thrown in its coverage limits.

Last to settle was John R. Morris Jr., MD, "individually and as an employee of Tri-County Medical," as Harry put it. Dr. Morris, unmarried and under-insured, lost his Porsches, his 401k, his second house, and he was still stroking a $3000-a-month note to Connor, secured by a trust deed on his first and now only house.

The year Dana died Connor turned forty. Martin left for college. Connor was alone. He decided it was time to make some changes. He began turning his general consulting almost completely to medical practices. In thirty-six months his accounts would all be doctors.

Harry asked him why.

Connor said, "I don't want what happened to Dana to happen to someone else. You and I know all professionals need help with information flow. Lawyers need it, doctors need it, architects need it. I do that, I fix the information flow, and I give help with time management. I take away the details of practice management, so doctors can focus on making critical decisions well. Harry, there are lots of excellent, caring doctors out there. I am making them even better. And, my friend, they are excellent clients. It's not hurting my back pocket."

With the malpractice money, Connor bought a new aluminum eighteen-foot Lund for the cabin, a small Franz Hals portrait Dana had loved, and two sketches which were studies for Bruegel's *Return of the Hunters*. Connor put the rest of the money into a trust for Martin, now a junior at Montana State in Bozeman. There hadn't been much left for the trust after the insurance people found out Connor wanted coverage for 16th and 17th century art on an island in Ontario you could only get to by float plane.

CHAPTER
FOURTEEN

Interstate 40 traffic was light. Judith was driving and thinking. The road was straight as an arrow. I-40 Nashville to Knoxville, then I-81 to Virginia, to Staunton. Then she would take I-64 over the mountains to Charlottesville. I really need this trip, she thought. Tom and Connor. What am I going to do? Two men. One dead, and one alive.

Grandpa Merchant was in her mind, too. Probably because of Tom, she thought. Tom and she had climbed Katahdin. Her first time at Katahdin had been with Grandpa Merchant. He had taken her up the Chimney Pond Trail. She had been fifteen. They had seen a moose. It was so big they had had to get off the trail, pushing themselves into the brush to let it pass. Big, loose-hocked, meandering, unafraid, close enough to touch, warm.

She had seen a cirque, a new word, her grandfather cupping his hands, showing her how glaciers had carved the bowl. The water at the bottom had been clear and cold. It made her think now of gin in a Waterford glass. She would have some gin tonight, she thought comfortably, but in a plastic motel glass.

Above the treeline, another word: cairn. She and Grandpa Merchant had followed the lichen-covered cairns, through fog across boulder fields, to a sign telling them they stood at the northern

41

terminus of the Appalachian Trail, so and so many miles to Springer Mountain, Georgia. Her grandfather told her she was standing on the first place in the United States touched by the rising sun.

The next winter he had died, a heart attack. The autopsy showed earlier damage. The doctor couldn't say when it had happened. Judith wondered if it had happened that summer on Katahdin.

Seven years later, she was a Radcliffe graduate, a first-year law student at Harvard law school, and engaged. Tom Scofield was finishing at Harvard Medical School, and had been accepted into a pediatrics residency program at Vanderbilt University Medical Center. Judith would transfer to Vanderbilt, "the Harvard of the South."

Before leaving New England, she and Tom had driven to Baxter State Park, to climb Katahdin. They had slept in a three-sided shelter at the campground the night before, zipping their sleeping bags together, making love on the board floor. They could hear other campers close by in their own shelters, talking, cooking by Coleman light.

At first gray dawn they got up, packed all their gear into their car, and stood before the trail sign. "Mount Katahdin. Danger. Extreme weather. Snow can fall in any month." Judith promised Tom a moose, a cirque, and a cairn. He got two out of three, and was delighted.

By five in the afternoon, they were back down, tired, exhilarated, proud. Judith could still remember how her feet felt when she took her boots off. Tom drove. They made it all the way back the same day, through Millinocket and Ellsworth, and on out into the country where Route One skirts the ocean, back to Grandmother Merchant's.

It was three in the morning when they got back. Judith smiled, remembering how they had tumbled in the tall grass across the road from the house, before going in. Grandmother Merchant insisted on separate bedrooms.

On the first of July, they left for Nashville. On the way, they had stopped in Charlottesville to see Monticello. They were in love, holding hands, walking the oval with its ponds, touring the house. The wedding had been set for the third Saturday in September. Tom hoped his brother would be able to come.

Judith was in the apartment in Nashville addressing invitations when the call came that Tom was dead. A three-car collision. Fog on I-75. No one's fault really. Not enough cairns, she thought immediately, not enough lichen-covered rock piles to save my man in the fog.

Harry had been there for her, said she should stay in law school. Harry from the apartment next door. So, she had stayed, not knowing what else to do. She had studied all the time, losing herself. She studied Jefferson's writings, thought about changing to a doctoral program in history, but didn't. She graduated first in her law school class. Harry Mather was second.

CHAPTER
FIFTEEN

Harry. What a job of work he is, she thought. A football player, an All-American center at Vanderbilt. Not to look at him now, she thought.

"Judith," Harry told her, "the coach used to say, 'Harry, you argue so much, you should go to law school.' So I did."

What a friend. They had talked about dating. "Why ruin a good thing?" Harry had asked. Harry Mather. She laughed out loud. One day he had come back to the law library from a Shell station and made her guess what were the four types of condoms for sale at gas stations.

"Ribbed," she had said. "Colored. Normal?"

"Pretty good," Harry said, "but 'normal' is known in the trade as 'extra-strong plus spermicide.' But 'normal' is acceptable. I'll give you that one. What is the fourth kind?"

"Flavored?" she guessed.

"Right! Very good, Judith, very good indeed. I can see you know a lot about condoms. Now the hard part: What are the flavors? I'll give you a clue. There are four."

She guessed vanilla, chocolate, and strawberry. "Right," Harry said, "the first three. But now, for editorship of the *Vanderbilt Law Review*, what is the last flavor?" She had no idea. "What is it?"

"Banana!" he said.

"That's gross," she said.

But, he said, here was the deal: There was a real marketing genius at work. Say you wanted a particular flavor, he said. You can only buy condoms with quarters. "Machine accepts only quarters" was written clearly on the machine. You had to "stack three quarters," the machine said, and put them all in at once. The flavored condoms were "sold in rotation." This was the marketing genius, Harry said. It meant that you had to approach with commitment. If you wanted, for example, a banana-flavored condom, and nothing else would do, you had to be ready with twelve quarters, be ready to spend them all.

Another day Harry had given her his McDonald's lecture. How the Egg McMuffin was a divine creation, as good as pecan pralines, better than Goo-Goo Clusters. An inspiration worthy of Michelangelo, if Michelangelo had cooked.

How the McDonald's french fry of old, not what they were serving now, mind you, had been a noble offering, poetry in a paper pocket, an epiphany worthy of ten thousand Frenchmen. How it was *de rigueur* for people he otherwise esteemed to throw off on McDonald's food. Pseudo-sophisticates. He was a McDonald's customer, by God, and a McDonald's stockholder, by God, and proud of it. He put his money where his mouth was.

She had teased him about the McDonald's drive-through 'Guarantee Zone.' "It's a guarantee zone, all right," she told him. "They guarantee that when you pay and drive off, you will have something in your bag. It might even be your order."

Harry had sniffed. "I speak of the food. Not of its packaging."

Even the five years after law school, when they had not practiced together, they had talked every week or so. After Vanderbilt, Judith had clerked for the state Court of Appeals. Harry had gone to the state Attorney General's office. "Always wanted to be a prosecutor," he said. Judith went with Nashville's largest firm for four years, after the clerkship. Harry left prosecuting after two years and started his own firm. Then one day he called her and said come with him, his new tort practice was going OK, he could feed her until something hit, she would have fun.

So they started Mather & Merchant. "M&M" they called it. They did personal injury and medical malpractice exclusively. Eating what they killed, and eating very well, thank you, from the very start.

While she was practicing with Harry, she had been nominated for a federal judgeship. That was eight years ago. The FBI had called the office of Mather & Merchant for a background check. They wanted to speak to "the senior partner." Martha the receptionist had told the man there were two senior partners, which one did he want? He wanted Mather.

"Harry," Martha called through, "the FBI is on line two."

Harry knew it was Courtney Pearre, his prankster friend. He picked up the phone and said simply, "I'm sending the cocaine back."

"Excuse me?" said the FBI man.

"I'm sending it back, don't worry."

"Is this Mr. Mather?"

"Yes, and I want you to know I take my debt to society very seriously."

"Thank you, Mr. Mather."

That had been the end of Judith's FBI background check. Well, Judith thought, it had been a long shot anyway. She'd probably been too young. And the Senator hadn't really known her, hadn't insisted on her.

Harry hadn't wanted Judith to go on the bench, not then, not ever. "Look Judith, I don't want to lose you. I'm not pure here, I don't deny it. I want you as my partner practicing law at M&M. But I have to tell you, the way you work, the way you care, you're going right into harm's way if you become a judge. You don't cut corners, you don't duck when it gets hot. You'll be a target."

When the governor called to nominate Judith for the state circuit court, she had asked for Judith. Harry hadn't gotten the call, thank goodness. So he hadn't been able to send any drugs anywhere.

Judith made the blue-ribbon commission's cut to the final three, the governor picked her, and she was sworn in. That was twenty-five months ago.

But, at the swearing-in, Harry had beamed. He had put the robe on her himself. He even brought his own Pentateuch for the oath. Harry was getting out of the law. "Jude," he said, "without you, there's not going to be any fun left. I'm changing careers. I'm going to be a psychologist. Maybe it'll help me understand people. Who knows? It might even help me understand myself."

After Knoxville, Judith took the I-81 cut-off. Interstate 40 continued to the right, to the east, over the spine of the Appalachians to Greensboro, to Raleigh, almost all the way to the ocean. Judith headed north, up the Appalachian valley beside the spine.

CHAPTER
SIXTEEN

The whale was drunk again, skin damp, lying on the living room floor. He was playing "Tristan" on the pink RCA portable console. Richard, ten years old, was in the kitchen. He could hear it all, see it all whenever he peeked out. Love undying, love resplendent after death. The whale's sweat wicked into the oriental pile rug.

The living room was hot, though all the windows were open. The whale was doing Wagner tonight, not Mahalia Jackson. Tonight was Karajan in Berlin, the "Liebestod."

Outside the windows, cicadas chirred their rising and falling song of mating, mating, mating. Isolde, Tristan, Isolde, Tristan. Up and down. Waves of volume. Love in the afterworld. Not here on earth. Not here, not now. The whale moaned. He was harried by small men in skittering four-oared boats.

Karajan was under the rug. His back was bowed, his gray hair hung into his face. He lifted his hand, he beat the time, he lifted the weave, the woven tale. He heaved the whale to bliss, to safety. The little boats fell back, they could not launch harpoons.

In the kitchen Richard whimpered, staring into the living room. He heard the songs of mating, mating, mating, songs of Tristan und Isolde.

Someone coughed. Richard looked out over the podium. "It took Wagner over twenty years to complete his *Ring*, four operas, extending from 1853 to 1874. While the *Ring Cycle* may in fact be Wagner's greatest achievement in scope and vision, and of course," he conceded, graciously, as though someone had interposed an objection, "it is his largest work by far. Some would argue that it is his 1859 *Tristan and Isolde*, or even the late *Parsifal*, which is more sublime.

"Whether you take the Liebestod as a specific reworking of Christian themes of death and salvation is unimportant. For Wagner, the Liebestod was the promise, no, the realization, of a surpassing state of blessedness, achieved at huge cost.

"Wagner's own life was compromised, erratic, as you know from Neumann. He was envied and harried by small men. But in his music, in the weaving of Germanic mythology, Wagner built structures of permanence, white-columned palaces of Teutonic splendor."

Someone hissed. It was a suggestion, fashionable that year on campus, that a professor was doing it again, getting lost in hyperbole. In the front row, Katherine Kelty had opened the gates. He saw thighs receding infinitely to heaven. There was a glimpse of panty.

"For Friday, then, either of the two short essays. Either *Volsung Saga* or salvation-by-death. They are in your handouts. The teaching assistants have extra sheets if you missed getting a copy last time."

The bell in University Hall began to strike noon. Richard liked to be punctual, to have the bell beginning its slow count just as he finished, continuing with the students filing out. He shuffled his notes together at the lectern, watching the skirts leave.

The creepy guy was in the back as usual, writing furiously in a three-ring notebook. Too old for a student, Richard thought. Doesn't have the look. A townie picking up culture? Oh, well. Richard put his glasses in his breast pocket and closed his notes. He wanted to get over to the Faculty Club for lunch. The guy looked like he wanted to talk, stood up. Richard turned and left quickly through the side door.

"Dear Connor," Judith wrote, *"this will reach you about the time I get back to town. I don't care. I want to spend these moments alone with you tonight. I want to imagine your face, feel your love. This is the only way I can do it here, in Charlottesville, hundreds of miles away from you."*

She sipped iced Bombay from the plastic motel glass. One of two, wrapped in Saran. I'm glad, she thought, there was not a Sani-Strip on the toilet, "to protect against disease." Queen Victoria looked benignly at her from the Bombay label. Judith continued her letter.

"My dear, I know you must wonder why I came here without you, without even asking if you wanted to come. At the time I wasn't sure myself, but now I am. It's because Tom and I were here before I started at Vanderbilt. It was my first trip to Monticello, my first time with Jefferson's ghost. It was special. I was in love. It was Jefferson and Harry who saved me in law school, after Tom was gone. I guess I've always linked Tom and Monticello, Tom Scofield and Tom Jefferson, in my memory."

She paused, read the sheet over, and tore it up.

"Dear One," she began again, *"I miss you. So I'm writing. My letter and I will probably get to you about the same time, but I have you with me tonight as I write. The house was wonderful, as always. The caracalla beans and the dolichos lab labs are high up the garden trellises. The bookstore was jammed. I got my new bookcase. It's in the back seat of the car."*

At Monticello when the house guide wasn't looking she had reached out and touched the original bookcase, Jefferson's own bookcase, felt its smoothness, imagined Jefferson's hand turning the mechanism. *"It will look wonderful in the study. I think it is a little darker than the one the man shot up."* Man. She didn't know the shooter was male, or even just one person. But she thought that he was. She had some candidates in mind. They were all men.

She would have to be careful, keep the farmhouse on patrol car drive-by for a month or so, hope the deputies would get the message out in Nashville that you don't mess with the judge. Chief Bolden's men had said the slugs from the bedroom ceiling were in good condition. The ones that killed the bookcase were useless for ballistics.

"My dear, some day we will come here together. I think I can do that with you, share my Jefferson with my man. But you'll have to be devoutly respectful. He and I go way back. He knew me before you did. Good night, my dear. All love, Judith."

She folded the note, addressed it, and took it out to the box on the corner of the state route, dropped it in, and looked up at the stars.

CHAPTER
SEVENTEEN

Connor was checking on Judith's house. Her driveway off Brayman Pike led off to the left from the road, over the creek. There was an open field on the right side of the road, with an open, honeysuckle-covered gate. That was where the shooter had fired from, the sheriff said, shooting up the hill, up the rise toward Judith's house. There had been vehicle tracks in the high grass, and .222 brass casings.

Connor stopped at the mailbox to get Judith's mail. She had been gone three days. He pulled open the door to the mailbox and a stench filled his car. A long turd was inside, baking in the summer heat. Connor rolled his car past, turned into the drive, and stopped. He broke a branch from a bush and fished the nastiness out.

He decided not to tell Judith, not yet anyway. But he would tell Harry.

"Ah, God," said Harry. "Some people. That's why I'm glad I'm a psychologist. Get a handle on the sickies."

"You're not a psychologist."

"Am too. I'm a Licensed Clinical Examiner. You may also call me 'Sir LCE.' And that's not all," he said, "I'm a doctor of clinical psychology *in spe*. As I used to say when I was practicing law and saying Latin things. All I need now is my dissertation. Then I'll be Dr. Harry Mather. As well as a Private Investigator."

"Harry, this country needs good lawyers, just like it needs good doctors. And with you gone there's one less."

"Yeah, well . . ."

"Harry, don't you miss practicing law?"

"I'm glad to be rid of it. God was good to me. He let me make so much money so I could get out of the law and do something useful." He paused, and then said, "Thoreau said to give of one's self, to leave the world a better place. to have played and laughed with enthusiasm, to know even one life has breathed easier because you have lived, that is success."

They were quiet. Then Harry added, "I tell you, Connor, the law can help people. I don't deny it. But it's slow. Mostly though, practicing law is a great way to make a living, provided you like constant anxiety, hemorrhoids, and the cold sweats at night."

"Cold sweats?"

"Yeah. You wake up in the middle of the night, thinking you've missed a statute of limitation. That means you've forgotten to file a pleading in time. My head keeps on working at night, you know, it doesn't give me any time off. So, when I knew Judith was going to go on the bench, that's why I decided to become a shrink. So I could figure out my head. Of course, I would have gone to medical school, if I could have. Instead of graduate school in psychology. But I didn't want to leave town, and I knew Vandy would never in hell let me in. Not after I cleaned their clock in *Peabody*. So I didn't even apply. I said screw them. It's the pseudo-science of psychology for me."

He grinned at Connor. "Harry Mather, J.D., P.I., Ph.D. Sounds good, doesn't it? All I need now is K.B."

"K.B.? What's that?"

"Knight of the Bath. Don't laugh, he said. "I know people in England."

Judith slowed for her driveway, turned in, and bumped up the hill, her headlights picking out blue periwinkle blossoms on each side of the drive. The Jefferson bookshelf rocked side to side in the back seat. At the top of the hill where the drive leveled out and went right, she saw gleams, bright sparkles in the driveway. She stopped the car, leaving the headlights on, and walked ahead. Nails.

"Besides," Harry went on, "because I'm a P.I., I still get to do the fun legal stuff. The small part of law practice that is fun. I drive around at night, detecting, with my gun. I get results. I help people right away. No waiting around, no trials, no research, no delays. No Judge Norton. 'Results now.' It's a motto to live by. I am going to put that in my ad."

Harry had applied for graduate school, and for his private investigator's license, the same day Judith had gotten the nod from the blue-ribbon commission.

Harry had told Judith it was OK, her being a judge, it really was, if she wanted to. He needed to make some changes anyway. It was time for changes. "Been needing to make them for a long time," he told her. No, he wasn't going to get a new partner. "Who would put up with me?" he had asked.

"Ah hell, Judith," he had said, flexing pudgy *On the Waterfront* arms and doing a Brando accent, "We coulda been contendahs."

"Harry, we are contenders, if you remember. We've made a lot of money, and we've changed some things for the better."

"Money we've made, yes. Helped some people? Yeah, some. But it's all too slow, too slow. I want results. I want them right away. That's why I'm going to be a P.I. You should try it, maybe."

"I think there's a problem with a judge being a private investigator. Something about ethics."

"See? The law is all screwed up. Rules, rules, rules. There you'll be, a judge, wearing black mourning robes, all proper, sitting on a rule book. I, on the other hand, will be driving around at night in Gotham City packing heat."

Harry's phone rang. He got up to answer. "It's Judith," he called to Connor. He put it on the speaker. "Judith, slow down. Connor is here. Tell us what's going on."

"Nails. Tacks. Whatever, all over my driveway up here at the house."

"Are you OK?"

"Yes."

"Is anybody over there?"

"I don't think so. I've got the gun."

"Good. We're on the way."

"Park in the grass. Don't drive on the flat part of the driveway."

CHAPTER
EIGHTEEN

David Branstetter had seen Judith at the campus screening of Leni Riefenstahl's *Triumph of the Will*. He had looked around as the lights came up, and there she was, where she shouldn't be. Here, of all places. It was obscene, her being here. David's head was still full of Third Reich greatness, all the bright promise, clean tall men. And there she was, the filthy woman. What was she doing watching purity? He knew she was Jewish. "Merchant" was a translation of Kaufmann. Who did she think she was fooling? Trying to hide a kike name in a translation. Really.

Being a professor wasn't bad, Richard thought. You got paid to read books and talk about books. Listen to music, talk about music. Go to plays, talk about plays. Not bad for someone like him, someone who'd been through what he had been through, someone with a father like his. A father who had sent him to the nuns when he was five. To play "Jack-Be-Nimble" with penguins. Richard had been terrified all that one horrible day. They were black and white, with cowls around their faces. He had wet his pants. Then his mother had come for him, said he didn't have to go back. They had walked home to the apartment, the apartment over the lady on the second floor who made scungilli. Richard was afraid of scungilli.

His father knew he had wet his pants. He said, "Tonight! Scun-gill-eee!" drawing it out, seeing the terror in Richard's eyes.

"Can you do DNA on turds?" Harry asked.

"Jesus, who would want to?" asked Judith.

"I do," said Harry. I want to catch this sick son-of-a-bitch."

"Yes, of course you can," said Connor. "Any bodily fluid. I just didn't think of it." They were sitting in Judith's kitchen, two pounds of roofing nails on the kitchen table. Connor had told Judith about the mailbox.

"Is there anything left where you threw it?"

"No, I threw it in the creek. The branch off the bush too. I even threw the paper towels in the creek."

Harry snorted and went to Judith's espresso machine. "Well, the long and short of it is, we've got three events. Which add up to precisely zero: the shooting, the nails, the turd. The turd is gone, the nails you can get at any Home Depot, and ballistics are no good without a gun.

"This guy is not going to quit. John Adams told the jury in the Boston Massacre trial, 'Facts are stubborn things.' Sometimes, Jude, facts tell us what we don't want to hear." Harry ran his hands through his hair. "You know, I'd like to see this guy's pre-school records, his pediatric records. See if he's got the triad."

"What's that?" Judith asked.

"Reliable predictor of violent behavior toward others. Bed wetting, fire setting, and animal abuse by age six."

"Huh," Judith said. Then she asked, "Harry, how common are .222s?"

"Not common, but not rare either," said Harry. "There are probably fifteen of them in Davidson County alone. And the out-counties will have a few too. It's a high-accuracy rifle, a 'varmint rifle,' throws a 40-grain Spitzer bullet 2900 feet per second. That's what your shooter was using anyway. It's classy. I had one when I was a boy in Georgia."

"Is 2900 feet per second fast?" asked Judith.

"Yes, very. Your .357 Magnum, Jude, the 158-grain jacketed hollow-point, is rated at 1004 feet per second. Lots of stopping power—the bullet weighs four times more than the .222, but the .357 doesn't have much velocity."

Connor said, "About the same as the basic .22 short. 1095 feet per second."

"How'd you know that?" Harry asked.

"Boy Scouts," said Connor. "We used them on the range in Boy Scouts."

"Hmph. They should have given you long-rifle cartridges."

Judith knew Harry was an excellent shot. One of the many contradictions in my partner, she thought. My former partner. She knew Harry kept a gun in his golf bag. He had told her it was, "Just in case. You never know."

Another contradiction was Harry's Judaism. He was taking instruction. His closest New York friend was a rabbi who lived on Tenth and C, in the alphabet jungle. Harry had told Judith he intended to convert, not soon, but some day. He said he admired the black-coated, ring-locked Hassidim. He said their "systematic removal of ambiguity" was a successful struggle against life's problems.

"So, are you going to move?" Connor asked Judith.

She didn't answer.

"You have to move," said Harry. "It's that simple. A no-brainer."

"Where would I go?" she asked. "I have to live in Davidson County. It's a requirement of the job."

"It doesn't matter where you go in the county," Harry said. "But you have to go. It's how you go."

"What do you mean?" asked Connor.

"It means Judith doesn't own her next house. And she doesn't have a phone in her name. All her mail goes to the courthouse or to a PO box. She has no home address in any database. She changes all her credit cards to the neutral addresses. No judicial plates on the Volvo. No more judge.merchant@davidsoncounty.gov. It's phonyname@hotmail.com for her from now on."

"Hmm," Judith said.

"Judith, will you do it?" Harry looked at her seriously. She said nothing. Connor could hear the creek.

"You know, you chose this job," Harry said.

"Yes, and I love it. I guess this is part of it. Yes, I'll do it. But I'm angry."

"Angry is good. Smart is better."

"How do you own a house and not tell your name?" asked Connor.

"Set up a trust, a straw man," said Judith.

"Or two trusts," said Harry. "The Island Mountain Trust, which then deeds the property to the Valley Slope Trust. Made-up names. Paper fictions. Judith retains all the equitable interest off the books, by separate unregistered deed. The only thing filed in the registry of deeds is the legal interest in a couple of paper entities."

"I'm glad I have lawyer friends," said Connor. "I lack basic survival skills."

"Classic first year law school insight," said Harry.

Judith nodded. "When life gets sticky, you really do need an edge," she said.

CHAPTER
NINETEEN

David Branstetter had found a superb website. It was about parental alienation, what Jeanie was doing to him, keeping him from Joey. There were links to other fathers, other men who were going through what he was, men who through no fault of their own were being taken advantage of by ex-wives and judges. He would have to put a link to this website on his own page. So all the men reading his website could find out about parental alienation. The acronym was PAS. It made David think of Easter eggs, and Joey, and the smell of vinegar.

These were fathers who knew the legalisms, the terms for the malicious things Jeanie was inventing. Such as telling Joey his father was too strict. Letting Joey do whatever he wanted. Letting him associate with a fairy.

He wrote in his laptop:

> *Treece is back. Jeanie lets him in her condominium.*
> *Lets Treece drive Joey to work. So she doesn't have to do*
> *it. That's Jeanie all over, unchanging, forever avoiding*
> *any output of labor for anyone else. She lets the fairy*
> *spend the night in Joey's room. Calls them "the boys."*

> *I drove all the way to Clarksville and found
> what I feared. I went to his employment, ready to
> watch him. But it was his day off. The young woman
> running the arcade, name tag "Rebecca" (couldn't get
> last name), says Treece is thirty and has three interests:
> video games, Star Trek, and young boys. Says she hears
> Treece lets those he likes play for free in the arcade, that
> he loads free games into the machines for his pets. Says
> that he tells everybody about a girlfriend killed in a
> freak accident, how he "just isn't ready" to date again
> yet. The old story fags use.*
>
> *My son's mother is asleep at the switch, and she
> says I am the problem! What can I do?? "The boys" are
> sixteen and thirty!! My son is getting his penis sucked
> by a parasite in her house!*

Some of the on-line fathers had Jewish judges, too, just as he did. There was one father in Pennsylvania who even had an honest-to-goodness Cohen. No attempt to hide it with a translation. Right out in front of God and everybody. Jewish judges for American children. It was really bad. They had to work together, fight back.

Richard was in his office at the university, thinking about sex in literature, sex and literature, literary sex, Gloria. He could still see the view. He had been lying on his back, Gloria on top, squatting up and down on the Pony Ride, moaning, the suitcase in the corner of the bedroom, as always, open. Her clothing inside.

He remembered how she would not unpack her suitcase after their trips, just leave it open on the floor. If she needed something, she would get it out of the suitcase. Richard didn't know whether any items ever went back into the suitcase. He didn't think so. But the suitcase never became empty. Maybe she did put stuff back in. Or maybe the contents just spontaneously regenerated. Fruit flies.

The first time the suitcase had shown up on the bedroom floor, it only stayed for a few days. Richard had said to himself, well, OK, she's just slow about unpacking. The suitcase had sat there, lid up, clothes inside, waiting. Normal perhaps, he had thought, she's just slow. Dilatory.

But he had been wrong. After the next trip, the suitcase stayed for weeks. Soon, it was there all the time, lid raised. When the cleaning lady came, Gloria would close the lid, leave it sitting there. The cleaning lady vacuumed around it. Every week. Once, Richard had asked Gloria could he help her, could he help her put things away, did she have enough room in her bureau, could he take the suitcase to the attic? "No," she had said, "It's fine."

Perhaps, Richard thought, she doesn't see any net improvement in moving things from the suitcase to her bureau. Because her desk, her bureau, every storage place she had, was filled with dingy, crumpled items in no order beyond stratigraphic succession. At the back of shallow drawers, or at the bottom of deep drawers, were items Richard had never seen outside the drawers. Things from Gloria's high school years, junior high school. Magenta halter tops from a K-Mart of twenty years ago.

Why, Richard would ask her, don't you just give that to Goodwill, or to the Salvation Army? "Oh," she would say, "I might wear it." Or, more often, "I'm saving that for . . ." and here would fall the name of a toddling niece or nephew. Who might in twelve years or so need a magenta halter top. No items ever came out of the drawers.

There had been a time when Richard wondered if the suitcase might be a mute testimony to the unhappiness he caused her, to mistakes he was making, mistakes he had to correct. An accusatory mouth telling of his neglect.

He tried believing that for a while, tried feeling guilty. But he had foundered on her desk drawers crammed with ten-year-old phone bills, foundered on her boxes of molding cloth, old elastic from high school sewing classes. After all, he wasn't making her keep all this, the detritus of her life. The shoes with no soles, moccasins with the sides gone, leftovers spoiled in the refrigerator. Could he make himself believe he caused all her problems? She wanted him to do just that, accept all blame, be her alibi for fecklessness. Cunt. Cunt. Cunt.

CHAPTER
TWENTY

Several weeks had gone by since the shooting. Judith had found a builder she liked, Jake Pridden. She had called and learned he had three houses going. She looked at all of them, and chose one on the very edge of the county. The most expensive one, two bedrooms, definitely upscale. It shared a hundred-acre lake with three other new houses. If I can't live where I want, she thought, I can at least live how I want.

She had gotten a condo downtown as a transition until the new house was finished. A month-to-month lease. No personality, no view, and she could walk to work. Harry had stayed with her at the farmhouse for three weeks, and then told her he was tired of it. It was time for her to move, he said. "I may not have much social life, being a big man and all, but I've got more than this." So she had put the Brayman Pike farmhouse on the Multiple Listing Service and moved.

She and Connor were designing her new kitchen in the evenings now, after work. Granite countertops, double ovens. An icemaker. Two dishwashers. A separate freezer in the kitchen. He told her he still had sixty pounds of halibut and forty of coho salmon from his Alaska trip. She needed to have a big freezer, he said.

She looked at him when he said that. Then she asked, "Are there fish in my lake?"

"Probably," he said. "Want to learn to fish?"

"I think so."

The next night, with the plans spread out on the kitchen table in the condo, Connor fixed baked stuffed halibut with miso sauce. Judith moved appliances and cabinets around on the plans, using cardboard cut-outs. "The vinaigrette won't blend right," Connor said. He was fussy about salad dressing.

"It'll be fine," she said, "just put in more blue cheese." She put the icemaker on the other side of the kitchen, near the dining room. It didn't fit. "I love it that you like to cook. Same as me."

He smiled. "Cooking for me is like art. It is a creative process." He paused, putting in the blue cheese. "I never considered it to be a manhood issue. You know what I mean, 'Men don't cook.' All that." He got out the plates and napkins. "Well, we know men do cook. Chefs cook."

She loved talking to him, loved hearing him moving about. They talked about art history, about fishing, about food, about her work. He told her about the cabin in Ontario, and how her lake probably had bluegills in it, and maybe largemouth bass. He told her that fishing for halibut was like pulling up a log from the bottom of the ocean.

"I'd like that," she said. "If you're going fishing, it seems to me you should focus on productivity."

"There are some people who fish like that," he said. "They're called 'meat fishermen.'"

"Well, I think I'm a meat fisherman."

"Some guys would use Rotenone and electric shock if they could get away with it."

"I wouldn't do that," she said. "But I still want the poundage. I just wouldn't do the illegal things. I mean, if you're going to step up to the plate, you should score as many runs as possible." She paused, "Like that economist at Harvard says, the one who does Markov analysis on hitters, 'NERV' he calls it. 'Net expected run value.' I think he's right. I believe in maximizing scoring, maximizing fish poundage."

Connor laughed long and hard, and then hugged her. "Lawyers," he said.

After he left, she realized she had been thinking of the new house with Connor in it. Thoughts of permanence, she smiled to herself.

But it also worried her. She knew love depended a lot on luck, on traffic on the interstate not killing your man. On chance, undeserved fortuity. On beauty walking in, coming to live in your house.

"Judith," she had written in her diary, *"you can do all the things, the good things, the caring things, the acts of devotion, that are necessary for a man like Connor. But they are only necessary, they are not sufficient. Not for Connor, not for any man. Omit them, and you have no hope at all, but even with them you cannot make Connor love you."*

She thought of how Connor laughed, a stream rippling over stones, trout flashing in glacial outwash. She knew she didn't understand the chemistry they had. She liked the Greek idea of the missing half, the part that had to be found in order to be whole. When she was with him, him drawing her to him, fingertips, wrists, shoulders, embracing her, him smelling her hair, saying, "Oh, yes, you're back, it's right again," she knew the half had been found.

Her pager vibrated. Seeing the jail's intake number, she thought of how people used the phone for many things. She could call Connor now. But instead, she would call the jail and talk of love gone bad, love gone violent.

She dialed the intake center, set the bond and appearance date for William Hensley who, tired of something, had broken down Dora's door, shown her a double-sided dagger, talked of permanence, and waited for the cops. He was in the holding cell now, doing his twelve-hour hold, calm and happy, Officer Fowlkes told Judith, waiting for the bondsman. Judith wondered if William Hensley had gotten through to Dora, if they would now be able to well and truly love, she knowing his intensity, his will to kill her, maybe, if she did not straighten up.

She thought of Memphis blues, how Momma don't love me no more, how the ice man come, don't leave no ice. She knew that her life was rich with the details of others' lives, that love was not a thing of definition, that William and Dora were part of life's laughter, pebbles in the outwash.

CHAPTER
TWENTY-ONE

Connor was thinking about language. He remembered Budapest. Three hours after getting there, he had still been in graduate school, he had felt disoriented, unhappy. It wasn't the landscape. That was the same as in Austria. And Budapest was a big city, like Vienna. It was not daunting. If anything, it was simpler than Vienna. But he felt terrible. He walked the streets, feeling worse and worse. He didn't know what was wrong.

He went from site to site, using his guidebook. Took some pictures from the hill. Drank a glass of tea. Even the tea failed to lift his mood.

At the summit of the hill was St. Stephen's cathedral. The guidebook said it was a must. Connor didn't care. He felt lost. He wanted to check out of his hotel, walk to the train station, and go back to Austria. Was he getting sick? He hadn't eaten anything odd, none of the sausages from the stands with names he didn't recognize. He had pointed to a roll, played it safe. He was lost inside a Bergmann film without words. Why had he come here, anyway?

He pushed his way into the cathedral, dropped a few coins into the collection box. He gazed at the stained glass windows. Immediately he felt better. There were words on the windows, words he could read! Latin! Wonderful Latin! It was in the windows, on the grave markers, at the stations of the cross, everywhere! That was why he had felt lost! He hadn't been able to read! Now he had recovered the Western tradition. No more impossible Ugric lumps, absence of cognates, the simplest everyday vocabulary beyond comprehension. He loved this church, its architecture. He loved Budapest. He was glad he had come.

Being with Judith was like that, Connor thought now. The three years since Dana died, he had lacked the language of women. Oh, he had liked them, had gone out to dinner twice, even fixed salmon in puff pastry once for a lady who delivered canvas to the gallery, but it had all been streets with signs he couldn't read. Now he was with Judith. Now there was language again. There was her beauty, her simple elegance, her bracelets.

CHAPTER
TWENTY-TWO

David Branstetter was reading the website of the father in Pennsylvania. The man with the Cohen judge. He was stressed out, you could tell, adding something to it almost every day. www. anotherfatherfkd.com, really. The taste of some of these people. But they were on the right side.

> Hizzoner, his Cohen-ness, his highness, whatever you want to call him, his kikeness, his rohyal kikeness, that's good, yeah. That sonofabitch said I had to take fucking parent skill classes, me, learn to be a father!!!!!!!!!!!!!!! Like taking fucking wood shop or something, jr high school. Get real, your royal kikeness. Just cause you can't find your ass with 2 hands doesnt mean I cant. Learn how to be a father in a class!!!!!!#### RIGHT. There are three of us here who say FUCK THAT NOISE!!!!!! YOU WANT TO KNOW WHOSE SAYING IT??? ME, AND SMITH, AND WESSON!!!!!!!

It sounded like the man in Pennsylvania either had a gun, or watched Dirty Harry movies. I hope he has a gun, David thought.

Judith always wore silver bracelets. They were gifts, she said, from her Texas side of the family. She had told him of her Spanish grandfather, her mother's father, the Benavides side of her family. Connor thought the bracelets must have come from him. They looked like Inca silver. Connor had seen pictures of the ranch in Nuevo Laredo, a grant directly from the king of Spain, Judith said, old and faded clippings in a scrapbook.

Judith had told him how her grandfather would take her to the plaza with him every day. There was a café in the plaza where he would meet his friends, drink a beer, and talk about the previous day's events. Judith would sit at the café's outdoor stand and drink lemonade while her grandfather kept her in sight.

Nights now, if she stayed with Connor, she took her bracelets off and put them on his sea chest. It was an old, scarred trunk Connor used as a coffee table. She knew it was old, she told him, because it only had six boards. It came from a time when pines grew that big, she told him.

Judith would put her bracelets down, the silver ringlets in a seeming tangle. When she put them down, they would ring out softly, and Connor heard bells and plaza pigeons, felt the sun of Mexico and years of wearing. He heard bells coming to rest on wood that had been to sea, and knew that here was a union, a joining of people and times and lifelines, a linking of people long dead.

Sometimes he saw her put the bracelets down, and sometimes he would come upon them later, see the intersecting circles, thin and lucent, each arcing over and through others, and he would think of Botticelli. He remembered John Keats had died at twenty-six.

Was his Judith even separable from the bracelets? Mornings she would pick them up and put them on again, the silver tangle sorting itself upon her arm. Pigeons flew, wing beats echoed off facades.

He knew he was getting over the loss of Dana. He and Judith were equals, each strong and incomplete, the bracelets needing the wood that had been to sea, the wide planks silent without their bells.

There had been a tiny grocery store in Judith's grandparents' town, Hancock, Maine, population 604. At the beginning of summer, Judith would go to the store with her grandfather. The store had treasure. Wax lips, big pink lips you could hold with your teeth and look glamorous. Big ugly teeth you could slip over your own. Black mustaches. Yo-yos, sometimes see-through yo-yos made of colored plastic. You could do walk-the-dog, cat-in-the cradle on the front porch of the store. Tubes of colored sugar water that were whistles once you had drunk all the liquid, once you had carefully nibbled out the liquid, not drawing too hard, or the walls would collapse.

Gliders, balsa wood gliders. Pieces you slipped together carefully. Ten cents. Sometimes one of the older boys would buy a folding-wing glider, really expensive, the kind you launched with a rubber band sling, high high up, where at the top the wings would snap open, and the plane would fly so far you might not find it, or it would land high up in a tree, and they'd throw rocks at it to get it down. Sometimes this would destroy the plane.

Judith thought about her domestic docket. Some men destroyed love to get it back, to get the airplane down. "We had to bomb the hamlet to save it." A boy would throw a rock at his plane, he had a plan, but his plan broke the wing, or crushed the body. And there would be the plane, spiraling down, gut shot, bumping branches as it fell, ruined. Might get taken home, get taped up, might not. Wouldn't fly right again, anyway, being too heavy from the tape and out of line. Dora Hensley. William.

CHAPTER
TWENTY-THREE

"Harry, she does this thing when she meets people. She makes them feel good. I don't know how she does it. It's like she just smiles all over them, and they know she likes them, that she's paying attention to them."

"Yeah, she did that with the clients too. I called it bathing-with-light. She made the clients glow." He looked wistful. "She was a real binder. I was a finder. God, we were a team."

"She'd be a killer in retail," Connor said. "If she worked at the gallery, we could hang a new show every week."

"Well, she won't. It's something about ethics. Judges can't do that. You know, be normal." Harry looked at Connor. "You guys getting serious? You and Judith? You going to get married?"

"Um . . .," said Connor.

"Marriage is heavy stuff. And I wasn't cut out for it. But you are, Connor. I think. Judith, I don't know."

"Right now, I think we'll just go fishing. She's never been to the cabin."

"The cabin. She'll like that. Show her my woodpile."

"I will."

"I got married," Harry said, "just to change things. You know, shuffle the deck. Invert the file. Not a good reason. But it worked out OK. I mean, it didn't work out OK, we got divorced and all that. But we get along now, Susan and me, and we've got Megan."

Connor knew that Susan was successful as a painter, not easy to do in Tennessee. She often talked to Connor about her work, and sometimes, after Dana had gotten sick, about other things too.

"Megan's a great kid, Harry."

"Yeah, she is. And she really likes you, Connor. You've even made her like fishing. Someone in my gene pool. I can't believe it."

"Harry, I taught her to fish. She liked it on her own."

"Whatever. Stupid sport." Connor didn't take the bait. Instead, he pictured Megan, long-legged in the bow of the Lund, or paddling the square-stern Grumman in the evenings, fishing alone.

"She really likes Martin," Harry said.

"He likes her, too."

Connor and Harry had been to the cabin twice with the two children. Megan was fifteen now. Martin was twenty.

"You think they'll get married?" Harry asked.

"Martin and Megan?"

"Yeah."

"God, no, Harry. Then you and I would be related. They'd never do that to us."

"No," said Harry, "I guess not. But if they did, we'd have to respect each other, be polite. Behave at the wedding." He grinned. "But you and Judith, that'd be OK."

"You sure are on the marriage thing today."

"Hey, I'm a psychologist. I deal in relationship issues. I think about these things. The complexity of humanity, the human comedy." There was a long pause in which Harry stared into space. Then he said, "I've been trying to figure out why I really did marry Susan. I mean, the books say it was creative and courageous for me to marry someone so different. An artist, a painter of watercolors. Now, though, she's doing mostly oils. Sells her stuff through a dealer in New York."

"I know."

"When I married Susan, I am supposed to have been looking for something I intuitively knew I needed. But I don't have a clue what it was."

"Regular sex."

"Well, yes. And maybe that's all it was. I'm standing there by life's highway, stick out my thumb, and get a fast bumpy ride in a sexy eighteen-wheeler? That's it? That's all?"

"Maybe."

"But, I mean, isn't marriage supposed to be more than just bouncing up and down on the highway, leaking seminal fluids?"

"Yes, Harry, it is, " said Connor.

CHAPTER
TWENTY-FOUR

Richard's trial management conference had gone badly. He didn't like this judge. She had sneered at him at one point, looking down her long nose, "Well, Professor Smith," she had said, oh-so-condescendingly, as if Richard just might be retarded, "your pension with the university is marital property subject to division, just as is your wife's IRA. Both were acquired during the marriage."

Gloria had twenty-six hundred in an IRA. Which I funded, for Christ's sake. I've got over a hundred thousand in my university 401k. I mean, am I hearing this?

His lawyer hadn't made a peep. Hadn't said, "Your Honor, Mrs. Smith hasn't worked to amount to anything. They have no children. It was her choice to stay home, to do volunteer work. That's why she has no pension, no real savings. She's a grasshopper. She fiddles all day, finds excuses not to work, she's a blight on society, a self-pitying worthless parasite." His lawyer hadn't said squat. His lawyer was a pussy. He had sat there next to Richard, taking notes. Notes, for God's sake. Gloria had smirked at Richard.

Her lawyer had stood up, oh, yes, Gloria's lawyer could talk. Had said, "Your Honor," emphasizing the 'Honor' part, drawing it out, sucking up, one cunt to another, "We intend to pursue more than equitable distribution at trial. We will show marital fault so egregious and so disparate as to justify permanent spousal support to Mrs. Smith. And to do equity, Mrs. Smith needs the award of the husband's entire pension to her."

Richard had seen black. He had pushed his chair back from the table, aghast. "Professor Smith is," she had gone on, "in the prime of his career. He has tenure, a handsome salary. He has published two books, and will write who knows how many more? He has a bright, secure future. My client, on the other hand," and she had looked pityingly down at Gloria, who sniveled, "has given him the best of her productive years, has worked little, due to no fault of her own, and deserves to be supported by this man for the rest of her life."

Richard had stood up. His pussy lawyer had tugged on his sleeve, pulled him back down. There was a black roaring in his head. Richard hadn't heard anything else.

Driving back to the house, a three-bedroom Victorian on tree-lined College Street, appropriate for an associate professor of Germanic Languages and Literatures, Richard turned over in his mind how to get rid of this judge, who was clearly biased, clearly not grounded in reality. Wasn't there something about recusal? A Middle English word, probably, from Middle French "recuser," Richard thought, about a judge withdrawing if you could show conflict of interest, or malice, or something? This judge was dripping malice. Oozing it. She would have to go.

He would ask his lawyer. No, he would ask a different lawyer. He was going to fire his present lawyer, the jellyfish, the pussy sleeve-puller.

At least Gloria wouldn't get any more furniture. No more oriental rugs. The jellyfish said that was a closed chapter. Because he and Gloria had made a list and signed it. The jellyfish said that was binding. Gloria had wanted the whale rug, but it wasn't on the list. Richard had thought, let her have it, maybe it'll get dear old dad out of my head.

The last meeting with Gloria at the house had been classic. It had started with a phone call: "Richard, it's Gloria."

"I can tell."

She always called him Richard on the phone. "Is this a good time to divide the kitchen things?"

They had spent five sessions dividing everything else, Gloria agonizing over each decision. They had left the kitchen for last.

"I guess so," he had said. "I've got some empty boxes. Come on over." She was out of his house at that point, renting somewhere, looking for a condominium, she said. They started in on the kitchen stuff. There was little of value except for a small color TV mounted under the kitchen cabinets, and the stainless tableware.

She wanted to divide the stainless in half. Richard referred to that proposal as a "nadir of stupidity." That hadn't helped the atmosphere. "So we can each go out and buy some more matching stainless steel to make a whole set? If we are lucky enough to find it? I don't think so."

"OK," she had said, "the TV is valuable, so is the stainless. Let's leave those two things for last." Fine, he had said. He was letting her set the rules. He watched her open a box of toothpicks, divide it in half. He didn't say anything.

They got together groups of things, put each group on the kitchen counter, chose single things out of the group alternately. He took the things she picked and put them in a box. He put the box by the kitchen door. She would linger over every choice. It was brain surgery. After a time, there were lots of boxes by the kitchen door. Only the TV and the stainless were left. She had had the last choice in the last group.

"So," he said, "I pick either the stainless or the TV, and we're done." He knew it wouldn't be that simple. She would try to con him. "Do you see anything else?"

"That's not fair! Just because I got the last pick in the last batch doesn't mean that you get the first choice now, the first choice of the only two valuable things."

"We've been alternating choices for two hours now."

"It's not fair."

"I don't care what we do," he said. "Let's just get this over. How about we flip a coin? Whoever wins gets first choice."

"That's not fair."

"Fine. You figure it out. What do you want to do?"

"Oh, all right," she said. "Flip a coin."

He got one out of his pocket, a quarter. "Do you want heads or tails?" he asked.

"Heads," she said. "Wait. I don't know. Tails." Richard started the toss. "No, heads," she said.

He flipped it up and let it land on the floor. It was tails. "I'll take the stainless," he said.

"That's not fair. It's worth more than the TV."

CHAPTER
TWENTY-FIVE

But that hadn't been the end of it. She still wanted to come back to the house, get inside, get inside his mind. She called him again.

"Richard, it's Gloria."

"I can tell."

"Ha ha. You said that last time."

"I did, yes." He paused, "What I say is uninteresting. Don't you remember? You told me that lots of times."

"I remember all too well. I was just wondering when we could get together to divide up the pictures."

"We already did that." Gloria had been out of the house four months.

"What do you mean? I don't have anything! You promised we would divide up the pictures! Two huge boxes in the basement!" She was shouting. "You've got everything! I would have stayed there and done it, but you said don't worry, we'll do it later."

She doesn't want to remember the real way she had left the house after Richard had in fact given her the not-on-the-list carpet, her yellow slit eyes gleaming, four feet splayed, balancing, gripping the carpet, her tail twitching back and forth, showing her vulva, the joy of possession.

"Oh," Richard said. "You mean the photographs."

"Of course I mean the photographs. What do you think I meant?"

"Well," he said. "Fine." He thought she had meant the framed prints on the walls, that she wanted to have another shot at those. How do I get out of this, he thought, having her over here again? "OK. But we're not *getting together* to do anything." Silence. "I'll just bring it all to you, both boxes. You can have everything."

"That's not fair! There's pictures in there you want, pictures of your family, I mean I hope you want them, but sometimes I wonder. Your mother, your grandmother."

"Look, you can send me back anything you think is mine. Or keep it. I don't care."

"Why do you hate me so much? What have I ever done to you?"

"Gloria, I have neither the time nor the interest to tell you."

"Well, I can see you're in a bad mood. This isn't getting us anywhere. I'll talk to you some time when you are in a decent mood."

"This is as decent as it gets," he said. "That's why we're getting divorced. Because I am unkind, because I have no honor, because I never think about anyone but myself." This didn't help. Gloria never understood sarcasm.

His father had been right about one thing. He had never liked Gloria, had responded most laconically when Richard and Gloria had gone to tell him they were going to be married.

"Shit," he had said. His father had always been a man of few words. This time he had forecast ten years of marriage in one Anglo-Saxon syllable.

"No, Daddy," Richard had told his father, "It'll be good. You'll see." The Goat Woman had nodded her head up and down.

"Shit," his father had said again.

This father was the same man who had no great relationship with his own wife, so what did he know? This was the man who had thrown Mahalia Jackson off the back porch, and it disqualified him, Richard thought, from opining on his son's marriage.

84

"So," he had said to ten-year-old Richard, "your Mother is bitching about my music? I can fix that."

And picking up the pink portable turntable, the RCA self-contained twenty-pound stereo console, tubes and wires and wooden cabinet, no transistors, no chips, no molded plastic, he had shouldered his way through the screen door, hipping the latch down, arms full of stereo, no hand available for the latch, in haste to do the deed, the brilliant symbolic launching. Stepping out onto the faux ante bellum tiled porch, columns soaring up into darkness, the noise of cicadas, his thigh to the rail, off he launched her, Mahalia, still rotating on the turntable as she fell and fell in darkness, crashing onto the lawn a full twenty feet below, a magnificent noise. No more "Deep River."

Judith was excited about the fishing trip. "I was wondering when I'd get to see the cabin."

"I hope you'll like it."

"I will. What's not to like? You'll be there."

"Well, it's pretty primitive. There is an outhouse."

"I love outhouses. I'm having Pridden put one in at my new place."

Connor laughed, and walked over to where she was sitting, put his arms around her. "Jude, we will have a good time. I know it. How about flying up July 2 for a couple of weeks? You'll really settle in, become a part of the North Woods."

"I'll talk to Norton about reassigning my docket. Connor, you honor me by taking me. You know that, don't you? To a place that means so much to you? A place with so many memories?"

CHAPTER
TWENTY-SIX

The creepy guy didn't miss a lecture. Every Monday, Wednesday, and Friday he took the same seat in the back. This Friday when Richard reached the podium, he found a note. In a very neat hand it said, *"Professor Smith: Please pardon this interruption. I need to see you after the lecture today. It is a matter of very great mutual importance. I'm in the back row, wearing a blue windbreaker. Thank you. David Branstetter."*

Richard looked up from the lectern across the crowd, found the blue windbreaker, looked into the man's face. Branstetter nodded seriously. 'Very great mutual importance.' I bet, thought Richard. A townie wanna-be intellectual. He opened his notes and began.

"The problems of presenting Rainer Maria Rilke in translation are manifold. To begin with, his meter is simple and direct. The lines are short. A translator has little room to move about, and is forced to choose all too often between preserving sense and preserving meter. A Hobson's choice."

"Hobson's choice," wrote four students, doubtfully. Who was this Hobson? Was he on the reading list?

"If the translator chooses to preserve meter, sometimes the word choice will do violence to Rilke's subtleties. And he is very subtle." Branstetter was gazing at Richard raptly.

"He was raised by his mother, as you know. A fine woman. A sheltered boy, sickly. Often terrified of his father. And despite all this he became the strongest visionary lyricist of pre-World War Europe." Branstetter was writing now. "That's pre-World War One, for those of you too young to remember." That drew some chuckles. Richard was hitting his stride.

"I want to present to you his 'Panther' today, both in translation and in the original German to show you what I mean. Take the opening lines—

Sein Blick ist vom Vorübergehn der Stäbe
so müd geworden, dass er nichts mehr hält.

For those of you who can follow German, so much the better. For those of you who can't, I know this is just sound, but listen to that sound. Feel it. It is lilting, mellifluous, simple. It must be preserved, if possible, for the feel of the poem.

"*Sein Blick* is, of course, the panther's gaze, in the first instance. But it is also his view, what he sees, his landscape. Or, arguably perhaps, also his countenance, his mien. What is the translator to do?"

Norton saw no problem in Judith being gone the first half of July. "If need be," he said, "I'll cover your cases myself. You've been through a lot. I don't want you to burn out."

Judith was grateful, and told Norton so. He made tut-tut noises.

"Judge Norton, there's another thing. One of my cases, Professor Richard Smith from CTSU. German Department. We had a trial management conference last week and, well, he acted very strangely. Muttered, stood up at one point, started talking. Looked furious. Thornton Tyler had to pull on his coat sleeve to get him to sit down."

"These professor types, these people, they can be high strung. It's a divorce?"

"Yes. No kids. Pretty significant assets, mostly liquid. Don't own their home, lease a big place on College Street. So we don't need to do an appraisal. Patty Palermo says she's going to hammer relative fault, go for permanent alimony. It could get nasty."

"Any affairs?"

"I don't know."

"Do you need extra security? When next you have the Smith case, you can have Bill." Bill was Judge Norton's superannuated bailiff. His strong suit was somnolence. "Or, we could get one of the young fellows from Cartwright's court."

"No, I'll be all right with Tommy. He's careful, and alert. Thank you for assigning him to me." Judith paused, and then said it anyway. "I was thinking more of what goes on outside the courthouse."

Norton's eyes went wide. "You don't think the professor is the person who shot into your house, do you? A university professor?"

"I know it sounds crazy. But if you had seen his look . . . I don't know. The case didn't get really bad until last week. In court at least. I don't know how long he's been angry." She looked out Norton's window to the river. "I wish you had seen him." Judge Norton had the best view in the building. Seniority is OK, Judith thought. I would like being the Presiding Judge. She went on, "If it's a long-festering wound, maybe I'm a catalyst. The one who tweaks the proud flesh."

"I take your point, Judge. Be careful. We don't want to lose you. And we will have extra security here in the courthouse. You have an upcoming motion day, I think, for *Smith v. Smith*, on May 10th?."

"Yes."

"About what?"

"Professor Smith has a new lawyer, William Terance Bailey. He wants some discovery that Palermo is fighting, so I've got a motion to compel. Looks like Bailey and Professor Smith are going to put up a fight. And Palermo is saber-rattling. She says she wants the good professor to have an involuntary mental examination."

"Let me leave you," Richard said to the class, "with this final thought from Rilke's *Duino Elegies*:

> *Denn das Schöne ist nichts*
> *als des Schrecklichen Anfang, den wir noch grade ertragen,*
> *und wir bewundern es so, weil es gelassen verschmäht,*
> *uns zu zerstören.*

In rough translation, it means

> *For that which is beautiful is nothing*
> *but the beginning of horror, which we can barely endure,*
> *and we admire it so, because it calmly declines*
> *to destroy us.*

"So, beauty as the beginning of horror. Is this the medieval 'memento mori,' which we have seen several times this semester already? That is to say, in the very midst of life lurks the seed of death? Even as we thrive, we decline? Or is this a vision of a superior, condescending evil which bides its time, waiting to do us in? I suggest to you that the latter was Rilke's opinion." Richard looked at his watch on the lecture podium. "On that happy thought, we will end today." The bell in University Hall began to chime. Perfect again, he thought.

Richard folded up his notes, watching Katherine Kelty's loose-limbed splendor recede up the aisle. He liked her blue skirt better. It was shorter. He put his small Manesse Verlag edition of the elegies and sonnets into his sport coat. Gloria certainly was the beginning of horror, Rilke got that right. He looked over to Branstetter. The man was rising, coming forward. Richard walked to the end of the stage, came down the four steps, and extended his hand. The affable state employee. "Richard Smith."

Branstetter took his hand. "Professor. I am David Branstetter. As you know from my note."

"Yes. What does this seem to be about?"

"Professor, first, let me say your Rilke today was brilliant. Your phrases. My notebook is full. I can't wait to transcribe my scribblings." He did seem genuinely excited. "But, Professor . . ."

"Yes?"

"It is portentous, I find it so anyway, that today you presented Rilke's panther-in-a-cage. Because that is our mutual situation, you and I. It describes the two of us. We are both trapped in cages, like the panther, pacing back and forth, looking for a way out. Powerful men, imprisoned artificially."

"I don't follow you."

"Judge Merchant. Judge Judith Merchant."

CHAPTER
TWENTY-SEVEN

Connor and Judith were tying fishing knots. She was having no problems. They sat in high-backed stools at his kitchen counter, short lengths of clothesline cord and two spools of eight-pound monofilament before them. The dishwasher purred, cleaning up the remains of broiled salmon with orange slices. Connor felt expansive.

"'Life is good, Edna'," he said. Judith lifted her eyebrows.

"What are you talking about?"

"Thomas McGuane. A line from Thomas McGuane's *Bushwhacked Piano*. I always think of it when I'm full of salmon."

"Connor, you keep coming up with these surprises. I didn't know you read fiction."

"I'm not just visual, Milady. I am also literate, and tactile, a veritable courtier."

"And very full of salmon. Or something."

"Ah," said Connor, feigning offense. "You sniff. You sniff at me, I perceive?"

"I sniff."

"You sniff. But do you also bite your thumb?"

"I do bite my thumb, sir."

"But do you bite your thumb at me, sir?"

She paused, looked warily around for Capulet backup, "Sir, I bite my thumb. But not at you, sir."

They laughed. Connor had to get up, wipe his eyes. He was still giggling when he came back. "That was a close call. Naked steel, daggers, right here in the kitchen."

"Poignards and monofilament."

"Speaking of which, you can still tie only two knots."

"Because you've only shown me two. And they're easy."

"They are not easy. The Palomar and the Improved Clinch are not easy."

"They are if you sew. And do cross-stitch."

"Do you bite your thumb at me?"

"No. But I do tie your fishing knots. Without difficulty. All you have taught me."

"Well, then, to put you in your place, we will now do the Helical Hell-Bender Stop-Slip knot."

"Sounds hard."

"It is hard."

"What's it for?"

"Airplane propellers. You don't need it often, but when you have to put one back on a plane, there's no substitute."

Richard thought Branstetter could be useful. He knew a lot about computers, email, and firewalls. They had gone out for coffee after the Rilke lecture. The man was intense, an anti-Semite, and boring.

"Judith is a Jewish name, of course. And people at the courthouse, I know people at the courthouse, they say her friends call her 'Jude.' A nickname. 'Jude.' He pronounced it the German way: Yooduh.

"You don't mean it." Richard was trying to carry his end of the conversational log.

"Oh, yes. And 'Jude' simply means 'Jew.' As you know, of course, know very well."

"Yes," Richard said.

They smiled at each other.

They met two more times after lectures. Richard had advanced
to calling Branstetter David. Branstetter had a lot of skills. He was
a computer wizard. He told Richard his job at Omega Computing
had to do particularly with the building of and, if need be, he said
slyly, the bypassing of security firewalls.

He suggested tentatively that he could just possibly, who knew?
perhaps get into the courthouse email accounts, find something
that could help Richard. Richard didn't say anything. He smiled
approvingly at him. Branstetter had glowed.

Richard told him what he knew about recusals, about the
circumstances in which judges had to withdraw from cases.
Branstetter was excited. Said he had to get that kike off his case,
thought he could find something. Said that his son would be ruined
if he didn't get custody of him.

"PAS is well known now. Jeanie won't get away with it. There
are these websites I have found . . ."

"What is 'PAS'?" Richard asked.

"Parental alienation syndrome. The mother alienates the child
from the father. Jeanie drives a wedge between me and Joey, makes
him hate me. Oh, it's poison. It demands extreme antidotes."

"I see."

"Extreme antidotes." Branstetter's eyes were narrow and dark.

"Like what?"

"Well, for example," he drew his chair closer to the café table,
leaned forward, "you read in the paper a while back about how that
Hebe's house got shot full of holes? Judge Merchant's house?"

"Yes."

"I did it."

"You don't say." Richard smiled at David. "Oh, David, you did
that?" Branstetter was going to be very useful indeed.

CHAPTER
TWENTY-EIGHT

To: mountkatahdin12345@hotmail.com
From: hmatherpi@yahoo.com
May 6, 6:07 AM

Jude—I like your new email address. Very Yankee. Very Radcliffe.

It's great you're going to the cabin. You'll like it. Make sure to see my woodpile. Megan says have fun, take some silk long johns. See you tonight? Harry

Richard was in fifth grade again. The new kid. His parents had just moved to the big house with the white columns. All the other children knew each other. He was the new one. He was all alone in his desk in a classroom of children. He had no pants on.

The class was doing long division. All the other children knew about long division. They had had it last year in fourth grade. He had never heard of it. He was ashamed. He was snuffling in his desk. They didn't know he didn't have any pants on, not yet. That would come later. He had brought home his report card yesterday, four A's and a C-plus in arithmetic. "A Cee-pluss in A-rith-muhh-tick!!" his father had roared, using the scungilli voice.

Judith was fixing supper for Connor and Harry at the condo. Harry had brought oysters.

"You guys think I'm stodgy, but see? I bring oysters. You were expecting maybe gruel. But I go to Kroger, see oysters, think 'Yes!' and I seize the moment. Very spontaneous. Very loving. They had oysters at Woodstock, I think."

"Harry missed the drug generation," Judith said. "But he likes to pretend."

After supper, they sat in the living room, which Judith had tried unsuccessfully to make look like her library at the farmhouse. A small wall of books, her rocker, the leather chair. Harry was cradling his espresso. Judith was drinking tea.

"So anyway," said Connor, "it was my fourth or fifth fishing trip with John Harcourt. He taught me to fish, and I'm getting pretty good at it."

"Harcourt taught you to fish?"

"Yes," said Connor. "Years ago."

"I know John Harcourt," Harry said. "Fine attorney. Lives in Cookeville, right?"

"Right."

"I thought all he did for fun was buy baseball cards, memorabilia, all that Yankees stuff they sell on TV," Harry said. "How about that? Harcourt is a fisherman."

"Well, anyway," Connor said, "it's just the two of us. On Rawak Lake. I'm going out by myself mornings while Harcourt's sleeping. This particular morning I'm throwing Fat Raps about half a mile from the cabin. I see a small float plane fly over. Sounds like it lands about a mile off. I don't think about it any more.

"In a little while . . ." Connor stopped, looked at Harry.

"You know, Harry, it really is beautiful in the early morning . . . the mist . . ." He stopped again. "I wish you liked fishing."

"I wish you liked golf."

"So," Connor continued, "then I hear and see a tiny little boat putt-putting toward me, an inflatable, and I think, what the hell? A dumpy little man in the back."

"Rumplestiltskin?"

"If only. Game & Fish. A guy from Ontario Natural Resources. Shows me his badge, asks me what I'm catching. I say bass. I'm catching bass and putting them back I say. No size, I say. He wants to see my license. Then he asks where I'm staying. I tell him at the camp on Grey Island. Any muskies? he asks. I say, we had some action yesterday, not much."

"Then," Connor said, "he asks do we have any muskies back at camp? I don't know what to say. I say, 'John does.' Because it was true. So, the Natural Resources guy says, let's go to camp, you lead me there. I say, yes, sir, thinking Harcourt's going to kill me, he's absolutely going to kill me, my buddy, my buddy who taught me how to fish is going to kill me. I need to go home now. I need to jump out of this boat and run screaming across the muskeg, get eaten by caribou, anything will be better than what is coming.

"See," Connor said, "I know the muskies Harcourt has on the stringer are not legal size. He was going to release them when he got some bigger fish. If he got some bigger fish. But we're out of bratwurst, and we're thinking Mother Hubbard's cupboard, so Harcourt gets some insurance on a stringer. Wait and see what tomorrow brings. But what I don't know, and Harcourt doesn't know either, is that muskies are not even in season yet on Rawak, not for two more days. Doesn't matter what size they are."

"Uh-oh," said Harry.

"So we get back to camp. Harcourt is up, thank goodness, must have heard the boats coming. Looks sleepy. He gets his license out, hands it to the Natural Resources guy. 'Understand you have some muskies,' the guy says. "Yes, I do," says Harcourt, very upfront. I'm going to turn them loose."

"Yes, you are, Mr. Harcourt,' says the Natural Resources guy. "Show me the fish." John takes him to the edge of the dock, shows him where the stringer is tied. The man kneels down, pulls the fish toward him, slips them off the stringer, gets out his citation pad.

"Mr. Harcourt," he says, "your hearing will be on the twenty second of July. If you do not wish, or do not choose, to appear in person, you may pay your fine at this address. Three hundred dollars Canadian." He tears off the slip and gives it to John. He's red in the face. "These fish are undersize and out of season. I could confiscate all your fishing gear."

"Yes, sir," says John, "I understand. I didn't know. I'm sorry."

"It's people like you who ruin fishing for everyone else," the man says. Then he gets in his boat and leaves.

"When he's gone, I tell John how sorry I am, that I didn't volunteer anything, that I knew the fish were too little, but he asked me a direct question and I couldn't lie.

"No," says John, "you did the right thing. I shouldn't have kept those little fuckers. I knew it was risky."

"I'll pay the fine."

"You will not."

So, we fish all that day, and come in late. We're drinking a beer, looking out at the lake, thinking it's time to clean our little bass, the pitiful ones we do have, and what do we see? Those two muskies have come back to us. They're swimming around, turning on their sides, bumping into the dock.

Harcourt looks at the fish, looks at me, says, "Connor, those fish are injured. The stringer hurt them. They're going to die."

"Yes," I say.

"So," he says, "since they're going to die anyway, and since there's about seven pounds of meat there, dressed out, I make it about thirty-nine dollars a pound, American."

"Yes," I say.

"So," he says, "let's eat." He gets the dip net. I dip them out of the water onto the dock. We pit them, clean them fast, throw the carcasses in the water. We have a great supper. Harcourt pays the fine, won't let me pay even half, and that's the whole story.

"I'm going to rag his ass the next time I see him," Harry said. "John Harcourt, ecological predator."

CHAPTER
TWENTY-NINE

"You know what I miss?" Harry said, "about not practicing law? I miss the war stories. Like that fishing story. But that's all I miss."

Connor looked at him. "What are war stories?"

"Oh," said Judith, "that's just what lawyers call funny things that happened on the job."

"Like the time," Harry said, "I'm cross-examining this lady. She can't answer a question with anything less than a paragraph. And she's got this terrible case of up-speak. You know, everything turns into a question?" Harry mimicked it, his voice rising at the end of each phrase.

"So after about ten minutes of this, I'm getting tired of it. I ask her, I ask, 'Mrs. Thornton, does the sun rise in the east?' Silence. Nobody objects. The jury is staring at me. Magic Beans is staring at me.

"And she starts right in: 'Does the sun rise in the east??? You're asking me, does the sun rise in the east??? Well, I don't know what you mean by that??? I mean, I do know what you mean, but I get up in the morning, see, and I ask myself, I look out my window, and what do I see??? I see the sun??? Sometimes I do, and sometimes I don't. I mean, it's cloudy sometimes??? And when it is cloudy, well, I wonder is the sun up or is it not??? I can't tell. And which way does my house face, anyway??? I don't know. Do you know??? I don't.'"

Connor and Judith were laughing. Harry was pleased. He said, "So, guys, I get up every day, happy to go to my modest P.I. office, soon to be my Ph.D. in psychology office, happy to drive by Kroger on the way, scope out the oysters, buy some bagels, and not go to the courthouse. But I do miss the war stories."

"Well, I can help," said Judith. "I can keep you in war stories. Last week I got a letter from a man who's at Northeast Correctional Center. His wife wants a divorce, he's been served with papers, and he doesn't think he needs to come for the hearing. So he writes me. Of course the warden wouldn't bring him anyway, but he doesn't know that."

She got up and went to her desk, came back with a folder. "I had my clerk transcribe the letter so it's easier to read." She handed it to Connor. "Would you read this out loud, my dear? It's a little raw."

Connor looked at the envelope. There was a red-stamped legend on the back:

> *Tennessee Department of Correction has*
> *neither censored nor inspected contents.*
> *Warden's Office*
> *N.E.C.C.*
> *P.O. Box 5000*
> *Mountain City, TN 37583*

"Well, the contents are officially uncensored, says so right here. I guess we've been warned."

Someone had written slant-wise across the front and back of the envelope, "LEAGAL MAIL." Connor looked at the handwritten lines marching across blue-lined notebook paper. They weren't that hard to read. He picked up the clean transcription and read aloud:

Dear Judge
My name is Anthony Macon
I am at the State Pen in Mountain City Ten.
I just want to write to say I
Don't Give a damn about my wife Getting
the Divorce So Give it to here!
I don't need to Be ther Because:
Just don't Give a Big Shit
what the hell you all do!
tell my wife Cherry to Kiss my
ass and Go to hell
I have 30 years to do and I
don't need A Bitch to Cry on my
Shoulder.
think you Judge Just
Please leave me the hell a long
and let me do my time
in Peace.
I don't need to Be there for here
to Get a Divorce So please Give it
to here as Soon you can.
She is a Bitch and She always will Be
I don't need here in my life I don't
need here are God are Know one I
have to do this time a long I was
the one that fuck up.

Anthony Macon

PS
think You Judge mrs Judith Merchant
for all the help You Give to me
and God Bless You Mam

"We shouldn't laugh," said Judith, "but . . ."

"No, we shouldn't," said Connor. "Here's this man, he's got thirty years to do, and he's writing you a respectful letter, a little crude here and there, but respectful of the court, and at the end he thanks you and begs God's blessing upon you. I'm impressed." He snorted. "Oh, it's a scream. I'm so glad I saw this." He wiped his eyes, 'Just don't give a Big Shit,' he read.

"'I was the one that fuck up,'" said Harry.

Motion day was coming up, May 10th. Richard had circled it on his calendar. He had exams to give on May 20 and 22, and then he would be off for the summer. Well, he'd be off once he got the grades turned in. It wasn't going to be much of a summer. The divorce trial had been set for October 3d.

William Terance Bailey, his new lawyer, said they had a lot of work to do. The jellyfish had sounded relieved Richard had a new attorney, and said he would "send the file right over to new counsel." No, he had said, there was nothing Professor Smith owed him. It had been a pleasure to represent him. And so forth. All mealy-mouthed pap.

CHAPTER
THIRTY

To: <u>dbranstetter@aol.com</u>
From: <u>tkp1953@charter.net</u>
May 7, 10:49 AM

Your right about the jews. There are jews in my state too. I live in Nevada, in Reno. It's a good place, except for the jews. Jews run the casinos here. Guess you must be in Tennessee huh? I mean, the woman governor you've got and all. Sorry about your kid. I do not have kids. Sorry, I really am. good luck to you and all the fathers getting screwed.

Tom in Reno

Harry and Judith were still trading war stories. Connor was thinking about fishing in Florida, in the Thousand Islands. He thought how men enjoyed fishing, even just fishing for baitfish, anchoring their boats on the grass flats. The boats would be in a line, close to each other, mesh bags of frozen chum hung into the warm ocean, releasing tiny morsels of chopped fish and oils, drawing clouds of little fish. The men stood in the sterns, using two-pound mono and little Christmas-treed hooks, fingernail-sized pieces of mullet on each hook.

Easy conversation between the boats. Ray had had his hip replaced, still lived in Miami. Pinfish seventy-five cents each at the marina. I'm getting rich, look at me, I may do this for a living. I got so many now I could retire, go to Jamaica.

The little pinfish were for snook. Serious fish. Put pinfish in the live-well through tide turn, and then move to your secret snook hole. Put out two anchors, set up to fish downstream. The largest pinfish goes on a forty-pound shock leader to a barrel swivel, a two-ounce slip sinker above the swivel. Put the whole thing on the bottom and wait. When he hits, keep him out of the mangroves and the oyster shells.

Connor remembered a fisherman in Saskatchewan at the end of a cold, rainy day. It was time, they both agreed, for a hot shower, a drink, a fire in the stove, "And," the man had said to Connor with relish, "time to play tackle box."

Connor had known immediately what he meant, though he had never heard it said before. He knew the activity well, the reordering of the multicolored arsenal. Time to put all the shallow divers in the left part of the upper tray, the crawdads on the right side, the Rattletraps to a less choice location. Time to sort the plastic grubs by color and length. Time to be anal.

William Terrance Bailey, Richard's new lawyer, looked at him intently. "Oh, yes, Professor Smith, it is entirely possible, let me change that, it is *theoretically* possible, that Judge Merchant could award a disproportionate share of the marital estate to Mrs. Smith. Equitable distribution is the guiding principle, and in Tennessee it has eleven statutory subheads. Many people think 'equitable' means 'equal' distribution, but it does not. That is only the starting point of a court's consideration.

"Equitable," Bailey continued, "means 'fair,' as you know. Fair distribution is what Judge Merchant, what any judge, must do in a divorce action. This is where it gets interesting. Judge Merchant is a new judge. I doubt she has ever had a case like yours. She certainly didn't in private practice. Mather & Merchant didn't do domestic work. They referred it all out. A lot of it to me, in fact."

"That means the judge must have a high regard for you."

"Well, it's good of you to say so. Let me just say no lawyer would ever place a client with someone he or she did not trust."

This was a good development, Richard thought. He hadn't known about Bailey's Mather & Merchant connection. Very good.

CHAPTER
THIRTY-ONE

Steve Alvarez in the Romance Languages Department had recommended Bill Bailey to Richard. "He ees what you call a 'corker,' Ricardo. He will clean her plow, the plow of your wife, you will see. Oh, yes." Alvarez liked American idioms.

"Women don't have plows, Esteban. Men have plows. Women have furrows."

"Furrows." He looked troubled. "Furrows . . . it is of the field . . . but of course, I see. How silly of me. He will clean her furrow, Ricardo, you will see. Clean her furrow. As clean as a whistle. *Muchas gracias*, for telling me this correct thing. I will not forget how to say this thing."

"So, when Palermo argues for more than half my pension, she won't get anywhere?"

"Hard to say. It's an uphill climb to get more than half. Judges like to stay at half. And fault won't be a factor, marital fault, in dividing the marital estate. The legislature has prohibited that, thank goodness."

"Thank goodness, indeed."

"Yes, but you and I do need to discuss marital fault, because fault can be a factor in deciding whether there is to be alimony. Alimony is the old word. The more current term is 'spousal support.'"

"So, fault is not a factor in dividing up the marital holdings, you say, but it can be a part of an alimony decision?"

"Yes."

"This is bad news."

"Let me be the judge of that. There is always marital fault on both sides. Maybe we can win the fault battle." Richard didn't think so. "And marital fault is usually boring. Judges don't like hearing about it. They're realistic, they know that most marriages have some rough spots. The fault has to be more than rudeness, the quotidian human indignities . . ."

"Like an affair?"

"Perhaps. It depends on how long ago. How many times. How the wife responded to it when she learned of the indiscretion. How you, if it was you, acted afterwards. You are telling me you had an affair?"

"Yes."

Bailey started taking notes. "Tell me about it."

"Well," said Richard, "it wasn't just *an* affair. There were several. Well . . ., there were many." He liked Bailey. 'Quotidian human indignities' was good. He wanted Bailey to know he was manly. "But only two she knows about. I think."

"You will be deposed."

"Do I have to tell the truth?"

"Yes." There was a silence. "And if I am certain, Professor Smith, I emphasize *certain*, that you are not being truthful, I must disclose the falsehood, or withdraw from your representation."

"I see." Richard didn't like this. Not at all. He had to be careful with Bailey, then. "Well, I can't remember very much really. It was a long time ago. In Iowa."

"Tell me about the two affairs she knows about."

"They were students."

"Not good."

"No. But grad students."

"Somewhat better." Bailey looked at the clock between them. "This could take a while," he said. " I think that is enough of marital fault for now. It is what it is, and we will return to it."

He took out a new legal pad. "Far more important to the question of spousal support, and I do think, Professor, that alimony is going to be the battleground in your litigation, far more important than fault is the parties' relative stations in life, their relative abilities to earn, the employability of the *potential* recipient of alimony. I emphasize: 'potential' recipient. Tell me about Gloria's work record."

The simple fact was that Gloria had had three jobs and failed at all of them. She had talents, but there weren't many jobs a professor's wife could do lying on her back.

"She worked in office jobs, the public sector, nine-to-five. Easy jobs. Couldn't keep them."

"Again, not good. But . . .," Bailey twirled his pen. It was monogrammed, Richard saw, WTB, ". . . if she is not actually productive, now, then we want her to be a paragon of possibility. Someone with untapped potential."

Richard saw where Bailey was headed. "She's great with numbers." But her favorite one is sixty-nine, Richard thought. "She looks good in public." And good in private, too, yes. Very good privates. "She presents well." And forcibly, he thought, she presents rhythmically, with sounds. "She likes accounting."

"Well, then," said Bailey. "Accounting. Let me just throw something out for consideration, just brainstorming here, just for discussion, the idea of rehabilitative alimony. Some training . . . brief, it would come to a definite end in a specified number of months. Training to enhance her earning power."

"Like to be a C.P.A.?"

"It's a possibility."

CHAPTER
THIRTY-TWO

Richard was in the dream again. He was in Europe, leaving Munich for Nuremberg. Trying to. But this was also his stable dream, he knew that, just another version of it.

His hotel room was the stable, no oxen, no guano this time, no swallows. He was trapped in a skein of impossible pre-departure tasks. He would never get them all done. The suitcase wouldn't close. There was too much to fit inside. He would have to carry some things in a shopping bag, no, in two shopping bags. One of the bags had a broken handle. No, a missing handle. The latch on the suitcase was questionable. The suitcase popped open. Now it was holding. The taxi, where was it? The taxi was late.

The taxi came, Richard got in. The driver didn't speak German, didn't know the streets, and Richard couldn't tell him the name of the train station he wanted. There were three in Munich. Richard had a street map. He could point to the correct station. Where was the map? In the suitcase, in the trunk of the taxi. Richard got out to get the map. The driver thought he was leaving, threw his arms into the air, gesturing, shouting. Richard made him understand, "Map, Karte, Strassenkarte," pointing to the trunk of the taxi.

The driver opened the trunk. Richard opened the suitcase, found the map, pointed out the station. The driver looked happy. They got in.

Drove two blocks, the taxi got stuck in traffic. Richard had to pee. He was going to miss the train.

He woke up, sweating. It was Gloria. It was she who made him have these dreams. He saw that with early-morning clarity. He would have to get rid of Gloria. And get rid of the judge, too, for good measure. A clean sweep. *A clean stable, stone floors washed by a river flowing through, new hay brought in . . .*

Then the dream would go away. The dream of Gloria the tree-climbing goat woman. Gloria, the beast who fouled his sweet-smelling barn. She was the leader of all of the oxen of Elis, the beasts who fouled the stable Hercules had had to clean. One of the twelve labors of Hercules. With her gone, the other oxen could just be oxen, simple, happy beasts. It was Gloria who made them shit themselves, foul his stable.

With her gone, he could load his suitcase on the backs of the happy oxen and travel. All his suitcases. He could put his life's load on their simple, broad backs.

They would arrive at the foot of Humanities Tower, shrug off the suitcases, and bray into the air, to the tower, he would bray with them, to the full professors waiting above, the Germanic arcana he knew, facts and theories of Rococo poetry, details of novelistic composition, dates, influences.

Then Richard would sit on the grass, watch his oxen, watch them graze peacefully in the sunshine, eating the grass.

To: mountkatahdin12345@hotmail.com
From: hmatherpi@yahoo.com
May 8, 2:14 PM

Judith—I've got these pants that would be perfect for you for the trip. I didn't show them to you the other night. Great meal. Thanks for doing the work. I'll bring oysters again next time? You've seen my pants in Megan's pictures, I know you have, the green ones I wear. From Travel Smith. Pockets and flaps and snaps, and places to put things. And I've got a perfect vest from Willis & Geiger you should get too. Ditto for storage pockets. Great for fishing stuff, if you go fishing. Hope you do, it will please Connor. He likes it so much. I can't see why. Golf is much better. Why won't you play golf? All judges play golf. Harry

To: hmatherpi@yahoo.com
From: mountkatahdin12345@hotmail.com
May 8, 2:18 PM
　　Harry, you don't like golf. That's why you do it.

To: mountkatahdin12345@hotmail.com
From: hmatherpi@yahoo.com
May 8, 2:21 PM
　　Yes, I do. You are completely wrong. I get to hit things. That's why I like it. Better than fishing. You don't get to hit the fish. You don't even get to see them, most of the time. With golf, you get results. Plant a radish, get a radish. Hit the ball, write it down. I like golf a lot.

From: mountkatahdin12345@hotmail.com
To: hmatherpi@yahoo.com
May 8, 2:32 PM
　　OK. Thanks for advice on clothing. Please send websites for Travel Smith, etc. You have a thing for Katy No Pocket? She had this need for pockets too, rampant social do-gooder, the Great Provider. Roosevelt taking care of all the animals, carrying

them around in her pockets. You have a big heart. I think you are a Democrat.

To: mountkatahdin12345@hotmail.com
From: hmatherpi@yahoo.com
May 8, 2:36 PM

You piss me off sometimes. I'm glad you're not my partner any more. I'm going to go out now and get over your rudeness by hitting lots and lots of little white balls.

CHAPTER
THIRTY-THREE

It was May 9. Judith looked out into her courtroom. The hearing was going to be difficult. David Branstetter insisted on representing himself. Why is it, she wondered, that the odd people, the quirky people, are the ones who decide to be *pro se* litigants? With David Branstetter, it was certainly not the absence of intelligence. He was obviously quick, and painfully articulate. Jess Carey, one of Palermo's young associates, had his hands full.

"Your Honor, with all due respect," Branstetter said, "my son does not need to be evaluated. And neither do I need to be evaluated. My ex-wife does not need to be evaluated. It is my ex-wife's *actions* which need to be evaluated. And that is your task. That is what you were appointed to do. To weigh the facts, and apply the law. The facts speak for themselves here."

The man was good. If he stayed this good, this professional and focused, maybe the hearing would accomplish something.

"I have objected," Branstetter said, "to the appointment of a court's own witness from the outset. That is why I haven't paid Dr. Orloff."

"Thank you, Mr. Branstetter. Mr. Carey?"

"Your Honor, it is a court order. This father is thumbing his nose at a court order. He fears what Dr. Orloff will find. He is simply being contemptuous of this court. My client has paid for her half of the evaluation, and she and the boy have been to three sessions with Dr. Orloff. It is time for the father to see the psychologist. Dr. Orloff wants several sessions with the boy and his father together. But he will not go forward until Mr. Branstetter makes financial arrangements with him."

"I object."

"Mr. Branstetter, this is argument. You cannot object." Judith paused, and said, "But what is it you wish to say?"

"I object to paying money for something I don't want. Something unnecessary. I want a trial. I want this over. I don't want sessions in a psychologist's office, sessions with someone I don't trust.

"Is there a problem with Dr. Orloff?"

"He can't possibly form an accurate *Gestalt*." Branstetter paused, looking at Judith, waiting to see the effect of his erudition. The judge showed no emotion at all. "He can't possibly form an accurate picture of the three of us. He's foreign."

"Excuse me?"

"He's not Christian."

"Just a moment." Judith thumbed through the earlier pleadings, back when Branstetter had been represented. The file was getting thick. But there was nothing anywhere about religious issues.

"Mr. Branstetter, there is nothing in this file, this fairly thick file . . . " Judith closed it briefly to look at the date on the jacket. She looked at the junk side of the file, the left side, to see if there was any correspondence on point. There wasn't. Nothing about religion. ". . . there is nothing in this file anywhere about religion. Why are you raising it now?"

"Orloff is Jewish."

"Yes?"

"His values, his traditions . . ." Branstetter waited. It seemed, she thought, that he was waiting for Judith to react. Judith stayed silent, looking at Branstetter.

Carey stood up. "Your Honor, my client is willing to pay for the entire evaluation, provisionally, until trial. Just to bring this matter forward without delay. Then at trial, Her Honor can assess costs as may appear just."

That breaks the logjam, Judith thought. Orloff couldn't opine on custody without seeing the entire family constellation, and Judith wouldn't compel him to work fifty percent unpaid. She could put Branstetter in jail for refusing to pay his half to Orloff, but that was heavy-handed.

"Mr. Branstetter, a generous offer. The Court accepts it. You will present yourself forthwith to Dr. Orloff, and timely meet all his requirements. The Court has great confidence in Dr. Orloff. He has testified in similar matters in this county hundreds of times, in many courts. He is highly respected. The Court sees no hindrance in a faith difference. If anything, it gives him more distance, more objectivity."

Judith wanted to change the tone. "Mr. Branstetter, let me speak personally to you." She paused. "Give Dr. Orloff a chance. I think you will like him when you get to know him." She turned away from Branstetter. "Mr. Carey, prepare the order."

"The man is a screaming racist, Judge," said Judith's law clerk that afternoon. "While you were at lunch, I went online, did a search on Branstetter, found he has a website. You're not going to believe this."

"Toby, I'm not sure I want to know. Do I have an ethics problem?" Toby Malone was bright, but sometimes Judith needed to push him to look at issues from her side of the bench. She liked working with law clerks, remembering her own experience at the court of appeals. Toby was only half hers. She shared him with Judge Weingarten.

"I don't think so, Judge. He's put it into the public domain. It's not an *ex parte* communication. It's out there for anyone to see. In fact, that's what he intends."

"You're right. I know it. But, Toby, I just don't need this." He looked crestfallen. "No, no, you did the right thing. It's just, well, when you're the judge and a case is already tangled, you really hate to see the hairball grow."

Toby nodded. "This case really is a hairball, Judge. You, for example, are, and I quote, 'a kike feminist judge,' and you are, quote, 'defiling a public trust.'"

"I was right. I don't need this."

"Well, Judge, the good news is that he doesn't name you. There are many such kike feminists on benches across the fruited plain. America is in danger."

CHAPTER
THIRTY-FOUR

"So what am I going to do?" Judith asked Harry after leaving the courthouse. She had stopped by his office on her way home. He was cleaning his guns. The office smelled of Hoppe's No. 9 Powder Solvent.

"Look, Judith, you can play it one of two ways. You can recuse yourself for unspecified reasons. Get Magic Beans to find someone else. Or you can hang in there. If some other judge picks it up, that judge will have to come up to speed. You're already there. I'm telling you what you already know."

"You think I should keep it."

"No, I'm not. I don't know the answer. Maybe you should keep it. Maybe you shouldn't. Maybe there are some more facts out there to help us. Let's see if there are. Have you done an ego surf?"

"A what?"

"An ego surf. Jude, come into the twenty-first century. Have you run your name through Google?"

"My name? Why? Harry, I don't know what you are talking about."

"You don't know Google."

"Of course I do. I use it. Or Toby does, mostly. Best search engine there is, he says."

"He's right. Better than Dogpile."

"Dogpile? Harry, please."

"An aggregation of quirky associations. I don't use it anymore."

"I'm glad."

"If I can't find something with Google or my *World Book*, I don't need it."

Judith knew that Harry bought a complete set of *World Book* each year. He had done it every year they had been partners, giving the previous year to Megan, and Megan's old set to a family violence shelter.

"Harry, you amaze me. When did you start doing online research?"

"I don't. I just use Google. That's all. A slight loss of virginity. I'm still basically true to print. The *World Book* forever, that's me. And the *New York Times*. Of course, the *Times* is not what it used to be, when you and I were in law school." He looked sour. "But it's still America's newspaper of record. I guess." He seemed disgruntled. "It really has fallen off. But, it's the only game there is for keeping up with American Judaism. About which you could give two squats."

"Harry, you were telling me something about 'ego surfing.'"

"Right. You should do it. And you obviously don't have a clue. So let's do it together."

He pulled the keyboard to him, got the Google screen. "Let's run Judge Judith Merchant first and see what we get. We can try other combinations, too." He typed it in. Out the window Judith could see it was raining.

This has been a bad day, Judith thought. *Branstetter,* then four jail cases, all order of protection violations, the men coming down the back hallway of the courthouse, past her chambers, ankle chains clinking. Marley's ghost on the stairs, Harry's talk of gruel versus oysters the other night.

"Oh, crap!" Harry said. "We're getting cites to Judge Judy's TV show. Look at this."

"Please. I don't want to."

Harry knew Judith hated all court TV, not just Judge Judy. But she particularly disliked being called "our own Judge Judy" in the *Davidson Tribune.*

"I'll put it in quotation marks. Then the search is only for the specific phrase. There." He waited. "Oh shit, Judith, you're all over the place. You're even in chat rooms. This is nasty. This is where people really vent. You don't want to see this."

"Yes, I do."

Connor and Megan flew to Manta on June 2d. "Will Martin be coming, too?" she asked.

"He couldn't work it out on such short notice. I'm glad you can."

"Me too."

Harry had suggested Megan go up with Connor, help him get the cabin ready for Judith. "Well, actually," Harry had said, Megan's mother thought you might need a woman's touch up there."

"Susan just wants me to keep Megan writing."

"That too."

Megan did have a gift, Connor knew. She wrote far better than any fifteen-year-old should. She had done an essay on fishing which Connor kept framed in the cabin. Last year she had told him that 'as a child' she had thought in the old days the world had been black-and-white, because it was black-and-white in the old films. "I mean, why not?" she had said. "It's a consistent world view, for a child. I mean, did the films lie?"

Clearly Harry's daughter.

CHAPTER
THIRTY-FIVE

The boats were up on the spruce skids. Megan worked the drain plug into the transom of the Lund. Connor got a Johnson 15 from the shed. He could have left the motor on the boat, back in the spring, but he hadn't known how soon he would be back.

Megan helped him get the mount over the transom, and they wound the clamps down together. She balanced the two clamps, then untied the boat while Connor went for a Duratank. He put it in the boat, and they stood on the skids.

"Ready?" Connor asked. She nodded. "One, two, three." They heaved the boat backwards. The stern floated free, the weight came off, and they pushed the bow into the water. Megan took the bow line and walked the boat to the dock. Connor got a paddle, a rubber dip net, and three rods.

Megan connected the fuel line, squeezed the bulb until it was solid, and looked at Connor. "Think it'll start?"

"First pull."

"No way." She pulled out the choke, swung her seat around so she could take the rope across her body. On the third pull the motor caught. She pushed the choke in. There was a cough, and the motor settled into a low burble.

"See? Three times."

"I'll take that."

"Me too. Remember the Mercury?"

She took them to Blueberry Island, where they put back three small bass. Connor said, "We're not holding our tongues right."

"Let's try Megan's Bay. It'll be warmer." Martin had named a broad shallow arc of water for Megan. It was weedy on the right, mud bottom, rocky on the left with sand and boulders. The bass would be bedding there before long, Connor thought, if they weren't there already. In the center of the bay's shoreline were two blow-downs, pines, providing good cover. "Where do we start?" Connor asked.

"The pines," she said.

Megan was lucky. Martin had said she could smell fish, particularly in this bay. That's why he had named it for her, he told her, in her honor. Megan's Bay made Connor wonder about his conversation with Harry. About having to be polite to Harry if Megan became his daughter-in-law.

She cut the motor forty feet from the pines. They waited, checking the wind drift. It was going to carry them past the pines, then along the rocky shore.

"Skip the trolling motor for now?" asked Connor.

"Yes. Watch this. See the little pocket? Oh, I hope I don't get a tree fish." Her line settled into the shady nook under the branches and she closed the bail. Waited. No action. She gave two twitches. Nothing. She turned the handle twice, and a silver-brown muskie, hooked in the side of his mouth, exploded up, out of the water, shaking the lure, tail thrashing.

"Oh my God, oh my God!" Megan wailed.

"Rod tip up! You're doing fine. Is he stripping?"

"Yes! Listen!"

"Let him strip. It'll tire him out. Your drag sounds good." The muskie ran left toward the weeds, turned, tried to go under the boat. Megan held the rod out, keeping him out of the motor. "If I can get past you," said Connor, "I'll tilt the motor up."

128

"Can we do it?"

"Yes." She came forward on the left, stepping over the benches. Connor stepped past her. She was in the bow now. He pulled up the outboard. The muskie started to tow the boat out into the bay.

"Oh, Connor, I love this! Can we stay forever and ever?"

Connor and Megan had been gone four days when Judith found a Star of David on her condo door. She wished for a cell phone link to Manta and Connor, but there wasn't any. She called Harry.

CHAPTER
THIRTY-SIX

Bailey told Richard about the medical depositions. "Attorney Palermo wants to depose two doctors who, she says, have treated your wife. One for lupus, and one for sinus problems."

"Red herrings," said Richard. "Disease-of-the-week. Gloria's been looking for a medical excuse for years, something, anything, to give her an alibi for laziness."

"Sinusitis doesn't worry me. But what's this lupus thing?"

"She doesn't have lupus. Two doctors have said she doesn't. The blood work came back negative. Twice. Gloria was very disappointed."

"So, lupus, no worry?"

"No worry."

But Richard was worried, all the same, when he got back to his office. He wrote exam questions, got the ones for German Literature in Translation done, and leaned back. The screen went into save mode after three minutes, with him staring at "and explain your reasons."

Gloria's reasons for wanting to be sick were clear enough. But what if she just pulled the scam off? What if she got that judge to believe it? The woman judge who would "understand" Gloria, the one who would give her permanent alimony. "Oh yes," she had said. He "would see."

Permanent alimony? Pay money to Gloria every month forever? Maybe upward modifications later, as Gloria invented new sicknesses? Bailey said that all alimony amounts were "written in rubber." As circumstances changed, he said, the amount could change, could go up or go down. "If your salary decreases, for example, and you are paying alimony, we can apply for a reduction." My salary won't decrease, Richard thought. It's locked in. With an automatic cost-of-living increase. But maybe Gloria really will get sick in a few years. I could be in deep shit.

He called David. It was time to wield the manure fork.

Richard drove out to David's house. It was his first time there. The neighborhood wasn't bad, exactly, but it wasn't headed in the right direction. David had a split-foyer. The house next door was vacant. There was a sign in the yard: "Recently Reduced."

David was pleased to see him, Richard could see. But he hadn't cleaned up for his guest. Branstetter was no housekeeper. Three PC's in the living room. A laptop on a chair. Clothes on chairs, some laundry on a dinette table. Unused connection cables, unused external modems, extra motherboards. The detritus of a geek, Richard thought. Richard heard a washing machine going in the back. He thought of Gloria.

David said, "I think the judge is taking a trip. Look at this." He pointed to one of the PCs. "This is the court's website. Look at Merchant's trial calendar. There's nothing scheduled for the first half of July."

"So?"

"So, that's why your motion hearing for July 8th got reset to August, and why my status report for July 10th got moved to August 15th."

"OK. I see."

"So, I start thinking, where's she going?"

"How do you know she's going anywhere?"

"I didn't. It just felt that way. So I did some digging, and . . ." He hit some keystrokes. "Here's her entire email file. Microsoft Outlook. Lake Mantakagis in Northwest Ontario. Her boyfriend owns an island there. They're going fishing."

"Holy shit, David. You're a genius."

Branstetter preened.

Connor was looking at an early sketch for *The Return of the Hunters*. The finished version was in Vienna, a huge oil, five feet wide. In the sketch, the outlines of the village below the men were only suggested, beyond the lead hunter's shoulder. Bruegel was working on the perspective from the cliff. One of the hunters didn't have legs yet. There were pheasants in this sketch, slung across a hunter's back. Megan was still asleep. It was first light.

Connor waited for the old Revere Ware percolator to finish. He's so good with animals, he thought, I wonder why he didn't do still lifes? Or did he do them and they are just lost? He had two Bruegel sketches, and was following two more. They were coming up for auction in New York in September. He'd ask Susan to look at them. She went to the city every fall. At least he thought she did. He'd have to ask Harry. No, Megan will know, I'll ask her.

Dana had loved *The Return of the Hunters*. They had made two trips to Vienna, to the Kunsthistorisches Museum, to see it, always going first to the Bruegel room. Dana said the hunters coming home made her feel safe and warm. There would be food that night in the village.

So much of their love had been wrapped in art, the viewing of paintings, the minute study of windows into times past. They had gone many places to see paintings by Bruegels and Hals. They particularly loved Naples, where Bruegel's *Blind Leading the Blind* hung in the Museo di Capodimonte. Art was something they had lived together, something they had loved together. Outside, a loon called, high, wavering. A second loon answered. I'm going to get moody, Connor said to himself, and put the Bruegel away.

He poured coffee noisily, hoping to wake Megan up.

CHAPTER
THIRTY-SEVEN

"Well," Harry said. "No surprise. We know he calls you 'Judge Kaufmann.' Toby found that on his website. The bastard thinks that's a real zinger. So him posting a Star of David on your door is right in style. No big deal for him. If it is him. We don't know that Branstetter did it."

"No, we don't. But somebody knows my new address. And how did they do that? I'm subleasing. Nothing of record. Anywhere."

"Maybe he tailed you. I tail people all the time. It's not hard."

"I took the judicial plates off."

"Yeah, but he knows what you look like. Waits for you in the parking garage, follows you home."

"Oh, Harry. I'm getting scared."

"Scared is good. Smart is better. Let's go to the range tonight. Get you back up to speed. I'll pick you up after supper."

"No, let's go now. I really need it. I'll meet you at the range. I'll make supper for us, after, at my place?"

"OK."

They hung up. Judith got her keys, locked the condo door carefully. It's good Harry taught me to shoot in law school, she thought. At least I feel like I am fighting back.

Megan yawned, sat up in the back bedroom. "Connor? That you?"

"I hope so, Meg. This island's not supposed to have anyone else on it. That's one reason I bought it."

"Oh, you know what I mean. I mean, is breakfast ready?"

"Yes. We're having scrod necks. Hurry."

"Connor. The scrod is a saltwater fish. A young cod or a young haddock. Either way, no neck. And not here. Manta is fresh water."

"OK, then. We're having Red River Cereal."

"What you meant was 'long necks.' You and Dad catch quite a few long necks up here. I've seen you."

"Ah. You mean the Molson Canadian Greenfish."

"Beer makes Dad fat. I wish he wouldn't drink it."

"Megan, your dad believes everyone has a natural shape, and that it is 'perverse and futile' to fight it. His words."

"Yes, he told me so. He said my shape is string bean."

"No," Judith said to Harry, "I'm not going to recuse myself. I'm getting paid to do a job. I owe it to the taxpayers to do the job, and not run from it." They were in the prep room at Southeast Shooters, cleaning their .357s. Once again, she smelled the Hoppe's No. 9. A combination of paint thinner and vanilla extract, Judith thought.

"Fuck the taxpayers. Let somebody else take the heat. Somebody who's not Jewish."

"I'm not Jewish. But, damn it, I may convert when this is over."

"Really?" Harry was excited. "I want you to meet my rabbi. Shulman is cool. I'm taking his classes. You could too."

"Harry, no, I'm not serious. But I'd like to make a good loud statement about anti-Semitism. And that would be one."

"Yes, it would. Hold onto that thought."

"But, partner," she said, "I am deadly serious about staying this course. If this guy runs me off, and I don't know it's Branstetter behind all this, but whoever it is, if he runs me off this case, then what does the rest of my judicial career look like? 'We know how to get rid of Judge Merchant. Cut out some little yellow paper stars. Call her a Jew, she'll get scared, call her a kike-in-a-skirt."'

"It's your funeral."

She swung the cylinder into the frame, raised the Smith, and dry-fired it twice, crouching. "I don't think so."

The plan had come to him as David was showing him the Judge's trip plans. If Richard was careful, very careful, it would work. Richard would drive to Canada. Nashville to Minneapolis to Winnipeg. He wanted a big border crossing, one where they would be in a hurry to move the cars through. He would stay the night of July 3 at the Fairmont in Winnipeg. The next day, he'd drive to Kenora, 127 miles, and take a float plane to a place called Mektu Lake Lodge. It was on the lake next to Mantakagis.

He had David's .222 in a seven-foot long, hard plastic rod case on the dining room table. The case was eight inches in diameter, plenty big enough for the rifle. There were two K-mart rods in there, too, brand new. When you picked up the rod case, it was a little heavy, but it rattled convincingly. He taped it up with silver duct tape. He didn't think he'd have any trouble crossing the border. He'd wear a fishing vest, have his tackle box on the seat next to him. He would ask: "Are they biting?"

I'll be there on July 4th, he thought, on site. To begin my personal declaration of independence.

Connor and Judith were in first class, seats 4A and 4B. The plane, it appeared, was going to take off on time, even though July 2d was a heavy travel day, in advance of the long weekend.

"I could get used to this," Judith said.

"So could I," said Connor. "I usually fly coach. I'm too cheap to fly first class, except to Europe. Then I fly first class, or business class if its available."

"This isn't coach. And this flight is to International Falls."

"Well, this is a special trip."

"Yes, it is. My first trip to your cabin."

"No, I mean really special." He reached in his pocket, took out a small box, and said, "I hope."

"Oh, Connor. Oh, my goodness."

City Cab picked Connor and Judith up from the little airport in International Falls and took them to Paul Beck's SuperValue. Connor arranged for the van driver to give them an hour to shop, then take them across the border for the 134-mile drive to Kenora and the floatplane.

"Of course, we could fly all the way to Kenora," said Connor, "and shop there, but I know where everything is in Paul Beck's, and the prices are lower in the U.S." He looked coy, Judith thought. Something was coming.

"Also, we get to hit the American duty-free store for forty ounces of what the Canadians call 'spirits.' Forty ounces each." He looked at Judith. "Right now, my spirit calls for champagne."

"Mine too."

They went up and down the aisles at Paul Beck's, loading the cart for two weeks on an island without re-supply. Bratwurst, English muffins, five pounds of frozen chuck, Gedney State Fair preserves, Read's German potato salad. "Buy it now or want it later," said Connor. "Harry loves this part of the trip."

"I bet," said Judith.

Judith was wearing the ring, and looking at it a lot. "First outing for the diamond is to a grocery store?" Connor asked. "Isn't that too humdrum? Too plain?"

"No. This is a perfect venue. Grocery stores are happy places. Besides, I'm not taking it off. Ever. If it gets dirty, I can wash it in champagne."

CHAPTER
THIRTY-EIGHT

Davey Barton's Flying Service in Kenora was expecting them. Davey himself pulled their cart out onto the dock. With four pilots and three planes, he could have had someone else make the flight, but he always tried to take Connor in himself.

"Ms. Merchant, good to meet you." Davey was being very formal, thought Connor. This may be hard for him. Davey had really liked Dana. Connor saw him look at Judith's left hand.

Davey and his dock boy loaded their gear into the back of the plane, and Connor and Judith climbed in.

"This is a DeHavilland Beaver, Ms. Merchant, the workhorse of the North. Very reliable. We'll be flying at just under 2000 feet. The belt is there, eh? " Judith was in the co-pilot's seat. She was so excited, Connor thought, she was almost bouncing up and down. She saw the sign on the inside of the fuselage, above Davey's head, and laughed. "Davey, is it true, 'Tipping Your Pilot Helps Him Remember Where He Left You'?"

"Absolutely. It's foolproof. Connor has always made it back to the states."

They taxied out onto the lake, the pontoons throwing shallow flat wakes. Davey brought the nose around into the wind, snugged his earphones, and pushed the throttle up to full power. The lake

surface rushed by, Judith glued to her window as the speed built.
Some of the luggage shifted slightly behind Connor as Davey rocked
one pontoon loose, and then they were airborne. As the plane came
around for Manta, Connor leaned forward and pointed out the
Lake of the Woods, huge and blue, extending out of sight, over the
horizon, toward the United States.

To: dbranstetter@aol.com
From: cgillespie@esper.com
July 2, 4:14 PM
David--

Hitler was poisoned. He had a quack doctor, gave
him little doses of that stuff, arsenic, same stupid
theory is around today, they call it homeopathy. I
read about on line.

You know all that. Your smarter than I am.
That's for sure. I go to sleep at night wondering how
the world would be different now if Hitler had of
lived. Maybe it would be better for me and my boy
Danny, I don't know.

I don't know about all the Jewish stuff, all the
hate stuff. All the Jews I know are nice people. But
I don't know many. You know a lot, I guess, so I'll
keep my mouth shut.

Well, I guess my Dr. Jack-Off is jewish, I don't
know. He sure screwed me and Danny.

--Charlie

Connor and Judith stood on the north dock, watching Davey
taxi into the expanse of water down lake, west of the cabin. Soon
he turned around into the wind, and ran the motor up to full. The
roar flattened as the Beaver gained speed. Then it was up, four feet
above the water, then twenty feet passing over them, gaining wind
speed before climbing up and over the ridge.

Connor and Judith turned toward the cabin. "Oh, Connor, it's beautiful," she said. "It looks like it has been here forever."

They walked through the rooms, the bedroom looking south toward Mektu Ridge, the kitchen, the big living room with a stone fireplace. The view from the big room was north and west.

"Wait until you see the sunset," he said. "Right over there across the lake. It's the most beautiful in the world."

"Bombay gin in a Waterford tumbler?"

"Even better."

She turned back into the big living room. "Oh, Connor, is that one of the *Hunters* sketches? Yes, it is . . . no, it doesn't look right . . . yes . . ." She was looking at a frame to the left of the fireplace.

"It's an early study. 1561, I think. Bruegel used some of it for the big painting in 1565. He never finished this sketch. The big painting is a lot different. So, from the point of view of the big painting, the sketch doesn't look right. I decided to hang the sketch in there for you."

She turned to him, putting her hands on his shoulders. She looked into his eyes. "Thank you, dear. The hunters are home now. They have found each other."

David didn't know the .222 was gone. That was the best part. And he had no use for it, the judge being out of town. He probably wouldn't even look for it before Richard got back and he could get it back under the couch. Richard had gotten the gun one afternoon while David was at work. He would put it back as soon as he got back to Nashville.

Richard had found Kenora using Mapquest, and his present lodgings, Mektu Lake Lodge, from the Ontario tourism website, "Northwest Ontario Dream Fishing Destinations." It had been child's play, really, locating Mantakagis Lake, where Graham had his cabin, and then a lodge on a different lake, near enough to Mantakagis to hike in with the rifle.

The drive up to Winnipeg had been long, but Interstate all

the way. He had spent one night in Madison, a city where he had interviewed for an assistant professorship, years ago. They had been snots, the German Department people. The interview hadn't gone well. He was glad they hadn't offered him the job.

At the border, the guards hadn't given his rod case a second look. He drove from Winnipeg to Kenora after a night at the Fairmont. The float plane was waiting. It was all going to be so easy.

CHAPTER
THIRTY-NINE

To: dbranstetter@aol.com
From: everyman666@hotmail.com
July 6, 3:12 PM

The enemy is no fool. But neither are we. "As for the beast that was and is not, it is an eighth but it belongs to the seven, and it goes to perdition." Revelation, Chapter 17.

To: dbranstetter@aol.com
From: kentsmith2273@earthlink.net
July 6, 8:46 PM
David—

The reason I did my website is kind of like you, only not so much politics and stuff as you. I want tell the whole world the truth how women Abuse MEN with their children! When I went to CTSU I took Comminication, the best thing it taught me was how to be more positive then negitive. So my website is positive about men.

The lodge served three meals a day. They did a box lunch for the boat if you fished without a guide. Or, if you used a guide from the lodge, the guide would fix a shore lunch for you. There were sixteen other guests. Richard went out every day, establishing a pattern of fishing alone. No, he didn't want a guide, he had a map, he loved the solitude. No, he didn't want his fish prepared in the evening. Catch and release, he said, always done it that way. Ecology.

The dock man had looked strangely at his lures, saying nothing. Must be the wrong kind, Richard thought.

It was now July 8th. He had spent three full days pretending to fish. He had found and hiked the portage trail to Manta. That was what the locals called Mantakagis. The judge and her boyfriend had been on the lake for six days. It was time to take a look at them.

The trail to Manta was a little over a mile long, rising gradually to a flat place on the ridge top, then descending steeply down to the lake. Richard needed a view of Graham's cabin, a good place to shoot from. Graham's cabin showed clearly on the topo map. It had to be his, because there was only one structure on the lake. The map showed a cliff some three or four hundred yards across the water from Graham's cabin. A good place for a man with a rifle? He would have to hike through the woods to find out. No problem, he thought.

The rifle was in the rod case under his bed, taped up, where Ellen the maid wouldn't find it. No, he wouldn't need his sheets changed while at Mektu, he had said. Ecology.

He would go to the cliff today, without the rifle, check it out. There were lots of islands in Manta Lake, most of them larger than the one with Graham's cabin. The judge and her boyfriend would be pinned down on a tiny island. Like shooting fish in a barrel.

They would have a routine by now, Richard thought. He needed to know it. If the cliff was good, he'd take the gun in tomorrow. The cliff would be good. He could feel it. Tomorrow was July 9. It was going to be so easy.

They did have a routine. Ham, English muffins, boiled eggs, Red River Cereal at first light. Then the little island, weed beds, shady shoreline until the bass bite fell off, then reading, lunch. Puttering or reading in the afternoon, or more fishing. Then getting the fish out of the live well, fish cleaning, supper, and watching the stars.

For the last three days, they had added canoeing in the afternoon before fish cleaning. Connor found out Judith was better with a canoe than Dana. Judith was as good as he was. She had a strong and steady J-stroke in the stern, matching herself to him exactly, the canoe holding a line as though on rails. "Need the exercise," Judith said, "what with no place to go running up here. Don't want to lose my girlish figure, being engaged and all."

"Well, we don't want headlines, 'Management Consultant Weds Woman With Bulging Biceps'."

"I can take that. Better that than 'With Bulging Bottom'."

They were on the fourth and last leg of the workout, twice to Blueberry Island and back. The fourth leg was always a full sprint.

Richard could see them clearly from the cliff. It was a good place. He would come back tomorrow with the gun. He would do her then, do her right. It would be so good, feel so good, like the first time he had done it to Gloria without a condom. Skin on skin, belly on belly, mucosae speaking the wonderful, wet, and joyous words. No more interposed latex, no more sheep bladder, fish air chamber, shoe protector, raincoat, inner tube coveralls. A real fucking.

David was reading his mail. He had a four-page letter from Wayne LaPierre. There was a lot of underlining, and the punctuation was strange.

> *Dear Fellow American,*
> *For years the NRA has asked patriotic Americans like you to join our cause* . . .

> *. . . Today I'm sending out this "Final Notice" to gun owners and freedom-loving Americans across the country to let you know that time is running out – unless you act now, your Second Amendment rights are certain to be dismantled and destroyed by anti-gun politicians.*
>
> *I urgently need you to sit down, grab a pen or pencil, complete the enclosed NRA Membership Application, include a check or credit card information for your NRA dues, place your Application in the postage-paid envelope provided and mail it right away.*

David Branstetter read all four pages. Then he sat down, grabbed his pen, grabbed his checkbook, and did what Wayne said.

Richard had hardly been able to sleep the night before. His prick had gotten stiff, imagining the canoe in the cross-hairs of the ten-power scope. And now it was show time. No more waiting. He had them. They were coming down the lake from that other island, paddling hard. There was plenty of time. He watched them getting closer and closer. Now they were even with him, heading for their own island, heading to the cabin. There was a humming in his head. He wanted to hurt the judge before she died, make her feel his pain, his fear, what she had been putting him through, make her bleed, see her twitching in the water.

She had the paddle forward in the water, pulling it back, back, all the way back, turning it out, holding it there. Now! He shot her in the right arm, between elbow and shoulder. He could hear her scream. He looked out over the top of the scope, saw her drop the paddle, saw her fall forward and to the right, upsetting the canoe. They were in the water. Graham was yelling.

Richard got back into the scope, shot again, kicking up water by her head. Spang! Again, on the other side of her head. Spang! Beautiful shots. She was screaming, looking for him, trying to find where the shots were coming from.

CHAPTER
FORTY

Connor heard the shot, heard Judith scream, turned, saw blood on the bright aluminum, Judith falling slowly, heavily, upsetting the boat, saw her left hand with the ring flashing. No, he thought, no.

The pain was indescribable in her right arm. She fought the water with her left, came up, got some air. "Connor! Connor! What's . . . what's . . .? My arm! My arm is burning!"

"Hang on to the canoe!" Connor was shouting. "Get behind it!" The canoe was upside down.

"Connor, I'm bleeding!" A second shot, next to her head. Then another on the other side of her head. "Connor!"

"Judith! Get under the canoe!"

The silver boat was upside down. Graham and the judge were under it. Richard was shooting it full of holes. I bet she's peeing herself now. I can feel the urine clouding out of her shorts, yellow, warm, her piss, it's getting on her boyfriend, it's stinking in the water. Brass fell down by Richard's elbows, tinkling on the rock as it rolled away, some of it rolling all the way off the cliff into the lake. He loved this rifle, the smooth bolt action. The roaring in his head was louder. The angle was getting bad. They were moving the canoe. They were under it, swimming it to the island. Trees on the cliff face were getting in his way now. He had to move, finish them off before they were behind the rocks by the dock.

"Judith! Hang on! We're going to make it!"

"Not, not, no . . . " She was moaning, a low constant sound.

Connor looked up into the canoe. Four holes. Now a fifth, the aluminum booming, and a sudden, sharp pain on the top of his head. They were inside a kettle drum. He was hit. Judith was gasping. This was going to be close. But she still had the strut in her left hand, holding her head out of the water beneath the canoe, kicking with her feet. Connor ducked under, put his head out on the side away from the shooter, and checked the angle.

"Stay as low in the water as you can," Connor said. "The water stops bullets better than the boat. I can see the dock! Just fifty feet more! Hang on, Jude!" Christ, it was slow going. The canoe had how many holes in it? The shots into the water made thunking sounds. The dock was getting closer. He stroked with his free right arm, kicked out with his feet, tugging the canoe onward. Judith was helping, not just holding on.

Now he had the bow of the canoe behind the jut of the dock, a two-foot high shelter. He ducked underwater and came up between the dock and the boat. Grabbing the dock skirting, he pulled the canoe all the way in, with Judith underneath. "Jude, we're behind the dock now." All of the canoe was sheltered now except the rearmost three feet. The nose was hitting the shore. He ducked under again, came up inside the canoe with Judith.

"Jude, we're going to go under now and come up between the canoe and the dock. He can't see us there, and we'll be safe." Until he starts shooting through the dock, he thought. They went under, Connor pushing her to the skirting. The canoe rolled over above them, righting itself, and settled low in the water. A gentle wind pushed it against them, pressing them against the skirting.

148

The shooter was holing the exposed end of the canoe now. Each shot vibrated the canoe. Then the shooter started on the dock planking, trying to find them. He seemed to think they were under the dock. The shots ripped into the planks, hissing into the water beneath. Judith had found a hand-wide crack in the skirting boards and was holding tight with her left hand.

"Hold on, Jude. Go under water and hold your breath as long as you can, then come up and breathe, then go down again. Keep doing that. I'm going to get to the cabin, get the rifle, and try to kill this guy. Stay here. I'll be shooting from the bedroom."

Did she understand? She looked blank. How much was she bleeding? "Jude, let me see your arm." She turned in the water. She had two holes in her biceps, but they were oozing, not pumping. "Do you understand about going under water, holding your breath?"

"Yes," she said. "The bullets."

"OK," he said, "I'm going."

He pulled himself along the skirting until his feet found bottom, then up the slope until he was crouching just below the top of the dock, in a foot of water. It was forty feet to the cabin door, up the bank, then over a big rock outcropping, but there were a few pines to make it harder for the shooter. The cabin door opened outward, he remembered. He'd have to go like hell, stop at the door, pull it open, and get inside fast. The gun was on the wall by the fireplace, and it was loaded. Thanks to Harry.

The shooter was back to working on the stern of the canoe. It must offend him that the Grumman wouldn't sink, Connor thought. Judith was staring at Connor.

Now, he thought, and scrambled up the bank, over the rocks, heard a shot hit the ledge next to him as he slid down the back side, rolled left, toward the shooter, and then crouched and ran through the pines, fast, stopped. Then fast again to the door.

The roaring in his head was louder now. This wasn't going right. The guy was running toward the cabin. Shoot him! Shoot him now!

Richard sighted down on Graham, just as he rolled, fired, missed. He's going into the cabin! Shoot him! Kill him! Richard shot five rounds through the open door, looked toward the dock. Can't see the bitch. Kill her. She's still in the water.

CHAPTER
FORTY-ONE

A bullet holed the door as Connor pulled it open. He dived inside. Shots came through behind him, angled, hitting the main room. He stayed left along the wall, got the rifle and ran into the bedroom.

One of the two windows was open. There was nothing on the right side but plastic mesh. He knocked out the mesh with the barrel of the gun. Oh, for a scope! The man was four hundred yards away, sitting on the cliff top, elbows on his knees, in a perfect shooting posture. Connor's vision was cloudy, why? He wiped his right eye, got blood on his hand, and touched the top of his head on that side.

Christ, I can't shoot if I can't see, he thought. He grabbed a pillow off the bed, wiped his forehead, sopped at his hair, and looked out the window again. The man was looking for him. Connor put the barrel slowly out the window, got down in the sights, moved them slowly toward the man's chest. The man saw him. He was shooting again. There was blood again in Connor's right eye. He held steady, moved the sights to the center of the man's chest, and the left window pane exploded just as Connor fired.

The man jerked, grabbed his side, shouted something, and got to his knees. The glass from the left window pane had cut the left side of Connor's face. He had blood now in both eyes. The man was up on his knees, shooting unsteadily, inaccurately. Connor couldn't see, but he kept trying to hit the man, a pink blur. What was that noise? Bullets were hitting the cabin, nothing close. What was that sound? There was a dull roar, getting louder. It was a plane!

The man stood up, looked over the island toward the approaching plane, and moved fast toward the woods behind him.

It was a float plane, low, behind the island, coming toward the island, coming straight toward him. Richard scrambled back from the edge of the cliff. The .222 scope hung itself in blueberry bushes and the rifle pulled out of his hand. Get down! he thought. Get out of sight! Get the gun when the plane is gone.

He held still. The plane passed over him, loud now, loud as thunder. The gun, the goddamn gun, was sliding off the cliff! He reached for it, couldn't get it, saw it slide off the edge and into the air, go out of sight, heard it splash into the lake eighty feet below. Shit. Shit. Shit.

"It's Davey! Oh, God, it's Davey! He's checking on us. I love you, Davey!" Connor looked up at Barton's plane as it cleared the cliff. The man was scrabbling backwards. He dropped the rifle. Connor saw the gun slide and fall. Davey was over the ridge and beyond now. The man stood up straight and ran into the woods. Connor shot twice more, then sat down on the bed. The bedroom smelled of gunpowder, the rifle was warm in his hands, he was bleeding on the bed.

Connor ran back to the dock. Judith was holding on to the skirting. She was very pale. She looked cold, dazed. He jumped into the water, put one arm around her softly, and kissed her. "It's going to be all right now, honey. We can go to the cabin."

Richard was on a train. The train was roaring down a track overgrown with trees and bushes. There was blood running down his leg, running into his shoe. Logs had fallen across the track. He was running, he kept falling down. He couldn't see out of his left eye.

The train had wrecked, gone off the tracks, and was rolling him over and over, across the ground. There were trees going by the windows, dancing left and right. The penguins were in the trees, their frocks whipping the branches. His father beat his huge black tail upon the water, scattering the penguins, making the gulls scream.

"You can't do anything right!" screamed his father. Again, drawing it out, "You . . . can't . . . do . . . any . . . thing . . . right!" stretching it, making it echo, last forever.

The bushes were cutting his face. He fell to his hands. His knees were cut open. Where was the trail? Had he missed it? His hands were bleeding. His suitcases were open, his underwear all over the ground. Gloria was in the trees. She had a frock on. It was black and white. She had pulled it up in front. "Little Dickey! Little Dickey! Little Dickey!" she called, rocking back and forth, her hand down inside her panties. "Come!" roared his father. "Come!" Gloria giggled. "My boy! My boy!" roared his father, "Come, let us ride in the Buick!"

He couldn't find the trail. He was lost. He'd run past it. No, he wasn't there yet. Yes, he had run past it. He didn't have any idea. He'd never get out of the woods, The plane was gone. So was the trail. So was the gun. He couldn't do anything right. Shit. Just like his father had said.

"No, Daddy, it'll be good. You'll see."

CHAPTER
FORTY-TWO

Connor got her to her feet. She was talking and crying at the same time, shivering from the water. They walked slowly to the cabin, a step at a time, the breeze chilling her. "Can he see us? Can he see us? He'll shoot us again."

"No, Jude, he's not there. He ran into the woods. His gun fell off the cliff into the lake. I saw it fall."

"He'll get another gun and come back."

"Maybe. I don't know. Let's go inside, honey."

Connor got her into a big chair by the woodstove. The windows in the great room of the cabin looked away from the cliff. He pulled off her shoes and wet pants and underwear, toweled her lower body dry, and wrapped her in a blanket. Her arm was still oozing. He found two pulses in her wrist, one on each side. No major blood vessels had been hit. He lit the fire he had earlier laid in the fireplace. She looked all right for the moment.

He took his binoculars and went outside, getting down behind the rocks. He studied the cliff and the woods beyond. No movement. He could hear the canoe bumping the dock, held there by the wind. It wouldn't sink, Connor knew, Grummans didn't sink. He lowered the binoculars. The planking on the dock looked like a millet field after harvest. Like the opening day of dove season.

He went back to the cabin and gently cut off Judith's shirt and bra with scissors. The arm was anatomically straight, but swelling slightly at both the entry and exit wounds. He held her shoulder in his left hand and put his right under her elbow. He gently moved the arm. Judith moaned. There was a lot of tenderness, but no evident fracture. Judith's pain said fracture, but the bone was straight. Maybe the bone is chipped, he thought.

Her bleeding had stopped. There was an entrance wound on the back of the biceps and an exit wound on the front. The guy had shot her at the finish of a J-stroke, Connor thought. It was a through-and-through, and looked clean. Judith moaned again. "I think the bullet is out, dear. That's good."

He got two Ampicillin, two Tylenol-3, and a glass of water. When she had swallowed them, he toweled her upper body dry, her hair, her face, and gently helped her to a different chair. A dry one. He put a hassock under her feet and wrapped a blanket around her legs. Then he laid another over her upper body and tucked it down around her. He needed to let the codeine take effect before working on her arm.

He went outside with the binoculars again. Nothing on the cliff, no movement in the woods. He went quickly to the shower house. There, the water high and hot, he washed his scalp and face, slowly, over and over, picking out metal and glass. He could see a scalp cut in the foggy mirror. It didn't look bad enough for stitches. His face had little shallow cuts on the left side, cheek and forehead. He took a Bic razor and shaved his hair away from around the scalp cut. Bullet fragment, he thought, after it came through the canoe. He turned the shower off, patted the site dry, and put a butterfly bandage on it. He'd have a scar. It wasn't the first. What was the Spanish for a dueling scar? *Cicatriz de duelo.* In Polish it was *pojedynek blizna.*

"I want some madeira," Judith said.

He got some Blandy's Rainwater, and poured a small amount. "Two of those pills were codeine. You'll be feeling better soon."

"Oh, I feel better already. Warm and cozy."

"I can't give you much madeira. You know, mixing alcohol and codeine, operating heavy machinery, all that."

"I know . . . I just want the taste . . . mostly." Her speech was getting languid.

He got a clean towel and laid it across the side table by her chair, putting hydrogen peroxide, Betadine, alcohol swabs, Q-tips, and compresses on it. He went to his fly fishing gear and got two hemostats, wiped them with alcohol, and laid them on the towel too.

"Let me take a look," he said. Her arm was resting on a pad of towels rolled up by her side. The two wounds had closed. He pried them open, and swabbed the holes with hydrogen peroxide, then Betadine. Judith moaned with each touch. "Almost done," he lied.

He knew bullets themselves did not set up infection, it was the clothing they carried into wounds. And Judith had been wearing a sleeveless blouse. But just the same, he put as much Neosporin into the holes as he could. Then compresses over the wounds, and an ice pack around the whole upper arm. The swelling was moderate at this point. It could get out of hand, he knew, set up compartment syndrome. He would change the ice every two hours for the next twenty-four hours.

Connor made an L-splint to hold the lower and upper arm as a unit. "We can use duct tape if you prefer," he said, as he bound the splint at her wrist, elbow, and shoulder with white adhesive tape. "I have both silver and black. You can make a convalescent fashion statement." He got a dish towel from the kitchen and made a sling for the splint.

"Done," he pronounced. "Ms. Merchant, I want you to know we've enjoyed having you here at North Woods Medical. Now it's time for Rudy here, come in Rudy, to take you to the front door of the hospital in a wheelchair. The wheelchair is so you don't fall down and embarrass us. Thank you for visiting our emergency department, and have a nice life. If you survive."

Judith giggled. "I think I want to sit up straighter," she said. Connor eased her forward and put a pillow behind her.

"That's better," she said.

"Do you want me to build up the fire?"

"Maybe just a little?"

Richard found the trail, followed it to the boat. He sat in the boat, shaking. The sun was still two hours above the horizon. The air was warm. He had blood on his arms, his face. Caked black blood. His pants were shredded at the knees. His side hurt like hell. Why did his side hurt? He smoothed the fabric of his shirt over the ache. That was a bullet hole! No, two bullet holes! That was why his side hurt.

He stood up in the boat, took his shirt off, and looked at his left side. There were two holes, two inches apart, just above his hip bone. In the slight amount of fat that Richard allowed himself. So Gloria could hold on, keep herself centered on the Great Unwobbling Pivot.

He wondered what to do. The shirt was bloody on the left side. Get the blood out of the clothes, he thought. I can't go back like this. He took his pocket knife and cut the fabric between the two holes in his shirt. One tear now. Then he took all his clothes off, threw them in the lake, and climbed in after them. He washed everything and spread it on big boulders. Then he waded back into the lake and washed himself. He had some Bacitracin back at the lodge in his Dopp kit. He'd be all right. Fill his side with Bacitracin, put on two band-aids. Big band-aids. Or compresses. He'd have to buy some when he got back to the car. Good as new in a week. He lay down by the boulders and went to sleep. No dreams. Too exhausted.

"Comfy," Judith said. "I like codeine. Tylenol-3 is a good number."

"I could make coffee for you," Connor said. "It might help."

"No."

"No, really," Connor said. "I read a Louis L'Amour novel once where the hero, a cowboy, kept getting shot."

"Was he in a canoe?"

"No. Cowboys ride horses. Not canoes. Pay attention. He would go hide away somewhere, maybe a cave, usually a cave behind a waterfall, and he would brew coffee. Strong coffee. And that would heal his gunshot wounds. It healed him over and over. It was amazing."

"Roborative."

"I guess."

"Means strengthening, a tonic."

"I know," said Connor. "*Roborare*, to strengthen. Has to do with restoring, or redness, or something. Latin."

"Thank you. Yes, Latin. Do you think we're getting punchy?"

"Yes."

"I love codeine. Worth getting shot for."

"We could do this every year," he said.

She giggled. "My ring is beautiful, Connor. I'm glad I got shot in the right arm, not the left."

CHAPTER
FORTY-THREE

Connor took his emergency signal, a big red cross on a white background, and took it to the other dock, laid it out on the smooth boards, and weighted it down with rocks. Well, he thought, if Davey comes back again, he can't miss it. It was a week before the scheduled pick-up. He had always resisted a satellite phone at the cabin but, oh God, how he wished he had one.

> To: dbranstetter@aol.com
> From: iowadad@hotmail.com
> July 9, 7:21 PM
> <<<Delete this when read!<<<
>
> Been following the string several weeks now. You and I have a lot in common. More than our legal problems with children. I found your listing in Who's Who in American Computing. Take a look at mine. I have some new techniques that might interest you.
> <<<Delete this file now! Delete all cookies now!<<

The sun was going down, its rim touching the tops of the spruces across the lake. Judith was asleep. It wouldn't be fully dark for more than two hours, but then the long Canadian twilight would yield to the darkness of tonight's new moon. A perfect time, Connor thought, for the shooter to come back and finish the job.

Whoever it was has had enough fun, if that's all it was, he thought. A plinker taking shots at strangers. I hit him at least once, I think, which reduces the fun factor. Davey's plane made him run. He panicked, dropped his gun off the cliff, and skedaddled. Northern shooting incident ends.

On the other hand, he thought, if this is not about fun, then the shooter is here to make sure we die. If that's the deal, he will come back. And the way things sit, we are little more than cut-outs in a shooting gallery. We don't have to go out in the boat for him. He can shoot us on the dock, he can shoot us in the woodlot, he can shoot us through a cabin window. Harder if we're in the cabin. Judith will not go outside until fly-out. And when I'm outside, I'll be moving fast.

But could the shooter get another gun? Yes. Maybe he had several guns, back at his cabin, his boat, wherever he had come from. But if he had to buy one, this was big game country. Parties went out for bear and moose every fall. In Northwest Ontario there were plenty of guns.

In the absence of more information, Connor told himself, you go with the obvious pattern. Occam's Razor. This is not about fun. This is not about plinking. This is about Judith. She has problems back home, she is the one whom the shooter shot first. The shooter had chosen her. Wouldn't a male ordinarily shoot another man first, then the woman second? The man who might have a gun in the cabin? Unless the woman is really the target? If he does know who we are, if he has a problem with Judith, he has to come back. He has to hope Davey saw nothing, or at least he has to watch to see if Davey sends in help. If no help comes, then Davey saw nothing, and it is time for him to shoot the tin cut-outs.

Connor worked on it: Figure the shooter needs time to get another gun, come back, see if the plane has sent help. If he's fast, well, then he comes back tonight. If it takes a while to get a gun, or if he wants to make it easy on himself, he comes back at first light. Either way, he comes in slow, looking for signs Davey has sent rescue. He'll see the red cross on the dock, know there's been no rescue, and finish the job.

It's not impossible that the guy could come tonight by boat. If he had already carried in a canoe from Mektu. There are no fishing boats on the lake except my two, and you can't get one in now, not in the summer. You have to wait for winter, use a snow machine, drag them over the frozen lakes and snow pack.

But a canoe was possible in summer, if the guy was in good shape. He had been tall and thin. He could do it. Perhaps the canoe's there now, hidden in the woods. Judith and he had fished that part of the lake yesterday. They had seen no canoe. But they hadn't been looking for one. And a canoe twenty feet back in the woods was invisible.

That's how I'd do it, Connor thought. Carry the canoe in from Mektu. Stash the canoe. Hike to the cliff. Shoot from the cliff, one, two, three. The canoe is ready for backup, in case you need to come to the island, finish things off. If you turn out not needing the canoe, fine, you were ready. Carry it back out with you. Carry it out one way or the other. Two bodies on the island, and an extra canoe on the lake? Too many clues.

But maybe, maybe, just maybe, this guy's not that good. Maybe he doesn't have a canoe. Maybe he's not a systems analyst. Maybe he doesn't plan for contingencies.

Connor stopped. He realized he was applying rational analysis to irrational behavior. Cardinal error, he told himself. A deranged person will continue to act consistent with his delusion, no more, no less. I must not count on him planning the way I plan. Unless of course his delusion does not reach down to tactics.

Who wants to shoot a judge? Someone angry. Or someone who needs to be important. Or someone who needs something concealed. Does Judith know something that has to be covered up?

Tomorrow is the most likely time. The guy will do it tomorrow, if he's going to try again from the cliff. He won't wait two days. Macbeth had it right, "If it were done when 'tis done, then 'twere well it were done quickly." The more time Judith and I have to prepare, the less he's in control. He has to limit our options. He comes in tomorrow with the new gun, brings the canoe if he hasn't already, hikes to the cliff. Watches us, and makes his plans. He won't shoot, won't give himself away, unless he gets a clear easy shot.

He won't be foolish enough to come by canoe in the daylight. Not with me and the thirty-thirty. So tomorrow daytime is his game time, but only on the cliff again, if he takes the daylight option. Or tonight or tomorrow night he comes by canoe right to the island. What he doesn't know, Connor thought, is that I have another canoe, behind the shed.

He looked in on Judith. She was fast asleep. He wrote her a note, telling her where he would be, and why. He laid out her next batch of pills and put fresh ice into the ice pack around her arm. She didn't wake up. The note told her to change her ice pack, if she could, whenever the ice melted.

Connor dressed in black, slung the rifle across his shoulder, and put the rest of the thirty-thirty cartridges in his front pockets. He went to the kitchen for his filet knife and the Leatherman with the fish scaling blade. He put them on his belt and moved quickly through the trees. At the back of the shed, he unslung the rifle, and knelt down by his Old Town canoe. Digging with his hands, he made a hole deep into the damp earth. He went to the lake, scooped up a double handful of water, and carried it to the hole, made a slurry, and spread it on his face and hands.

CHAPTER
FORTY-FOUR

Connor paddled slowly and quietly to the spot he had chosen, a pine tree which had fallen into the water but not uprooted. He put the canoe behind it, out of the shooter's line of vision, and went ashore. The Old Town was dark green. That was good. He was almost directly south of the cabin and two hundred feet from it. Connor climbed up a few feet and sat at the base of a cedar tree. He looked slowly left and right. The propane light in the kitchen burned a welcome for the shooter, to guide him in, and ruin the man's night vision.

The lake was narrow on this side of the island. Looking west to his left, he saw the main expanse of Manta, meandering away for miles to its outflow. Looking north north east, Connor could see the cliff face which was separated from the cabin by four hundred yards of water. If he's got a canoe, I will see him, he'll pass right in front of me, Connor promised himself.

He looked over to the cabin, quickly. The kitchen window glowed yellow. He thought of a story Dana had read to Martin, about leaving a candle burning for the Christ child.

Hours passed. Even without a moon, Connor could see clouds moving overhead. An owl called. His mind wandered. Muffled oars, he thought. Something from the American Revolution. "The patriots had muffled oars." Well, the shooter would have a muffled canoe paddle, black duct tape on the shaft. That's how I'd do it. Rational analysis.

Judith was at Monticello. She was part of the expedition to explore the Louisiana Purchase. Her arm hurt. It was in a sling. Mr. Jefferson was pouring glasses of madeira. She didn't tell the president her arm hurt, but he could see it was in a sling. The sling was made out of duct tape. The president asked her could she still go on the expedition? She said she could. Meriwether Lewis came over to talk to them. Lewis told the president Judith's arm would be no problem, it would heal soon. Sacagawea was there. Jefferson liked the silver duct tape. He had never seen duct tape before.

Judith gave Sacagawea some dollar coins with her picture on them. Lewis took one of the coins to the president, showed it to him. Jefferson liked it, too.

"They're not catching on," Lewis said.

"I can't see why not," said the president.

Sacagawea couldn't speak English. She smiled at Judith.

At 3:32, the first hint of dawn began uplake. Ten minutes later a loon called. Then the creavy bird started calling. By 4:00 it was clearly dawn. Thirty minutes later the sky was white all around. Connor got up, stretched, and went to the Old Town. He was cold and stiff. Time for food, he thought. Time for plan B. It was July 10. Six more days to fly-out.

At the cabin, he looked at Judith. Sleeping. He changed her ice pack. Connor figured he had forty minutes to get in place on the cliff, probably more. If the shooter was coming back today, he would start on foot at daylight at the earliest. He won't come in a canoe. He won't do that, Connor thought, even part way. His canoe would be in plain sight, or I could come looking for him in the Lund. More rational analysis.

He got out the percolator, put it on the back burner. If I should get shot today, he thought, I can take the coffee pot behind a waterfall and get well. He needed to go to the outhouse. On the way, he looked at the lake. Mist, low on the water. No canoe. Of course not.

There was a rough-winged swallow's nest inside the outhouse, above the door. She looked at him coldly, flew out, perched in the nearest tree, and watched him. Connor climbed on the seat and checked the eggs. Still three.

Back at the cabin, the coffee pot was beginning to thump. "Connor, I'm awake," Judith called. He went to the bedroom.

"You look pretty good," he said, "considering."

"You don't. Your face is dirty," she said. "Oh. You've been outside. All night?"

He nodded. "You didn't read your note."

"What note? Oh." She picked it up. "Yes, I did. I forgot. And I did change the ice pack. Twice. Connor, you look like something from one of those action movies."

"I know. I'll wash later. How do you feel?"

"I'm tired. I explored the whole Louisiana Purchase last night. And none of our money would work in the vending machines. We had to barter."

"Of course. Barter. Beads and things. Wampum. You took wampum with you?"

"No, just coins. And the Indians didn't want our coins. We had to trade our shoes for food. It was awful."

"The food?"

"No, being barefoot, no shoes, all the way to Oregon." She looked at him. "Connor, what are you getting ready to do?" He was packing food.

"I'm going up on the cliff where he shot from. If he comes back, I'll be there first." Her eyes opened wide. "Don't worry. I'll hear him coming. I'm taking the rifle."

He laid out the codeine and Ampicillin for her, explaining when she should take them. Then he handed her a walkie-talkie.

"This is Motorola's gift to fishermen. We use them when we're in two boats. Today, you and I can talk while I'm on the cliff. I'm going to stay there all day, unless you need me."

"I won't. But I'm going to be scared. Not for me," she said, "for you."

He turned on the Walkabout, set the volume on low, and turned it off. "Jude, if you are awake, turn it on at five before the hour, and keep it on until five after. I'll try to call you every hour. It's OK if you don't answer. Sleep if you can. If you need me, really need me, call for me at any time. I'll keep my unit on all the time. But don't call me unless you have to." She nodded. He put extra batteries in his vest pocket.

"Connor, if he comes, will you kill him?"

"Yes."

She looked at him.

"I thought so," she said.

Connor put more mud on his face, got in the Old Town and paddled west around the back of the island. He pulled the canoe into the woods and slung the thirty-thirty on his back. He climbed quickly through the woods to the top of the cliff. There was .222 brass all over the place. He put two in his pocket, and moved back into the woods, looking for a tree.

It was 8:00 A.M. He hadn't called Judith at seven, and had turned off his unit, because he had thought he heard movement in the woods. He turned on the walkie-talkie now and spoke softly, "Judith?"

"Yes, yes, I'm here. You didn't call at seven, I've been so worried. Are you all right?'

"Yes, nothing's happening. I'm in a tree."

"You're in a tree?"

"So I can watch the cliff top." He could see the brass winking. If the shooter came the way he was supposed to, he had him. Nothing but low bushes and moss for the last fifty feet to the cliff top.

"Judith, I'll try to call at nine. I love you. Out."

"I love you, too. Out."

No one had come. It was 5:00 P.M. Connor hated his tree. His legs hurt. He hated this whole plan. It was dumb. He was hungry. He had peed three times from on high. The guy would come tonight by canoe. If he came at all. He wouldn't come to the cliff top between now and dark. It didn't make any sense. Connor climbed down. He hurt all over. Could he stay awake tonight?

CHAPTER
FORTY-FIVE

Judith had looked worried when he told her he was going back out. They had a quick supper together, and Connor slept for two hours, with two alarms set. When he woke, Judith was in the kitchen, moving about stiffly. She had made fresh coffee and put it in a Thermos for him. He crossed the channel south of the cabin and took up his same station again. He thought about muffled oars.

Hours passed. He and Judith spoke a few times by radio. The first sliver of a new moon came up. Good for me, bad for him, Connor thought. I'll see the flash of his paddle. He drank some coffee. It wasn't working. He had to stay awake. He did an inventory: He had the rifle. He had the filet knife. His Leatherman was locked open on the scaling blade. He had his teeth. He had his rapier wit. He had a piercing understanding of European art history.

At 4:20, a creavy bird woke Connor. "Creavy! Creavy!" it said. It was day.

Richard woke up. Where was he? Oh, God, he had screwed up. He had tried and failed. His father in the trees was right.

His side was on fire. He got in the boat and ran it full speed back to the lodge. He got to his cabin without meeting anyone, took a shower, and put Bacitracin into the bullet holes. Then he decided to get good and drunk.

In the main building, at the bar off the dining room, he ordered Canadian Mist. Soon a man came in, another fisherman. Arne Paulsen. A fisherman, just like him. Fine man, remarkably fine man. From St. Paul. Heating and air. Practical line of work. Not like literature. Tactile. Ductwork, compressors, thermostats, things you could touch. More heating than air in St. Paul, but air was growing. Richard liked Arne, liked Canada, liked Canadian Mist. Richard told Arne he had fallen down today, hiking, had rolled down a slope, hit some rocks. Arne told Richard about falling down once, years ago. Arne had broken his ankle.

"I guess I was lucky," said Richard. "No more hiking for me. Gonna stick to fishing now on."

"Good idea, David," said Arne.

The next morning was July 10. Richard packed his things and took the morning float plane out. "We're sorry you fell, Mr. Branstone, so sorry. But please come back next year." His car at the airbase was hot and covered with dust. He rolled down the windows, put his bag and rod case in, and headed south to Fort Frances. He didn't need a busy border this time. No gun in the rod case. In International Falls he bought some compresses and Advil.

All in all, he thought now, it hadn't been such a failure. He had had such fun with the judge. And he was in the clear. Graham was alive, that was too bad, and Graham had seen him, but so what? He hadn't seen him well. Couldn't have, not while being shot at. Unless Graham had a scope. And the way he was shooting, he hadn't had one. The man had fired maybe ten times. And hit him only once. Barely. His side felt a lot better this morning. So it was probably a rifle with open sights. But still, he should be careful in Nashville. No trips to art galleries. No wine-and-cheese openings.

The judge, now. Was she alive? Maybe. But if she was, she'd

bang her gavel with the other hand now. And she hadn't seen him at all. That was good.

His gun was at the bottom of the lake. David's gun. On balance, that was good, Richard thought, maybe even an improvement. When David missed it, Richard would suggest a break-in. He would say he had seen a kid hanging about, a black kid. David would eat that up. The kid had been looking at the house. Richard hadn't thought anything about it then, he would say, but the kid must have come back. Richard would score the back door frame with a screwdriver, pop the mortise plate loose.

David Branstetter was a sycophant. A pain in the ass, but a very useful pain in the ass. If the judge was still alive, David would be able to tell him when she was traveling again. In June, she had been checking on flights to Munich and Frankfurt, David had said. Nothing booked yet.

Bailey. The lawyer was a jewel. As soon as he got back to Nashville, he would call Bailey. There was a deposition next week of Gloria's treating physician. The one who sought the nameless malady, the man on a quest for the sickness whose name was alibi. William Terrance Bailey would tear him a new asshole: "Tell me, Doctor, all you have here is speculation, isn't that true? You have no name for these so-called symptoms? Doctor, tell me, couldn't all these complaints be subsumed under an umbrella term, perhaps? The term 'shiftless'?"

Gloria. Ah, Gloria now. Her deposition had been wonderful, just before Richard's trip north. She had worn her beige knit skirt. She had kept crossing and uncrossing her legs. Avoiding Bailey's questions. But he had kept after her, had made her squirm, and had made her answer. Gloria was hard to pin down, but easy to nail. Slippery deposition. He had sat there watching her answer Bailey's questions. He bet she was slippery between the legs, up there under the beige skirt, even now, looking at him, answering Bailey. Slippery where she should be, slick where the nail went in and out, where sometimes the old Irish airline went in and out, she moaning, screaming don't stop, don't stop, oh, oh!

Well, he thought, she's been nailed for the last time by me. Probably by anyone. He was going to kill her. He decided that, fixed upon it, as he drove south. It had been fun with the judge.

It was the middle of the afternoon. July 11th. The shooting had been the day before yesterday. Judith felt better. There was no swelling, no compartment syndrome, Connor said, and no fever. But her arm hurt like hell. Five more days to fly-out. "Have some more coffee," Connor said. He had had a long shower, washed all his mud off, and then slept for nine hours.

"Unh-uh. I'm swimming in coffee. Been to the outhouse twice already."

"There's a rough-winged swallow nesting in there. Did you see it?"

"Oh. That's what it was." Judith laughed, "No. I mean I saw something. Something saw me, anyway. There was a whole lot of fussing and flapping."

They smiled at each other. "How's the arm?"

"It hurts. When can I have more codeine?"

"In two hours."

"Connor, what's going to happen? He's got to kill us now. You've seen him. What did he look like?"

"All I could tell was he was white and tall. Sort of thin. My eyes were full of blood. I'd never pick him out of a line-up."

"He doesn't know that. He might think you got a good look."

"He might."

"Will Davey come back today?" She had asked this twice already.

"Not likely. I'm sure he didn't see anything on the fly-by, just that there was no signal out on the dock. I've got the red cross out there now, on the other dock."

"Why did he do a fly-by?"

"He does that when he's in the area. If I need something, I put a red cross out on the dock."

"Oh, yes. I remember now. You told me that yesterday. When will he come back?"

"Five days at the worst. He's taking us out on the sixteenth. That's our scheduled fly-out day. Maybe he'll check on us before then."

She yawned. "Am I going to be all right?"

"Yes. Your wound is clean. We have Neosporin in it. You are taking 250 milligrams of Ampicillin four times a day. The humerus is splinted, because it may be broken or may be chipped. I can't tell. I know it aches like everything, but you'll be OK." He didn't tell her she could still get an infection or spike a fever. Oh, Davey, he thought, come back. So much could go wrong. Look what had happened to Dana.

"Connor, how do you know all this about trauma? Why do you have so much medical gear?"

"Well, sometimes people get hurt fishing, get cut, or snagged with hooks. I want to be ready. And the docs I do work for load me up with stuff."

"Well," she said, "I'm glad."

CHAPTER
FORTY-SIX

Richard's compresses stunk now when he changed them. He had made it past Madison before stopping. The skin surrounding the wounds was puffy and the wounds were beginning to drain. He thought it might be a good sign, the draining. But the redness worried him. He felt awful. I've got to see a doctor, he thought. I've got a fever.

Connor took the Lund, looking for a canoe, or signs that one had been there. Nothing. The guy either hadn't brought one in, or he had stashed it somewhere else.

When Connor got back to the cabin, Judith had Megan's fishing essay, the one Connor had framed. She was holding it and smiling.

"This is pretty good."

"Yes, it is. I think she should keep writing." Judith handed him the little frame, and Connor hung it back on the wall. He read it over again.

> *The best time on the lake is early in the morning, just before the sun rises. The air is cool and everything is still and quiet. An eerie mist hangs over the water. To take the boat out and disturb the flat, glass-like look*

of the water almost seems wrong. At first everything remains silent, and you feel like you are the only one alive. As the morning progresses, the loons begin to make their calls, letting the world know that they are there too. Their calls are eerie and drawn out. Along with the still mist along the surface of the water, the whole scene sends chills down your back.

Nothing else seems to matter as you bait your hook and let it drop down into the water, watching it as it fades out of sight. The world stands still while you wait. Then the fish attacks the bait, and the fight begins.

From years of fishing I have learned the importance of patience and perseverance. My friend Connor used to tell me, "The fish aren't going to jump into the boat on their own . . . if you don't have a line in the water, you don't even have a chance."

This holds a lot more meaning for me now. If you don't make an effort, you aren't going to get a result. So go ahead and put a line in the water. If you don't catch anything, at least you know it is not because you didn't try. Some days are good days, and some days nothing happens. You just have to keep going, and hope that a fish will strike eventually.

"She wrote that last year, and I framed it over the winter. When she was here in June, she found it."

"Was she pleased?"

"Yes."

"I'm glad," Judith said. "Some young girls can be so sensitive. A lot of them just don't want to be noticed."

"She said she had been doing a lot of writing, and that one of her essays won a prize at Harpeth Hall."

"Really?"

Connor went to his briefcase, got it out. "I think I am becoming an unofficial mentor. Here's another Connor-inspired essay. She wrote this in April, in her English class." Judith took it, settled down to read.

Connor taught me how to cook, at his cabin in Canada. He started with fried eggs. I was seven or eight years old then, and didn't know how to cook anything. No one else had bothered to teach me how to cook. I guess it hadn't occurred to them.

There was a wood-burning cook stove. The first thing you had to do was slap it fast to see if it was hot enough. If it wasn't then you balled up a half sheet of newspaper and poked it down through the stove eye, and put kindling in on top of the ball of paper, and struck one of the big red-and-white-headed matches, the ones from the box behind the door. You struck the match on the stove top. It made a soft rasping sound and flared and smelled like cap pistols. You could watch the kindling catch fire down through the stove eye for a while, and then you had to put the lid back in place so it would get hot.

The small black skillet was the one to use, Connor said. It went right on top of the stove eye over the place where the kindling was. Connor kept bacon grease in the coffee can on the counter. What you needed was a whole tablespoon, rounded on top, one of the big spoons from the drawer.

The white, semi-soft, brown-speckled grease would start to melt in the skillet, getting clear as water around the edges of the lump, and the water would expand and expand, the lump sinking down and disappearing, until the whole pan bottom was covered with melted fat. Then you could push it around with the pancake turner, or shake the skillet, but you had to use a pot holder if you did that.

Connor showed me how to break the egg open, and you have to do it just right, or you have a disaster. If you hit it too hard, you get yellow and white running through your fingers. But if you don't tap the shell hard enough on the stove edge, you can't slowly and carefully open the doors with your thumbs and let the yolk out. You have to push your thumbs in, and that's when like as not they go all the way into the egg and break the yolk, and you can't do sunny-side-up then. You have to do hard-fried, like for a sandwich at lunch.

You put the egg softly on the warming bacon fat, and it just sits there, the yolk self-assured, glowing, a glistening peach half, an upside-down oatmeal bowl, and you can't even see the white yet. It looks just like the bacon grease. You can see right through it to the black skillet bottom. And then a little film of white starts to appear, like an image coming up in a photographic tray, just a suggestion, outlines coming, a picture of egg landscape emerging, the edge reaching to here, curving around to here, coming close in to the yolk down here, time to jiggle the skillet a little, make the yolk get more in the middle. It moves some, slides back some, moves again, sort of stays there.

And then the best part, sliding the pancake turner around the edges of the white, lifting them up while they bubble and whisper and flap up and down, hissing about being a beautiful egg, while turning brown and crispy in places, and the yolk starting to film over and get a duller yellow. At this point you can change your mind on sunny-side-up and poke a little cut in the yolk and a puddle will leak out and flow over toward the hot bubbling edge of the white, fall off the cliff into the

> *hot black ocean, and fry up light yellow, right next to*
> *the white, an annex, a different colored stepping stone*
> *off the white iceberg, a porch into the ocean.*

"Connor," Judith said, "this is just wonderful writing. I can't wait to see Harry, talk to Harry about Megan. Wow."

Nashville. Richard was exhausted. He was feverish. He smelled bad, even though he had changed his compresses four times and taken long hot showers. A Red Roof Inn outside Rockford, and a Budget somewhere in Evansville. Cash both times. The draining had stopped, and there were firm, hot areas around the wounds. When he walked into his house in Nashville, he threw the rod case and all his stuff on the floor, stumbled to his study, and lay down on the floor. He was too tired to climb the stairs to his bedroom. It was nine o'clock at night, July 12th.

"Nail gun," he told the doctor the next morning at the walk-in clinic. "I was so embarrassed I didn't tell anyone, not even my wife. Treated it myself. She didn't want me to build the deck myself. Said we should get a contractor."

"She was right, Mr. Branstone," said the doctor. Richard was lying on his back. The doctor was irrigating the wound, and clucking. "Why did you wait three days to come in?" The smell was bad. The doctor used a long scissor-like instrument to open both wounds further. Richard saw yellow stuff, baby custard, coming out. His pain lessened. There were red places in the custard. "You are just shy of hospital admission, Mr. Branstone. In fact, I probably should admit you now."

"I can't do it, Doctor. No insurance. I mean, unless I'm dying."

"No, you're not dying, but you could. You have bacteremia. It is not a killer. But it can quickly move toward sepsis, and sepsis is a killer. For now, and I emphasize that I am saying for now, it is acceptable procedure to pack the site with iodoform gauze, that is what I am doing now, and load you up with antibiotics." It looked to Richard like the doctor was putting a yard of the stuff into his side. When the doctor finished, there were little tails sticking out of each hole.

"Change these compresses twice a day. The iodoform gauze will wick some moisture out to the compresses. Here is a prescription for Keflex. 500 milligrams. Fill it immediately. Take it four times a day, every six hours. That is most important. I want to see you every day for the next three days without fail. We'll watch this day by day, and see how it goes. Do you understand? Every day."

"Yes, sir. Every day for three days. I'll be here, Dr. Patel, I promise."

Richard paid cash and left.

CHAPTER
FORTY-SEVEN

Connor sat by Judith in front of the fire. It was the morning of the fifteenth. There was wind in the trees. Waves were lapping against the dock.

"Davey will be here tomorrow," said Connor."

"Yes, or maybe even today if he does a fly-by and sees the cross," she said.

Connor got up. "Can I get you anything?" he asked. He adjusted her lap robe, and pulling it up, let his hands rest upon her breasts.

"Just checking?" she asked. "Making sure everything's still there?"

"Yes," he said. "Its important to check now and then. Sometimes breasts fall off during the night."

"Really?"

"Yes," Connor said. "You get out of bed, don't know they're gone, cover them up with the bed clothes, and during the day they just deflate, gone, nothing left when you find them except little limp membranes, which you probably don't notice when you make the bed. So, the breasts are gone forever. That's why you have to check now and again, make sure all the parts are still there. Or have someone like me around, to do it for you. Sometimes twice a day."

"So, what should I do, if I'm alone, and I find out that my breasts have fallen off during the night?"

"Well," he said, "of course you have to find them, blow them back up, put them on again. But quickly. Before they get completely deflated. When they're totally flat, sometimes it's too late, you can't blow them up again."

She looked at him and laughed, "What would I have done without you, without this information? I've been at risk all this time."

> To: dbranstetter@aol.com
> From: iowadad@hotmail.com
> July 15, 4:46 PM
> <<<Delete this when read!<<<
> Eternal vigilance is the price of liberty.
> With our computing skills we can go anywhere, read anything, and remain always vigilant. Prepare to take the enemy down.
> Liberty and freedom from oppression will be the product of our journeys through the neural pathways of America.
> <<<Delete this file now! Delete all cookies now!<<

Davey's plane came in from the west, facing into a light east wind, the motor still steady at high rpm's, then lower pitched. The most welcome sound in the world, Connor thought. He had all their gear on the west dock, the shorn millet field. The rifle was on top of their bags. While Davey turned around and headed back toward them, Connor went to the other dock and rolled up the red cross.

He could hear Davey coming on a fast taxi. He had seen the red cross. He waved urgently at them through the windshield, spun the plane around, and let the wind blow him to the dock. Then he cut the engine and stepped out onto the left pontoon. He looked at Judith's sling, at the chewed up dock, at Connor's thirty-thirty.

"Christ, Connor! Ms. Merchant! What happened?"

"It's a long story, Davey. I'll tell you while we're flying. Let's get Judith into the back. I'll sit up front with you."

As the plane rose above the island, Connor looked down at the cliff top. The .222 casings were winking in the sun. He took the two casings from the cliff top out of his pocket and looked at them.

It was July 18ᵗʰ. The antibiotics were working. Richard was feeling pretty good. He asked himself: What will happen when the Canadian thing becomes news here? Because it will. "Local Judge Shot in Canada," and all that. A media event. She'll do interviews, how horrible it was, how brave her boyfriend was.

No one can point a finger at me. No one knows anything except David, and all he knows is he told me the judge's travel plans. Well, he knows we both dislike the judge. But why would anyone go talk to David? They won't. I'm in the clear. Unless, oh hell, unless they decide to look at the judge's caseload, find David, and then find his website. If they find that website, they'll definitely want to talk to him.

But David will never volunteer anything about me, even if he puts two and two together about Canada. Which he won't. Not David.

I'd better call him, go see him. When I called him on the 13ᵗʰ he sounded fine. I'd better go see him. Today if I can. Go early, before he gets home. Damage the back door. Jimmy it open.

Richard's new attorney Bailey reached him at home. He wanted to talk to him about the approaching deposition of Gloria's doctor and "some tactical things." Richard drove downtown to the law firm.

"Palermo has filed a motion to have you mentally examined."

"You've got to be kidding."

"No. The judge will probably grant the motion, given their

theory of extreme mental cruelty. They want to make you out as a really bad guy."

"They want me mentally examined, get a shrink to certify that I'm crazy? When is this supposed to happen?"

"It hasn't even been scheduled at this point. The judge hasn't granted the motion. May not grant it. And I'm not sure Palermo is for real on this. You've put your finger right on it, Professor, the whole problem of their approach: It won't work. You are clearly not 'crazy,' as you put it. And if you were, well, you wouldn't, you couldn't, be held responsible for your actions.

"Then, even worse for them, if you are 'crazy,' you can't continue to be a university professor. And believe me, they want you earning productively year after year so you can pay alimony. So they have to be very careful not to push this too far.

"Palermo thinks either that you will be forced to settle favorably with them, because you don't want to go through with the examination, because you don't want any bad publicity, a negotiation tactic, or she thinks that the examination will make your hypothetical bad deeds more credible."

"The two grad students weren't hypothetical."

"No, you admitted those in your deposition. Those are factual. I mean your 'sadistic, demeaning language,' as they put it. That is still hypothetical as far as I'm concerned. And I believe the same is true for Judge Merchant. They are going to have to prove it to her, and that can be a long hike."

Richard thought of the trail, the trackless woods to the cliff. "A long hike?" he said.

"Yes. Ugliness, like beauty, is pretty much in the eye of the beholder. Palermo is going to have to take Gloria through the statements, the miles of statements she says you made. The 'sadistic,' words. You have already denied such language. You said you were frank at times about her laziness, but that you were candid. Let's see. You used the word 'compassionate,' I think."

Bailey scanned the index to Richard's discovery deposition.

"Here it is, page 37. Yes. 'Candid but compassionate,' is what you said. That was well put. You were frank in your assessment of your wife. You told her the truth, but you were helpful to her as well."

"Yes."

"So, as I see it, Palermo is going to have what I call a 'whiny witness' problem. When is her complaining just too much for the judge to take? When has the client gone too far? When will the judge tire of hearing that Gloria's laziness was all your fault? Pretty soon, I think."

Here Bailey swiveled in his chair and looked up at the wall over his desk. "I've always found that it doesn't work to blame other people for our own failures. It is a hard sell to yourself, for one, and it is a hard sell to others."

"Gloria said the judge would understand what she's 'been through,' because she's a woman." Richard used air quotes.

"I don't accept that for a moment. That's just victimology. It's nothing but whining cant. 'I'm a victim, don't you see, I'm not responsible for my own life.' Judge Merchant is a hardboiled, successful woman. She believes everyone, including your wife, has to pull her own oar."

Richard thought of the judge's oar, the wooden canoe paddle, floating by the canoe, bullets tearing into the water, while he laughed and held her in the scope, watching, firing again and again. Graham yelling at her, getting her under the canoe. More fun with them under the canoe. Shoot holes in the canoe. Bam! Bam! Like a big can floating in a river. Richard was a teenager again with a pellet rifle, plinking a line of cans in the river, one after another, making them sink.

The canoe was larger, made more noise when you hit it. Why wouldn't it sink, the big ugly can? Lots of holes in it. They were underneath it now, holding it upside down. It wouldn't roll over, their floating shield, carrying them to the dock.

It was Gloria all over again. Yellow eyes gleaming, rising above the subdivision on her carpet, naked. She had the wet canoe paddle between her legs, riding it like a hobby horse. She was sliding up and down on the shaft of the paddle, it was slick and gleaming. She was chanting at him while she moved back and forth on the handle, jerking her hips in time to the words: "Wom-an-judge, wom-an-judge, wom-an-judge!"

". . . and neither do you, I expect," said Bailey.

Richard had lost the thread. He looked around Bailey's office.

"She's a woman," he said.

Bailey looked confused.

"And the Pope's a man," said Bailey. "So what? Palermo's going to have to build the case, just the same. Brick by brick. Professor, would you like some coffee? You seem distracted."

"Yes, please."

Bailey picked up the phone and called his secretary.

"So this mental evaluation is a gambit. A risky gambit. If you're impaired, if you are 'crazy,' as you say, they lose. Of course, you and I know you are not crazy, and they don't want to go there. They have to hit a small target: They have to prove that your particular bent of mind makes it more probable than not that you would say the things Gloria alleges. It's a long hike, as I say. Or putting it another way, it's using a three-pound hammer to drive a tack. Their aim had better be good, and their touch light, or they'll make a mess. I'm betting on the mess."

CHAPTER
FORTY-EIGHT

Connor called Harry from the airbase at Kenora. As soon as Harry heard what had happened, he said, "Put Judith on. I have to hear her voice." They talked for a long time. Judith was crying. She gave the phone back to Connor.

"Unless you know someone better," Harry said, "I think you ought to use Tim Kelly, here in Nashville."

"I was going to suggest him," said Connor. Kelly was both the Vanderbilt team orthopod and Connor's client.

Richard's side was scabbed over, and the red areas and heat had almost disappeared. Dr. Patel told him to come back in a week. Richard was planning to go backpacking in the Smokies at the end of the month. He thought he could make that. It would clear his head. Prepare for the questions at his mental evaluation. If it ever took place. And prepare for possible other questions. Just in case those other questions came up.

The clinic in Kenora took X-rays and e-mailed the images to Dr. Kelly. The orthopod got back to Connor in Minneapolis between planes. "We can do it. Looks like a non-displaced, incomplete oblique fracture. It probably won't even require surgery, unless there is blood vessel damage or infection. But I want to have a look at it as soon as you guys land. Here at the Med Center. Call me from the airport, and I'll meet you in the E.R."

"Tim, we'll do it. Thanks."

"Hey, it's what I'm here for."

It was a good thing they were in first class. All the movement was giving Judith a lot of pain. Connor was telling her stories again, trying to keep her mind off of her arm. He could knock her out with the codeine, but didn't want to. He was down to cat stories.

He told her about Rubens and Monet. He had trimmed beef one night for a stew, and he had saved the trimmings for the cats.

"So, I put the meat in the microwave, and went outside to move the cats' bowls from the wooden deck to the concrete walk. See, leaving the bowls on the wooden deck was a problem, because Rubens liked to take his meat out of the bowl, eat it on the deck, and make a mess. I told them that food was on the way, and went back inside."

God, Connor thought, there's not enough here to keep the mind alive. I really love this lady.

"So when the microwave chimed, I got a fork and separated the brown lump into bite-sized pieces again." A flight attendant looked at Connor and smiled. "I took it outside. The cats were excited. Not the usual crunchies. I put it into their bowls. They stared at it. It was too hot."

"Is this *The Three Bears?*" asked the flight attendant.

"Even better," said Connor.

"So, I knew they would wait until it cooled, walking around the bowls, sniffing at it now and then, trying to take bites. So I went back into the house. In a few minutes, I looked out. Monet was eating out of the bowl. He had his foot in it." Judith laughed. "Rubens had brought his beef pieces up from the concrete walk, onto the deck, and put them down where his bowl had been. Where he wanted to eat. He was eating them there, making the deck greasy."

Time for the grand finale, Connor thought. "So the point of the story is: When it comes to cats, you're never in charge." The flight attendant smiled faintly.

Judith said, "Connor, dear, if it's all right with you, if you don't have any better stories than that, I think I'll go to sleep."

They had been back in Nashville for five days. The surgery had gone well. Judith wasn't even grumpy any more. Connor told her so. He figured it was time for an outing. They went to Tootsie's Orchid Lounge.

"You really know how to impress a woman," Judith said, looking around. "Get her shot, get her a first-rate surgeon, get her almost well, then take her to a redneck dive."

"I want to keep you guessing. I don't want our love to be routine."

"It isn't," she said. "You know, I've heard a lot about this place, just never been here. Sheltered life." She looked around. "Well, it certainly isn't routine, not for me anyway. I'm from Maine. The rock-bound coast. I went to Radcliffe."

Sunlight slanted through the open door. There were pictures of singers taped to the walls, writing on the photos in black ink. A bottle of pickled eggs sat on the bar. Someone had stuck a Polaroid of a stringer of fish into the edge of the back bar mirror. There was a sign that said "The singer plays for tips," a white cardboard sign, hand-lettered and sitting by a jar stuffed with dollar bills. It had probably been a pickled egg jar in its first life, Connor thought.

He smiled at Judith. "I've always loved redneck beer joints," he said.

"You really do keep me guessing," she said. "I had no idea. I've known you, what, for three years? You're a management consultant. A systems analyst. An art scholar. You never told me about this side of you before."

"I'm starting to feel secure in this relationship."

"That's good, Connor. I've got your ring on."

Connor thought it had something to do with not having any real roots. Something that came from bouncing around all those years.

Mostly he had been in Boston his teen years. Maybe these juke joints amounted to a Tennessee homecoming for him. His childhood. Probably that. He'd ask Harry.

"Jude," he said, leaning back and throwing his arms wide, "as I sit here in this plebeian commercial establishment, pickled eggs in a jar, I feel an unspoken acceptance welling up, an unvoiced gathering-in, an approval of all I have been through."

"I think you should have another beer. What have you been through? I'm the one who got shot."

CHAPTER
FORTY-NINE

"Harry, Connor said 'humerus.' He was wonderful. He had Tylenol-3, and Ampicillin, and he made a splint from a branch. And best of all, he said 'humerus.' I was impressed."

Connor looked sheepish. "You learn a lot of anatomy in art school," he said.

"Common doctor tactic," said Harry. "Name the problem in Latin. Patient thinks the doc knows what he is doing."

"Connor was so sweet. Yes, you were, dear. You sat with me all day, talking to me, making me drink water, making me laugh, giving me medicine. He didn't even go fishing." Harry laughed at that, and so did Connor.

"He told me stories. Stories about his childhood. Stories about how his attorney friend Harcourt taught him to fish. He has great stories about Harcourt," Judith said. "I laughed and laughed."

"She was on painkillers," said Connor. "It was an easy house to work."

"Tell Harry the story about you guys drinking all the beer, that one."

"I will sometime," said Connor, "Harry will like it. Harry likes beer."

"No, tell him now. I want to hear it again."

"Well," he looked at Harry. Harry nodded. "It was eight years ago. Bright and Looper and Harcourt and I fly into Rawak Lake. This is maybe my third fishing trip, I don't know much. Looper and Bright are real fishermen, but they've never been to Canada. So Harcourt is telling them all about lake trout."

"No, not that one. The one about the beer and the motor."

"Oh, OK."

"No, finish the lake trout," said Harry. "I can't stand it. The tension. I may have to go hit golf balls."

"OK. Lake trout first. I tell Bright and Looper on the airplane to Minneapolis, 'There are no lake trout.' Of course there are, really. At that point, I had just never seen one. My first two trips, Harcourt and I trolled up and down in the sun, back and forth, hour after hour. Miserable. He loved it. After a while I took to referring to them as 'hypothetical lake trout.'

"So, I announce on the plane that there are no lake trout, and that if anyone catches one, I will eat the head."

"Eat the head?" said Harry.

"The head," said Judith.

"So what happens? I catch a lake trout. Oh, my God. Big scene before supper. 'Graham's gonna eat the head. Ooh, look at it. The eyes.' All that."

"Did you?"

"Listen. So, Bright and I are outside cooking the trout on a sheet of tinfoil on the grill. I say to him, 'I can't do it. Help me,' and he says, 'Connor, cut the head off and put it in the lake. I'll swear you ate it.' I do it, and he does. I still owe him."

"Perjury," said Harry.

"Yes," said Judith. "Now, the motor and the beer."

CHAPTER
FIFTY

"David, look at this," said Richard. He was inside Judith's PC at the courthouse. "You've taught me well, my friend. I'm having a lot of fun."

David came over from his own computer, looked over Richard's shoulder. "My, my, she's on a roll isn't she?"

"Looks like she's working on an opinion in a custody case and the mother's going to lose."

> *This mother has misled many people, including herself. The Court gives great weight to her mendacity. She is an accomplished and successful liar. It may be that she is convinced of the truth of some of what she says. But her world is imagined; her facts are non-facts. This mother successfully creates confusion as to almost every topic which she finds uncomfortable. If she doesn't like the topic, then the cumulonimbus clouds roll in: ambiguous, rambling, misdirectional gambits, by which she exhausts her questioner. Whether she knows she's deceiving as she musters her ambiguities is not material. The fact is that she does it. This is lying by*

evasion, lying by indirection. However she does not scruple to lie directly whenever it suits her purpose.

The court also gives great weight to the fact that this mother knows and uses the vocabulary of victimhood. She has made herself a poster child for victimhood in her own mind. She has misled many people, many good, dedicated people who know full well that women are victimized daily by men. She knows the postures and buzz words, and she uses them to great advantage. But her victimhood is utterly fabricated.

There is marital fault to spare on each side of this marriage. But when it comes to the hell of living, it is the husband who has been the real victim. She has cowed him; she has reduced him to servitude. He tried and tried to please her. Did he warp and cow his wife? No. But he threw her world of martyrdom into chaos by entering a twelve-step program, by apologizing to her for the purchase of sexual favors, and by becoming faithful to her for the last seven years of the marriage.

This was immensely threatening to the wife because the husband was no longer a villain. What was she to do? She re-created the villain for herself and for her son. She denied her husband's rehabilitation; she denied his last seven years of fidelity. It did not fit her view of herself, so it could not be allowed to exist. She painted the father as a sexual predator who would feed upon anyone. The mother has no recognition of her destructive effect upon her son. Her needs come before her son's need for a father.

The onset of reality, this litigation, was horribly threatening to this mother. She had two excellent lawyers, one after the other, and fired them both, precisely because they were bringing her to reality. She wanted the lawsuit to be postponed forever, to last

forever in stasis, her denunciations hanging in the air
unrefuted.

"You know," said David, "it is vexing that this Merchant woman makes some correct decisions. I would really rather she be consistently wrong. It would help me feed my wrath."

To: <u>dbranstetter@aol.com</u>
From: <u>iowadad@hotmail.com</u>
July 22, 7:21 PM
<<<Delete this when read!<<<
    You are right. There is no substitute for decisive action. Talking is ersatz.
<<<Delete this file now! Delete all cookies now!<<

CHAPTER
FIFTY-ONE

"Well," said Connor. "Same trip. I may not know about lake trout, but I know which beer to buy at the border. I tell Bright and Looper to buy LaBatt's Blue. Important decision, a case of duty-free beer. Harcourt buys a case of Molson Canadian, says it's much better. 'Can't get it in the States. You guys'll be sorry,' he says to us. I buy LaBatt's. Bright and Looper buy LaBatt's."

"The float plane drops us off at the cabin. The Rawak outfitter is already there to meet us, show us the cabin. He tells us that this particular motor over here under the cabin, be careful, it seized up with the last people. That's why it's under the cabin. Sounds OK to him, he says, he ran it a while, but he wants to get it checked out. That's why it's under the cabin. We've got two boats, two motors in perfect condition. And this extra motor. Might work, might not. He leaves.

"We're standing on the dock. Four cases of beer. Harcourt's Molson Canadian is on top. He opens one, asks do we want to try a real beer? We say sure. He gives us each one. It is good. Very good. Harcourt looks at the motor under the cabin, and goes and puts a third boat in the water. Then he goes and gets the questionable motor. Puts it on the third boat. Gets a new beer, cranks up the motor. Sounds OK to him, he says. He's the veteran fisherman, see, Alpha Dog, he knows.

He takes the third boat out for a short spin. Comes back in, says, shit, the motor's fine. We all drink some more Molson. Harcourt says he's going to go out in the third boat. He'll unpack later. He gets his tackle box, one rod, some beer for the boat. We say we're going to finish unpacking. Harcourt takes off straight down the lake, out of sight.

"The question is: How far can an outboard run with no impeller to cool it? How far will it run before it seizes up? The answer is: about four miles. Harcourt gets stranded four miles out, has to paddle back against the wind, finally gets a tow from another fisherman.

"We don't know why he's gone so long. The Molson Canadian is very good. 'He must have gotten into some good fish,' we tell each other. We're talking, rigging up all our poles. Harcourt's been gone for hours. We're unpacked, fishing from the dock. The tow boat comes into view, drops Harcourt off. He's beat, dead tired, wants a Molson. All the Molson is gone. We tell him he was right, the Molson Canadian was better than the LaBatt's. Would he like some LaBatt's?"

Despite Judith's hospital admission under a different name, the newspapers found the story. "Judge Merchant Shot in Canada." They put in all the details they could get, including that the Royal Canadian Mounted Police had called Metro Nashville's Chief Bolden to tell him they had a rifle, perhaps used in the assault on Judge Merchant. A dive team had gotten it from sixty-five feet of water at the base of a cliff. The Mounties had taken the rifle and a canoe "with multiple bullet holes" out to Kenora, and were holding both as evidence.

What the papers didn't report, and what Metro Nashville's Chief Bolden told Judith, was that the rifle was a .222. The Canadians were running ballistics, and would fax him the results.

Connor and Judith were having breakfast. He was holding *The Davidson Tribune* in front of his face, and reading to Judith.

> *Local art dealer and consultant Connor Graham, forty-three, handsome, is incredibly lucky. On a recent Canadian fishing trip, Graham, who some years ago became moderately wealthy by inventing a blood filtration process, pulled a large-biceped mermaid from a Canadian lake. They intend to marry in the somewhat near future.*

"One large bicep," said Judith. The other one is atrophied and in a sling."

> *. . . pulled a mermaid with one large bicep,* Connor read on, *from a Canadian lake. One arm is atrophied and in a sling. They intend to marry in the somewhat near future. The bride will carry flowers in her left hand.*

Judith grabbed the newspaper from him. She pretended to find the story.

> *. . . the bride, according to some accounts, found Graham, a merman with a dirty face, on a Canadian lakeshore. Bemused by his dusky countenance and extensive quantities of Tylenol-3, she consented to marry.*

"Well, either way," said Connor. "Who cares about journalistic accuracy?"

"Not *The Davidson Tribune*," said Judith, "that's for sure. 'Focus of dislike,' 'our own controversial Judge Judy.' Pah!"

There was a touring Andrew Wyeth exhibit at the Cheekwood Museum. Judith and Connor went to it. The exhibit started her thinking about her house in Maine. Maybe it was time to go there, take Connor. He'd never seen it. Magic Beans would give her some time in the fall. He had told her he felt "somehow responsible" for her injury.

The Wyeth exhibit had brought it all back, how the house had looked when she had bought it. A wreck. Empty rooms, broken panes stuffed with rags, the remnants of years of coastal living pushed into barn lofts, clapboards askew, cellar door falling in, the cistern with animal bones in it.

She thought about the famous painting of Christina Olson, crippled on the ground, looking uphill at the house. The Olsons had been Wyeth's neighbors from the thirties until their deaths in 1969. Their house could have been Judith's house.

If she had it to do over again, would she buy it again? The house had been in her family. Rufus Merchant had built it in 1835. After him, it had passed out of the family. But when it had come up for a tax sale, Grandmother Merchant had called her, and Judith had gotten it for very little. Now, one hundred and ninety thousand dollars later, it was a place she could take Connor.

She knew it was a place of intense history, without words. Oh, she knew words had been spoken there. Words of her bloodline, in that house, and throughout the small town. The Merchants and the Murphys were the two oldest families.

In my house, Judith thought, people of my bloodline have loved and argued, rejoiced, been shabby to one another, scrabbled out an existence. They did it by farming, putting vegetables in the root cellar in the fall, cutting ice in the winter for the icehouse, going down to the sea to fish, to clam, to pull pots, to dig bloodworms for Boston twice a week, the big truck coming through on Route One. Hard work. Impoverished dignity.

Now here she was in Tennessee, rooted here now, instead of Maine. About to marry. The Wyeth exhibit at the Cheekwood

Museum carried her back. Her heart ached for the empty sweptness of Maine, for the desolation that said, "Here, for hundreds of years, your people survived. You are part of us."

Judith needed to be tough now, needed to survive. Whoever had shot her was not finished. Could not be finished.

CHAPTER
FIFTY-TWO

"Judge, I think I've got something. Maybe." It was Detective Jay Blake, from Chief Bolden's department at Metro. He had called Judith's clerk, asked to stop by. Judith was in chambers. She came out from behind her desk, and they sat together at the round table. He looked at her sling.

"Judge, this may be nothing, but I've been thinking . . . A .222 is not that common."

"I thought it was a varmint rifle. That sounds common."

"Well, yes. But it's loud, and it's fairly expensive to shoot. Not many people use it for regular range shooting. Well, anyway, I may be way out of line here, but there is a man at Cumberland Rifle & Pistol where I go, a strange bird, shoots a sweet Remington .222, ten-power scope, an old Model 722D, on the three-hundred-yard range. Branstetter. David T. Branstetter," Blake said, consulting a slip of paper.

That fits, she thought. "David Branstetter is one of my cases," she said. "He doesn't like me. He has a website. Take a look at it, Detective. It's pretty bad." She wrote down Branstetter's website address and handed it to Detective Blake.

Connor thought about knowing that *humerus* was the name for the upper arm bone. Harry had something there, the thing about Latin and posturing. John R. Morris Jr., MD, his magnificence, had used the Latin for migraine. Dana had *"Hemicrania extremis,"* he had said. This after Dana had been in the E.R. for thirteen hours. This as he sent her home to go blind, to go irreversibly into a coma. He had put a fancy name on what he didn't know, what he hadn't bothered to test for, had walked out, felt important, had gone on to the next patient. God walking on water.

Well, doctor, Connor thought, you've lost your Porsches, your *automobilia celerissima.*

"Judge, we've had a break in your case."

It was Sheriff Bolden. The ballistics for the Canadian gun matched the slugs from her bedroom ceiling. The Chief was keeping the detail privy to the investigation, but he wanted Judith to know.

He told Judith that Detective Blake and his partner were going out to Branstetter's place at 6:00 PM, to ask him some questions. They would try to catch him at home, after work. They would ask for permission to look around, see if he had a .222 rifle. If he refused to cooperate, they'd get a search warrant, and keep him under surveillance until the warrant got there.

"Sheriff," Judith said, "this Branstetter guy is a racist, and he hates me. He thinks I'm Jewish. He hates Jews. But he doesn't strike me as a killer."

"Judge, with all respect, they only look like killers in movies and on TV."

"Professor, it's David. The police have been here to see me. About that thing up in Canada, Judge Merchant. They think I did it!"

"David, that's terrible. Terrible. Are you at home?"

"Yes."

"Stay there, I'll be right over."

The Tennessean said the rifle had been found at the base of a cliff on the lake where the judge had been. Not good. But still, things were moving faster than Richard had thought they would. This was really not good.

Richard parked around the corner from David's house. He was wearing a brown herringbone jacket with a rep tie. Blue button-down shirt. Conservative, academic, understated. He walked slowly to the front door. Zinnias were blooming across the street. The house next to David's still had not sold. The grass needed cutting. It never would sell if they didn't keep the grass cut.

David let him in before he knocked. He had been drinking. His hair was standing up in the back. The house was worse than usual. David started right in, even before shutting the door behind Richard,

"They wanted to search the house, talk to me about guns. They asked me a lot of questions, about Canada, about Judge Merchant."

"They looked at my thirty-thirty, my thirty-aught-six, my hand guns. That was all fine. No problems. Then they said, 'Mr. Branstetter, where is your Remington .222?' 'Right here,' I said, going to the couch." David went to the couch. Spread his hands. 'Right here,' I said, and I reached under the couch. David showed him how he had done it. "It wasn't there! My .222 was gone!"

David looked like he was going to cry.

"I told them, 'Yes, yes, I have a .222. It's not here. I don't know where it is. It's missing.' They said, 'Of course it is, Mr. Branstetter. It's in Canada. Tell us about Canada, Mr. Branstetter.' I didn't say anything. 'Don't lie to us Mr. Branstetter,' they said, 'We know about your website.'

"I didn't know what to say. I was thinking about you. I thought maybe you might know something. I thought maybe you had done something. I didn't want to say the wrong thing. So I said I wanted a lawyer. They became hateful then. They arrested me, they took me downtown to their headquarters place. They made me get finger-printed. It was awful, just awful!"

"David, I am so sorry."

"They put me in a cell with a man who threw up. I got emesis on my shoes. I had to throw my shoes away."

"David, let me fix you a drink. You really have been through hell."

"I had to post bond. My mother posted bond for me. My mother had to post bond for me! I thought I would die. Scotch, please, Richard."

Richard went to the kitchen. He would have to handle this right. There was a bottle on the counter, a glass next to it. He sniffed it. Scotch. He filled the glass half full and took it to David. He went back to the kitchen, got a beer. When he came out, David was sitting on the couch, staring, tears in his eyes. Richard sat down next to him, said nothing, and hung his head, not drinking his beer. David drank quietly, looking at Richard.

Richard raised his head after a while, and looked into David's eyes. "David, I have to apologize to you. I'm dreadfully sorry. Abjectly sorry. I have done something which turned out badly. I took your gun. I took the .222. I went to Canada. I didn't want you to know. I was trying to protect you." He stopped, took a sip of the beer. "I care about you. I didn't want you to know, to get involved." There was a long pause. "David, I was trying to keep you out of it."

David said nothing.

"I was going to put the gun back under your couch. You wouldn't have known anything. You would have been in the clear. You hadn't given me the gun. You'd be perfectly innocent if anyone asked questions."

"If I didn't know you had the gun . . ."

"Exactly. There would be a killing in Canada. 'Local Judge Dies in Canada.' Your gun would have been here all the time, in its place, under the couch, if any odd questions were ever asked. I mean, they know you don't like the Judge. But there'd be no possible ballistic connection, all the slugs would be at the bottom of a very deep lake. It was perfect. It was going to be perfect."

He drank some beer. "But, oh, David." Here Richard allowed his voice to crack, tears to come into his eyes. Histrionic, he thought. Don't go too far. He cleared his throat, spoke in a deeper register. "David, I lost the damn gun! It fell off the cliff, into the lake. The judge's boyfriend was shooting at me. Graham was shooting at me. He hit me. I dropped the gun. It must have been found. The papers say they found a gun."

They sat silently. David's Scotch was almost gone. Richard sipped his beer.

"I'm in trouble, Professor, because of you."

"David, we're in this together from now on."

"We?"

"Yes, 'we.' We're a team, from here on out."

David exhaled loudly, ran his hand through his hair. "I feel better already."

"I knew you would. David, you are my friend. I have a plan for us. A very good plan. Now listen." Richard outlined his plan.

CHAPTER
FIFTY-THREE

Judith was reading what had become her monthly alumnae magazine, *Harvard Magazine*. There was no Radcliffe College now, no Radcliffe publications. There was only Harvard College. And something called Radcliffe Institute, whatever that was. She had graduated from Harvard, it seemed. It was as simple as that, her college having been ingested in 1999 by its larger partner. She remembered from college biology, at Radcliffe, that amoebas did that. Phagocytosis.

"Toby," Judith asked her clerk, "do you know anything about Markovian analysis of events?"

"Wow," he said, "let's see. Something about sequence. Yeah, that's it, you look at the present in terms of what came before and what comes after."

"That's right, 'a chain of possible events in which the probability of each event depends only on the state attained in the previous event.' So, Markov theory concerns events that are conditional upon those that precede them and affect those that come after.'"

"OK."

"Well, we've had four events so far," she began.

"Right. There's been the shooting, the feces in the mailbox, the roofing nails, the Star of David. Yes, I see where you are going . . ."

"Each event," said Judith, "may have been conditioned, under this theory, by something I did before it. And each event may have influenced something that came afterward."

"Every event influences something afterward. There is no action without a consequence of some kind. We know that without Markov."

"Yes," she said. "But maybe we can look for a skein of Markov events. You and I know which cases we think are the problematic ones. There are several of them. But do we have any litigation where I have acted four times in a similar proximity to the four, um, harassments?"

"No," he said. "I've already looked."

"I hoped you would say something different. I happen to agree with you."

Richard went to Bailey's office the first thing the next morning. A criminal defense lawyer for David was part of the plan. Richard told Bailey he needed a recommendation for 'a friend with a criminal problem.'

"Serious problem?"

"Yes. I don't want to go into it. I just need a couple of names."

"I need to know more," Bailey said. "For instance, is it white collar crime?"

"No. More in the violence line. They say he threatened someone with a weapon."

"Well, then. Two names come immediately to mind. But first, you need to know that all this sort of work is retainer work. Up front. Can your friend pay a retainer of several thousand dollars, perhaps more?"

"Yes." Richard would do it himself, if need be, if David's mother did not. Somebody had to.

"Then I'd say Martinson, Ray Martinson. Or Benny Levitt. Now, Martinson is a showboat, likes high profile stuff. He'd defend anyone, even a confessed child rapist." Bailey stopped, shook his head. "In fact," he said, "he did just that. James Willetts. Got the confession suppressed. Went to trial. Hung the jury. Before the second trial, he pled the guy to indecent exposure, got him twenty months. Willetts was out in eight. And three little girls are still in therapy."

Richard was taking notes.

"Levitt on the other hand is principled. Quite different. Thomas Benjamin Levitt. He needs to believe in your friend, either in his innocence, or that the state is overreaching. As bright as Martinson. No, he's brighter. But not showy. Very effective with a jury."

Richard made a show of taking more notes on Levitt, asking questions about him. Said, "Sounds like Levitt is perfect." He knew David would never use someone named Levitt.

"Mr. Branstetter," Martinson said in his first meeting with his new client, "I don't want to know whether you did this thing the state says you did. I don't want you to tell me. It is the state's job to prove beyond a reasonable doubt that you did it. And it is my job to prevent them. I will prevent them. I will use every possible legal means. You may be assured of that."

"I have heard that about you."

"I will hammer the very hinges off the doors of hell to protect you. I will attack the Pope's virginity, if it will help you."

"Please don't do that, Mr. Martinson. I am a Catholic."

"I am being figurative. The point is, I will do anything— *anything*—to protect your freedom."

"I believe you. Thank you."

"Then let's get down to business. The state says your gun was used to shoot and wound Judge Judith Merchant in Canada. And that the same gun was used in April to shoot up Judge Merchant's house on Brayman Pike."

"The detectives told me that. Detective Blake, and somebody else. His partner I think. They were rude to me."

"I am sorry. The minions of the state are often rude. We will attack the state's ballistic evidence, first of all. We will prove it is possible that there are two different guns, the one used in Canada and the one used at the judge's house. We will show that neither one is the gun missing from your home. I'm sure you don't happen to have any ballistic data on your missing gun. That would be most unusual."

"No, I don't think so, well . . ."

"Very good," Martinson said quickly. He was pleased. "We will hire our own ballistics expert. I have a good one. A man who often works with me. He will impeach the Canadian results, whatever they are. He will create a reasonable doubt. If need be, we will demand to test the Canadian weapon ourselves. It is also possible that during those tests, or during shipment here, the Canadian weapon will disappear."

"Really?"

"Oh, yes. Stranger things have happened. Life is odd. I have had it happen." Martinson looked smug. "Time is on our side. Father Time is the defendant's best friend. Witnesses die, or move away. Memories become inaccurate. Evidence is lost. I will interpose every possible delay in the trial calendar. The state will tire first, I assure you. I will not tire. Judge Merchant will grow weary of seeing herself in the newspaper month after month. She may even ask the state to drop the prosecution."

"That would be wonderful."

"Yes, it would. Of course, we must remember, it's not her decision. It is the District Attorney's call, but he'd feel pretty awkward forcing a judge to go to trial."

"I see."

"In fact, this whole thing may just blow away, with enough delay. Wait until you see me filing motions! Father Time is on our side, Mr. Branstetter! Entire slash pine forests will be consumed to produce the flood of paper I will file. I will challenge every tenet of the state's case. I will challenge the rotation of the earth, if need be, to delay your trial."

"So, I told Martinson about the gun being stolen months ago. As you said I should, Richard. Just as you said. That I had forgotten the break-in. That my .222 had been stolen, and a pistol, and my confidential files. I called them, 'the supremacist folders.'"

"What did Martinson say?" Richard asked.

"I didn't even have to use our next line. He said, 'Well, Mr. Branstetter, I can see why you didn't file a police report. Those files, I assume, were very sensitive.' 'Yes,' I said, 'embarrassing.' 'Quite so,' he said, 'exactly. The jury will understand, if we have to get to a jury, which I doubt. This is very helpful. This alone creates reasonable doubt, in my opinion.'"

"David, this is wonderful news."

"Yes, yes, it is. And he's very thorough. He said my website might be a problem, but that there were lots of outspoken websites. He talked about First Amendment rights, our freedom of expression. The Constitution. I felt very comforted. He even asked about my computers, both at home and at work, which I thought was very thorough. I said there was nothing interesting on them, and besides, Richard, no one, I mean no one, can get through my security."

CHAPTER
FIFTY-FOUR

Judith and Harry were having lunch. "Do you still read the *New York Times* every day?" she asked.

"Every day except when my partner is in the hospital, and her house contractor can't talk to her, and her landlord can't find her, because she's in the fucking hospital under a fictitious name, and her damn fishing date won't leave her bedside, and I have to feed his cats. Which is beneath me."

"Poor Harry."

"I tell you, back when you were in the hospital, it was almost enough to make me go back to the Y, do my famous Mather workout. Two sets of mirrors, a steam bath, and then a massage. It was almost enough to make me take up swimming again. Which was good for me back when I did it. Good for stress."

"I remember."

"But it didn't change my natural shape."

"No."

"Fat guys are good at swimming," he said, "and golf. Nicklaus would be fat if it were natural for him."

"I'm sure he would."

"And then my attorney said to me, 'Mr. Branstetter, you must have been very upset when the detectives came to your house, asking questions.' 'Oh, yes,' I said.' He said, 'It is perfectly understandable that you went to the couch, where your gun had always been, to show it to them. In fact it indicates your innocence.'"

"Which in fact it does," said Richard.

"Yes," said David.

"Only you couldn't tell him why."

"Oh, my goodness, no," said David.

Richard went into David's kitchen to get them two more beers. He sliced some cheese, and put bread on a plate. David was working at his newest PC. Richard could hear the key clicks. He found some olives and put them in a bowl.

"Richard, look at this. This may help you."

There was nowhere David couldn't get to, it seemed, inside the judge's computer. He pointed to the screen. "I just found this. It's an opinion she's writing."

> *The husband freely admitted to the wife's psychiatrist that during the course of the marriage he from time to time struck the wife. His testimony in this cause has been disingenuous, straightforward, punctiliously insistent on accuracy, even when it places him in a bad light.*
>
> *The wife's testimony has been skewed and biased, certainly vituperative, with internal contradictions. It has impaired her credibility. The Court has given great attention to the demeanors and credibility of these parties. Indeed, the demeanor and credibility of parties is the bedrock of today's finding with regard to relative fault.*

"Isn't Gloria trying to say your marital fault outweighs hers?"

"Oh, yes," Richard said.

"Well, then make a clean breast of it. Merchant likes that. And look at this, it gets even better."

She has abused him and his family, his extended family, in all of its ramifications with a vituperation which is rare even in domestic litigation. The Court is going to depart from its usual policy and place some of this in the Memorandum Opinion. The Court finds that for hours she would berate her husband as "a prick, a pussy, a wimp, a piece of shit, a mother fucker, a pathetic human being." Later she would pretend that such disputes and occurrences had not taken place, or she would excuse her conduct with various explanations.

She called the husband's father "a wimp and a pussy." She spoke of the husband's sister in gross sexual terms that the Court will not place in this opinion. She spoke of the husband as tied to his mother's apron strings, and suggested that he needed to have her come over so that he could "suck her titties."

The experience of living in this maelstrom of abuse warped the husband. He became a part of his wife's world. He did small, mean things to her at times, in response to her wildly creative nastiness.

The relative fault of Mr. and Mrs. Farmington is ninety percent wife's, and ten percent husband's.

"Wow," said Richard. "A slam dunk for the husband."

"Hasn't Gloria berated you in 'gross sexual terms'?"

"You bet she has."

"Richard, 'Don't you remember,' as my ever-helpful attorney Martinson says, 'her calling you some of these exact words'?"

"Counselor," said Richard, "I believe I do. In fact, I will remember entire conversations. They will come to me in the next few days. I am going backpacking in the Smokies for five nights, starting Tuesday."

"Do you have to have a written permit?"

"Oh, yes. They don't let you just go hiking any more. You have to tell them each night where you will sleep. It's all planned out and on their computer."

David looked happy.

CHAPTER
FIFTY-FIVE

To: dbranstetter@aol.com
From: iowadad@hotmail.com
July 29, 9:28 PM
<<<Delete this when read!<<<
    Your thoughts are clear. Your purpose is pure.
It is now time for decisive action. As we have shared
with each other many times, vigilance is the essential
foundation of all success. Then action follows. The
elephant is loose.
<<<Delete this file now! Delete all cookies now!<<

It was August 5. Richard had just gotten back to Nashville from the
Smokies. He was relaxed, dirty, and tired. He needed a shower. He
would go backpacking more often. Even when he didn't have exigent
reasons to do so. He stopped at a convenience market for bread,
milk, and a cup of coffee. Then he saw *The Tennessean's* headlines:
"Professor's Wife Killed in Belle Meade." He bought the paper, and
hurried to his car.

By KELLY THOMPSON
Staff Writer

Gloria Jean Smith, 31, wife of Professor Richard T. Smith of Central Tennessee State University, was brutally murdered two days ago at her home in Belle Meade. According to Metro Nashville Police, Mrs. Smith's body was discovered only yesterday by a deliveryman, at her 112 Kingsdowne Circle home.

Metro Medical Examiner Jane Crenshaw has preliminarily indicated the cause of death as multiple gunshot wounds to the head, pending a complete autopsy. The exact time of death has not yet been established.

Metro Police Chief Larry Bolden issued a brief statement: "It appears that the victim was shot several times with a high-powered gun, possibly a handgun. She had no chance. Whoever did this made sure she died. We are actively pursuing our investigation."

Neighbors speculated the assailant or assailants stood in a flower bed beneath a side window, shooting Mrs. Smith from there. Police declined to comment. Mrs. Smith had only recently moved to Belle Meade. She and her husband separated in November of last year, shortly after she filed for divorce. The divorce trial was scheduled to begin before Circuit Judge Judith Merchant this coming October 3d.

Professor Smith, 38, is an associate professor of Germanic Languages and Literatures at CTSU. He could not be reached for comment.

So, Richard thought, travel has its benefits: It's not just broadening, it's liberating. You go away for a while, come back, and your wife's dead. He wondered if Gloria had been doing drugs and not paid her supplier? This sounded like a professional hit. Brutal. An object lesson? Could drug addiction have been Gloria's nameless malady? He thought about it. It was possible. It would explain why she wouldn't keep a job, even easy ones. My God, he thought, the nameless sickness. It not only existed, it finally killed her. Now the judge couldn't give her alimony, permanent alimony. Gloria was dead.

This meant he was free. The oxen were free. If David kept his mouth shut.

> To: dbranstetter@aol.com
> From: everyman666@hotmail.com
> August 6, 2:02 PM
>
> When the devil wants to destroy a family, he focuses on the man. For if he can neutralize the man, he sells the family into bondage.
>
> The family without its shepherd wanders lost in foreign lands. What are these lands? Verily, they are the Babylons of modern un-civilization:
>
> (1) video game violence,
>
> (2) whoring television entertainment,
>
> (3) so-called "low rider" trousers sold in shopping malls to display the buttock-clefts of maidens.
>
> Go not unto these lands. Shield and protect your children from them. Do not let the devil take your family.
>
> The damage that takes place when a man's family leadership is neutralized is beyond calculation.

CHAPTER
FIFTY-SIX

"Professor, I don't know what to say," Bailey began, "but let me start by saying I'm sorry. It must have been a terrible shock to you."

"Yes, " said Richard. "It was. Thank you."

"I saw your statement in the paper today. I thought you handled them well, the ghouls of the press."

Bailey had the paper on his desk. He had circled a paragraph in the August 6 *Tennessean*.

> *Reached at his home last night, Professor Richard Smith said, "This is an unspeakable tragedy. I don't know what to say. Gloria and I had our differences, but she was fundamentally a good person. She didn't deserve to die this way."*

A well managed interview, Richard thought. The stricken husband, with functional but simple words. Sensitive. Of course, what I wanted to say was, "She had good areas." That would have been fun. But pushing it. It was enough to speak of her good fundament. That was honest. Gloria's fundament was very good.

"It's a wonder I was coherent at all."

Bailey opened his file, took out a sheet of notes. "There are several things we should talk about. First of all, there is the suggestion of death."

"Excuse me?"

"I'm sorry. That's lawyerese. I should have said, we should now dismiss our divorce action, our countersuit to Gloria's original filing. And suggest to the court, by reason of death, that her initial suit has died with her."

"Yes. I suppose so."

"Of course, we will end up with our court costs. And Gloria's estate will get the costs for her action. Which takes me to my second point. Her estate. Did she have a will?"

"Yes. We both did. She left everything to me. As I did to her." He paused. "I still haven't changed my will. I don't know whether she has. Had, I mean."

"Well," said Bailey, "if she didn't change her will, clearly her estate passes to you. And her court costs, too. And the attorney fees for Palermo, if there are any still owing. If she destroyed her previous will, but didn't write a new one, the same result takes place. Everything passes to you by intestate succession. So far as I can tell, it does not appear that there is a new will. I talked with Palermo this morning. Gloria had not mentioned it to Palermo."

"What an irony," Richard said. "The woman hates me. Someone kills her. I get all her money. And I pay her debts. The dutiful husband. No, the dutiful widower. It's something straight out of Thomas Hardy."

"Palermo thinks you killed Gloria."

"I don't doubt it. Let her. I bet some of my colleagues at the university think so too. The fact is, I didn't. Screw them, and screw Palermo."

Bailey sighed. "You can't control what people think," he said. "But be prepared for inquiries. The police will surely want to talk with you."

"Yes, they already have."

"You met with them without counsel?"

"Why, yes," Richard said. "I don't need a criminal defense lawyer, Mr. Bailey. I'm innocent."

"Professor, with all due respect, you're being naïve. You have to be the prime suspect."

"Mr. Bailey, I didn't kill my wife. Between you and me, attorney-client privilege and all that, I'm glad she's dead. Very glad. But I didn't kill her, I don't know who did, and I don't care. Personally, I think it was a drug deal."

"That's not impossible. The autopsy did show Oxycontin in her system. Palermo told me, hush-hush. The papers don't have that. Not yet. It's a pain pill, but you can also crush it and snort it."

"There you are."

"Perhaps," said Bailey. "By the way, in case Palermo asks, where were you, as they say, on the night of August 3?"

"Hiking in the Smokies. From July 31 to August 5."

As he might have added, his on-line backcountry reservation would show. Issued to rtsmith@ctsu.edu. Which Metro Police had already verified. And they had also found the earlier, more important, reservation for July 1 to 12. Richard looked Bailey straight in the eyes and said, "Counselor, backpacking is a good, clean, celibate activity for a man going through a divorce. I go hiking as often as I can."

CHAPTER
FIFTY-SEVEN

Several weeks had passed. Richard toted up his mental ledger. The divorce was over. That was a blessing, that much was clear. Gloria was dead. Bailey was doing estate wrap-up. That was fine.

So what was wrong? Richard was trying to give himself permission to think about Katherine Kelty, and would she take one of his classes in the fall semester? But he couldn't get there.

Things might not go well in the next few weeks. David was a problem. David might not go well. The whole thing could come unglued, even with Martinson helping him.

David was getting edgy. He had graduated from being a potential problem. He was now an imminent problem. He had entered imminency. Have I created a new word, Richard wondered? Imminency. 'An imminent explosion.' Not whether, but when.

Richard could clearly see how it would come unraveled: David would tell Martinson everything. Richard got up from his desk, and paced back and forth. He was in his faculty office, pretending to work.

He'll tell his lawyer, I know he will. He'll get that sniveling look, that mincing way he has, and tell Martinson, 'My friend, the Professor of Germanic Languages and Literatures, didn't exactly tell me his plans about Canada, but . . .' And it would all come tumbling out in a jumble of self-congratulation and relief, exculpating David from everything except misdemeanors.

Harassment of a public official, a misdemeanor. Big deal. Martinson would get him probation for that. Or immunity for testifying against Richard. David wouldn't do a day of time, and Martinson would be front page. Where he liked to be, his element. Richard knew Martinson would deal him to the D.A., that he wouldn't hesitate a minute.

The problem was that David was so weak. He wasn't sufficient in himself, as Richard was. David was derivative; his worth came from elsewhere. Being of Pennsylvania Dutch descent, from his few quotable snippets of German culture. The wrong snippets, of course, the Aryan nightmare, the worst of the German tradition.

And on top of it all, on top of being wrongly accused of shooting a judge, David was obsessing over his son. The boy's probably better off without David, Richard thought. The idea of Branstetter, of all people, complaining about a nance was rich. "A popcorn vendor has his hand in my boy's fly." It was almost poetry. Not Rilke, but maybe Ginsberg.

David had told Richard, "I am the man, the only real man, who cares about Joey's future. I am his father, his progenitor. The father-son relationship is not a starfish, Richard, it does not re-grow." Here he had swelled up pompously, "If the father-son relationship loses an arm, it cannot grow it again. I have lost an arm. I must look at the stump where my arm was, every day of my life. It is unbearable, Richard."

David couldn't carry the load. He couldn't be a criminal defendant and a suffering father at the same time. He was going to crack.

CHAPTER
FIFTY-EIGHT

"I was dredging up old fishing tales, anything to keep Judith entertained, to keep her from thinking about her arm, or thinking about when the plane would come back."

"Sounds like you did a good job," Harry said. "What would a psychologist say? You were training for the senior years of marriage, for the times when wife Judith, old and gray, will drool on her bib and . . ."

"Harry, shut up. Connor, tell the story, please." She beamed at him.

"Well, if Harry can stand another fish anecdote."

"I love fish," said Harry. "I just don't like fishing. Tell the story. I will focus on the fish *per se*, as I used to say in the law."

"Actually," said Connor, "it's just sort of a moment in time when I was fishing down in the Thousand Islands in Florida . . ."

It was August 13th, a good day for a killing. Richard had figured out the *Endlösung* for David. He rather liked the sound of it: a "final solution" for an anti-Semite. As he drove over to Richard's house, he thought of David's devotion to the CTSU German film festivals. There were two festivals a year, and David was always there. David's favorite film was *Triumph of the Will,* and then anything else by Leni Riefenstahl.

Richard wondered whether David had seen *Das Boot.* He hoped so. It would help if he had. Richard needed David good and drunk tonight. He needed to stage a drunken evening like the one in the movie, the crew of the submarine downing schnapps and beer, schnapps and beer, over and over, to oblivion.

Richard had 100 ml bottles of Jägermeister and Vollkorn in a plastic bag, along with three six-packs of Beck's beer, and a roll of paper towels. Richard had given David a small bottle of Jägermeister for his birthday in June, and the man had beamed. David kept the empty bottle on his desk now, beside his favorite PC. Richard intended to play that card again tonight. But the Vollkorn was sham. Richard had poured out the clear alcohol and put water in.

Judith's file. Harry looked at it. So far, his investigative notes had led nowhere. He sat down and pulled the file toward him.

August 13

> **Metro and the Mounties are getting no match on the Branstetter photo with any flying service. How did Branstetter get to Manta, if not with a flying service?*

Harry put the end of his plastic pen in his mouth and chewed on it. He looked at the framed photograph of his senior year team, big Vs on their helmets. The games and scores were at the bottom. A 5-4 season.

> **Maybe it wasn't Branstetter at all? Metro says the RCMP are still checking, but so far no hits from any service in the range of Mantakagis Lake. No one recognizes Branstetter. They say July is the busy season, the flying services might not remember one person.*

**Maybe Branstetter was disguised?

**Maybe he didn't use a commercial flying service at all, got a private pilot to fly him in. RCMP says there are lots of private pilots glad to make a little money.

**No one at Mektu Lake Lodge recognizes the Branstetter photo. It is the nearest lake and lodge to Manta.

**Metro says no hit on photo does not rule Branstetter out.

He picked up the phone and called Davey Barton, Connor's pilot in Kenora. "Davey, this is Harry Mather, down in Tennessee."

"Harry! Good to hear from you. How's Ms. Merchant?"

"Pretty good, Davey. She's been going to physical therapy every other day, and hasn't missed one. Her arm is going to be OK."

"Great. Are you and Connor coming up? I got the windows fixed at the cabin. The dock's still a mess."

"Maybe soon. Can't tell. Davey, if a person wanted to get to Manta but not fly in, could he do it?"

"Oh sure, with a canoe. You'd have to portage up four lakes. Take you two days if you're in good shape. Three if you're not, or if the wind is bad."

"Could he rent a canoe?"

"No problem. Lots of places."

**Called Ogden's. Ordered topo maps FedEx for Mektu, Manta, and portage lakes.

CHAPTER
FIFTY-NINE

"Why the paper towels?" asked David.

"I got them for the windshield. Bugs on it. Should have left them in the car."

David's three PCs were all up and running. That was good. Richard had been prepared to ask David to show him things on each one, get him past his passwords.

"Your face is bruised."

"Yes," said David. "Embarrassing. Don't ask. Well, I'll tell you. Some shelves fell on me at work. I was standing on a chair, pulling on them. Me, an engineer. Oh, you brought Jägermeister. Lovely. And Vollkorn for you."

"Yes."

"But isn't Vollkorn, Richard, well, just a little common for a tenured professor?" He smiled at Richard, shyly, proud of his friend, pleased he could take a liberty, tease him just a little.

Richard played along. "Yes. Of course. But . . . David, well, the simple truth is that I am in many ways a common man. I really am. From Iowa. Sometimes, with a good friend, I like to drink a little much and go back to my roots."

"Oh, are we going to drink 'a little much' tonight?"

"Well, it is a hallowed German tradition," Richard said. David nodded sagely. "There's that great scene in the submarine movie, *Das Boot.* Have you seen it?"

"No."

"Pity. Well, there's a wonderful drinking scene in it. Schnapps and beer, and lots of laughing. Richard opened the Jägermeister, pretended to break the seal on Vollkorn, and poured a round. They raised their glasses to each other. "Prost, my friend," said Richard.

"Prost, lieber Freund," said David.

Richard tossed his ounce of water back, smacked his lips, grimaced, and reached for his beer. David poured himself another shot of Jägermeister, tossed it off, and proceeded gravely to read aloud the legend running around the edge of the label:

> *Das ist des Jägers Ehrenschild,*
> *dass er beschützt und hegt sein Wild,*
> *weidmännisch jagt wie sich's gehört,*
> *den Schöpfer im Geschöpfe ehrt.*

"What's it mean, Professor? I mean, I can tell it's poetry, and I know it's about a hunter."

"You really do read very well, David. Excellent pronunciation. Yes, it is poetry, rather archaic language. It is an awkward little bit, and hard to understand."

Richard looked happy. "Schöpfer is 'the creator,' isn't it?"

"Very good! Let's see, let me try. Of course this is not Rilke. In fact, I'm afraid it's pretty much doggerel." Richard studied the label. Then he translated:

> *It is the hunter's badge of honor*
> *That he protects the creatures wild,*
> *And hunts them wisely, as he should,*
> *Advancing his Creator's good.*

David clapped. "You even made it rhyme, the last two lines."

"I took some liberties," Richard said, pleased in spite of himself. I'm a very literate killer, he thought.

The drinking had been going well. Richard had had three beers and nine shots of water. David had had three beers and nine shots of Jägermeister. They were playing Lotte Lenya on the stereo. Loud. "Noch ein Bierchen?" Richard shouted.

"Ja, bitte!" shouted David.

Richard poured. "Und ein Schnaps dazu!" said Richard, and poured them another round. David eyed him. Literally. He had only one eye open. He reached for the glass and upset it. Richard poured him another. "Prosit!" he shouted. They drank. "And a caboose for that train!" said Richard, pouring another round. "David, do you know what 'Prosit!' means? What 'Prost!' means? They're the same thing." David looked at him with his one eye.

"Didn't think . . . thought just . . . toast, you know. Word."

"It's Latin. It means, 'May it be sufficient!'"

David was asleep, head back in his armchair, snoring. Richard spoke to him, shook him. Nothing. He went to David's three PCs, and did a search on each one, deleting all files containing "professor," "Richard," or "Smith." It took twenty minutes. He only found ten uses of "professor," about twice that many "Richards" and four "Smiths." None of the files referred to him in any way. Thank you, David, he thought.

David was still asleep. Richard announced loudly in his direction, "Muss jetzt pissen! Muss jetzt Wasser machen!" David did not stir. Richard shook him. No response. "Jetzt! Wasser machen!"

Richard went to the bathroom off the living room, peed with the door open, watching David. He flushed the commode loudly, clanking the handle, and cleared his throat. Still no movement. He wrapped toilet paper around his hands and stepped quietly through the bath into David's bedroom. He got David's Luger from the bedside table, pushed the drawer shut with his knee, and returned to the living room. He turned the stereo up louder, wrapped David's hand around the Luger, put the barrel in his mouth, and pulled the trigger.

Moving quickly now, he shed his toilet paper gloves into the toilet and flushed it, wiping the handle with the paper just before dropping it in. Then he put his own glass, the Vollkorn bottles, and all the Beck's bottles into the grocery bag, and wiped all the room's surfaces he had touched using paper towels. Last, he wiped all the Jägermeister bottles and, holding them by the neck with a scrap of paper towel, he rolled all of them over David's hands and fingers. He put the last one into David's left hand, rolling it over his palm and fingers. He looked around, nodded, stepped quickly through the front door, locking himself out, and walked the two blocks to his car. It was 3 AM.

CHAPTER SIXTY

Harry was making notes.

August 14.

**To Branstetter's early to look around while he was at work. He was dead.

**Bad scene. Luger in his hand.

**Little time. Dangerous. Looked for links to verify Canadian trip. No notes on his desk. Bills, filing, computer magazines, "Hacker's Monthly."

**A few German books.

**No PDA. No diary.

**Found a laptop in the bedroom, under the mattress of the extra bed. Took it, hoping for leads. Could not take big PCs. Afraid to be seen.

Judith got the news from her law clerk. "Judge. I hate to call you at home, but I had to. David Branstetter killed himself."

"Oh, my God, Toby."

"It's on Channel Five right now. You may be able . . ."

"Hang on," she interrupted him, going to the TV. The story was finishing up. A shrouded body on a gurney, doors to the EMT van closing. "And that's all from the scene, Randy, back to you." The anchor was on the screen now, "More detail on this apparent suicide in our six o'clock coverage."

"It's over Toby. What did they say?"

"Just that a body was discovered at the home of engineer David Branstetter, such and such address. Hadn't gone to work today. Boss went to the house in the afternoon. Valuable employee, that sort of thing. Linked to the, I quote, 'recent controversy involving a local judge.' They didn't use your name. Bet they do at six."

She called Connor from her car. "I'm on the way. Turn on Channel Five and record it. Branstetter's dead. Killed himself, Toby says."

"I'll get it, Judith. Drive carefully."

She got there before the coverage began. The anchor led in: "The body of David T. Branstetter was discovered today at his home at 3563 Lanscombe Way, the victim of an apparent suicide. Mr. Branstetter was a computer engineer who had worked for many years at Omega Computing on Nolensville Road, rising through the ranks from assembler to Administrative Vice President."

The screen showed a man in a brown suit, while the anchor continued in voice-over, "Mr. Branstetter will be missed by his colleagues." The man in the brown suit began talking. Script under the picture read, Joseph Pierce, President, Omega Computing. "David had been with us for twelve years, since our very beginning. He was loyal, very loyal. This is terrible." The camera panned from the brown suited Pierce to the company's front walk, then to the sign

240

over the entry, then to employees looking out through windows on the second floor.

The anchor again: "Metro Medical Examiner Jane Crenshaw has ruled David Branstetter died of a single gunshot wound to the head. A gun was found by his side. Mr. Branstetter had apparently been drinking."

Chief Bolden was next, a light bar flashing, crime scene tape in Branstetter's yard. "At this point," the Chief said, "it appears to be a suicide. Ray Kenworth, the personnel manager for Omega, found the body. He had come to check on Mr. Branstetter, who hadn't reported to work, and saw the body through the living room window." He pointed to the house.

The anchor was back: "David Branstetter had been charged in the July shooting incident involving Circuit Judge Judith Merchant. Judge Merchant was shot while on a fishing trip in Canada. The indictment filed in Davidson County Criminal Court alleges that Branstetter followed Judge Merchant to Northwest Ontario, and shot her while she was canoeing. Mr. Branstetter's trial date had not been set."

The screen changed to show the anchor and his co-anchor. He turned to her. "Charlene, it appears now there will be no trial."

"No, indeed, Randy."

"A tragedy."

"A tragedy." She nodded gravely. Then Charlene's face brightened, and she said seriously, "It must be a great relief to Judge Merchant."

"Yes, indeed, Charlene."

"Airheads," snorted Judith, turning off the sound. She looked at Connor. "But they're right. It is a relief to have it over."

"If," said Connor. "If it's over."

"Whatever can you mean, Connor?" Judith was angry. "The man was whacko, a Jew-hater. He thought I was Jewish, and he hated me for it. I'm glad he's dead. One less anti-Semite breathing the air of good people. I'll bet there are swastika flags in his bedroom."

"Judith, I don't mind that he's dead. I'm glad too. But did he shoot you?"

"Of course he did."

"How did he get to Canada? They haven't found any plane reservations."

"I don't know. False passport. Or drove, I guess. I don't know. He took some time off the same time we were gone."

"Whoa. When did the cops learn that?"

"I don't know. I learned it yesterday." She walked to the window, looked out. She could see Harry parking his car in the condo lot. "Connor, he shot up my house. He put nails in my driveway. He put . . . feces in my mailbox. He got in his car, and drove, or flew, or teleported to Canada, I don't care how he got there, and he shot me. He ruined our time together. It was his gun in both places. He's the shooter, and he's dead."

They were silent, staring at the TV screen. There were cats looking at jewels in a litter box, talking to each other. Then there were people suffering from "moderate to severe" things of various kinds, while the screen showed beautiful scenery. Connor went to her, took her in his arms. "You are right, Jude, it's over."

"I need a trip," she said. "I need to get out of town."

"How about Europe?"

"How about Monticello?"

They stayed in Charlottesville at the Boar's Head. For three days they wandered Monticello's gardens, browsed the bookstore, and bought seeds from the Jefferson Center for Historic Plants. They took the house tour twice. Judith touched the bookcase again.

While they were there, the Metro Medical Examiner called. "Judith, it's Jane. Sorry to bother you, but I figured you'd want to know this. It's just so weird."

"No, thanks for calling. It's Branstetter, right?"

"Yes. I've never seen this before, except in books. He's had a surgical reversal of circumcision."

CHAPTER
SIXTY-ONE

Harry was at his office. He was worried.

> To: crgrhm@my2way.com
> From: hmatherpi@hotmail.com
> August 19, 2:03 PM
>   Connor, suicide doesn't feel right. This guy
> would have left a note. He was a verbal guy, verbal
> diarrhea, look at his website. He would have gushed
> all over the people left behind. Also, he thought he
> was the only one who could protect his son.

He hit "send." Connor would get it on his pager at Monticello. Or on the drive home. Judith's file folder lay on the desk in front of him. Harry opened it and added:

August 19:

**Metro is headed toward finding suicide by Branstetter acceptable; they see no reason to think otherwise. They are going to do some more poking around, but it feels like they are happy closing the case. No suicide note,

they say, but the guy lived alone, was stressed out by his custody fight, stressed out by his arrest for shooting the judge. They call the suicide 'virtual admission of guilt' for the shooting of the judge.

**Bullshit, so that the cops can wrap the case.

**If Branstetter didn't kill himself, who killed him? Why would someone else kill him? A drug dealer, a burglar. Who else? A lover? A jealous lover? Man or woman? Got to see if cops have anything that points to a lover.

**Someone killed him because he knows something? What could he know? Is it on the laptop?

**I can't get to all the laptop. Tried "encryption" on Google. No help. World Book failed me too. Essays on the history of codes, code breaking. Nothing on hiding files on a hard disc. Connor needs to look at the laptop.

Connor and Judith had just gotten in from Monticello. It was August 20. They had spent the night at the Hotel Roanoke on the way back. Judith was at the courthouse.

"I've got to clean off my desk," she had said. "Pick me up in a couple of hours?"

"Sure. I'm going over to Harry's office. He's got some ideas. I'll call you when we're done. Or you call me when you are ready to leave."

"Chicken on the grill tonight?" she asked.

"Sounds great."

"Bring Harry?"

"Yeah, probably," Connor said. "We've been gone for four days. He needs to bring us up to date on Vanderbilt football."

CHAPTER SIXTY-TWO

When Connor arrived at "H. Mather Investigations, Results Now!" Harry was fidgeting with his pens.

"Hey, Connor."

"Hey, pal. Jude wants us to come over for supper tonight at her place."

"Good. We've got some talking to do." Harry got up and walked around the office, looking out the window at Second Avenue. Connor watched him. "Connor, I know Judith thinks it's all over. Thinks that Branstetter shot up her house, shot at her in Canada, and then killed himself. Maybe he did all that. I don't know. I don't want her to worry. She's got enough on her. But I've got to tell you, this suicide thing doesn't feel right. That's why I emailed you. I wanted you to be chewing on it."

"What do you mean?"

"I'm a psychologist. I'm supposed to have a sense for these things. I can't always read people, but I know this guy was a coward. He pulled his prestige from outside, from his Nazi worship, his anti-Semitism. He had a deep sense of unworthiness. Connor, cowards don't kill themselves."

Harry sat down, got up again. He ran his hands through his

hair. "Ah, shit, Connor, I've gotta tell you. I went out to Branstetter's a couple of times."

"Oh?"

"Informally. Mostly, just, you know, looking around. Trying to get some leads, trying to see if I could get the case to make some sense. The second time I went out, he was supposed to be at work. That was my plan. But he was dead. I found him with his brains blown all over the living room. I didn't tell the cops, didn't tell you, didn't tell Judith. I looked around some. And I took this." He got up from his desk and picked up a laptop computer. He handed it to Connor.

"God, Harry, this is evidence. What if Metro finds out we have it?"

"We're in a world of hurt. I lose my P.I. license, for starters. And you won't be allowed to sell paint brushes."

"It's worse than that."

"I know. Believe me I know. This scares me more than when the coach called 'Mather!' and put me in the UT game, freshman year. I didn't think I was ready for that then. I'm not sure I'm ready for this either."

"I know I'm not," Connor said.

"Connor, sometimes in life you have to break the rules. Normal police channels are not efficient. I can tell you that as a lawyer, I can tell you that as a P.I. It's a fact. Doing business as usual can let your friends down. Sometimes your friends need results when they need them."

He stopped. Connor said nothing.

"Anyway, I can't get anywhere with this laptop. The files I can see are all about Branstetter's work at Omega Computing. There's nothing personal. Nothing useful. But I'm poking around on this thing, and I see the hard drive has ten gigabytes of capacity, and it's sixty percent used up."

"So?"

"The files listed only take up four gigs, not that even. Less than forty percent of the drive."

Connor pulled the laptop to him, started punching keys.

"See what I mean?" said Harry, "Over half of the hard drive is full, fifty-nine percent. What's going on? Nineteen, twenty percent of the hard drive is missing."

"There is such a thing as hidden files or hidden partitions," said Connor.

"Yeah, I've heard something like that. But I don't know how to find them. Don't you do a lot of stuff with computers at your business?"

I can find them, thought Connor. But it doesn't have anything to do with management consulting. He pushed the laptop away, stretched his legs out, and looked at the ceiling. "Harry," he said, "All this . . . all this risk . . . this interfering with the state's investigation, we're doing it because the case doesn't feel right to you?"

Harry looked unhappy.

Connor went on, "I mean, it doesn't feel right to me, either. I said that to Judith, and she jumped all over me. She said it was Branstetter's gun in both places. End of discussion. She was angry."

Harry said, "Well, let me help you out, make you feel worse. While you guys were gone, the autopsy report on Branstetter got finished. I got a look at it. No bullet wounds on Branstetter."

"So?"

"You said you hit him."

"I said I thought I did. I shot, and he jerked. But I had blood in my eyes. I can't say for sure."

"Connor, tell me, does the absence of bullet wounds make you more suspicious?"

"Yes, it does." Connor sat quietly, turning it over, the risks. The risk of doing nothing and Harry being right. The killer still out there, after Judith. "I'll take a look at the laptop. You're right. I work with computers in my business. Maybe I can come up with something."

Connor picked up the laptop and walked to the door. He said to Harry, "You remember the guy who wrote to Judith, the guy at Northeast Correctional Center? Anthony Macon?"

"Yeah, the guy with the wife. 'You tell my wife Cherry to Kiss my Ass and Go to hell'?"

"Yeah, that guy." Connor said. "We may be going to see him, you know, as cellmates."

Harry grinned. "No, not we. Just me. Like he said, 'I was the one that fuck up.'"

CHAPTER
SIXTY-THREE

After Connor left, Harry pulled out the wide center drawer of his desk and took out Judith's file. He opened it and wrote:

August 20:

**Branstetter had the motive. He hated Judith and wanted to blame her for his problems with his son.

**He had the means. His .222.

**Did he have the opportunity? Yes, if he did the planning. He took eight days of "personal leave" right before July 4th. But a trip to Canada with a rifle? It takes more than time. It takes border documents. A picture ID and a formal declaration of the firearm. Or it takes deception and a customs agent who doesn't search your gear.

**If I were doing it, I'd be a fisherman. I'd take the rifle apart and tape the parts into the bottom half of two different rod tubes. The big black ones Connor

has. Fill the tubes up with rods. Or, I'd just tape the rifle parts under the frame of the car. No worry then if they search the luggage.

**Did he drive to Canada? Possible. Probable, given airline security these days. Two hard days up, two back. There aren't any airline reservations out of Nashville for "Branstetter." Or Knoxville, or Memphis, or Jackson, or Atlanta.

**Different name? False photo I.D.? He's a computer wizard. He could make one. Or find out how to get one. You can get a false U.S. passport if you have enough money. But all you need for Canada is a photo ID.

**Where did he cross the border? The RCMP say no "Branstetter" is on their records at Fort Frances, Rainy River, Pigeon River, Tolstoi, Angle Inlet, or Sprague. I asked them about South Junction and Piney too. Zip.

**So, he didn't drive, or he drove and just got waved through, or he drove and used a false ID.

**John Adams was right: "Facts are stubborn things." Even more stubborn when you don't have them all.

Connor found Branstetter's diary in the hidden part of the laptop. It talked about Rilke. He went online. There were two people named Rilke living in Tennessee. Both lived in Obion County. Near Reelfoot Lake, way in the west part of the state. From Mapquest, he looked at the location. Right on the Mississippi River, 201 miles away by road. This is a dead end for now at least, he thought.

Connor went back to the diary, and read again a strange part:

And we could have been there together, R and I, in another life, swimming naked, swimming with beautiful boys, swimming with young blonde men, just like in the Riefenstahl films. Afterwards, R and I would be on the rocks above the water, warm in the sun. Looking at the gorgeous young men. All of us nude, easy with our bodies, proud of our bodies.

The little boys, so adorable, their little peckers all tiny from the cold water, lying on their backs on the rocks. R and I, my panther and I, we are both panthers then, real panthers, lying in the sun. No more bars on our cages. He is purring, asleep. I have my head on his chest, staring at his glory.

Harry dialed the number for Detective Blake.

"This is Blake."

"Jay, Harry Mather. I need some help."

"If it's the Judge's case, you got it. Just don't get me in trouble."

"I hear that. I'm wondering about passenger names similar to 'Branstetter.' Sometimes these guys get just half-way clever. 'Randolph' travels as 'Rudolph.' I wonder whether the Mounties did a 'sounds like' when they talked to the flying services?"

"I don't know. You want me to ask them?"

"No. I'll be a lot happier if I call the flying services myself. Only I don't know who they are. I don't have the list the Mounties came up with. Do you guys have it?"

"We might. I'll check and call you back."

CHAPTER
SIXTY-FOUR

Blake called back. "Harry, there's fifteen of them. Fax them to you?"

"Yeah."

Ten minutes later Harry called Connor. "Connor, I've been calling the flying services. I've got a 'Branstone' at Remote Flying Services out of Kenora into Mektu on July 4. I called Mektu Lake Lodge, and they have a "Branstone' staying with them from July 4 to 10."

"Wow. You think it's him?"

"I don't know. I'm going to fly up there tomorrow, take the photo, talk to them about it, see what they remember. These things are better done in person."

"Before you go, we need to talk. I've cracked the laptop. There are some things you need to see. Can you come out here?"

Connor's office was across the Cumberland River. Harry drove up Second, took the Woodland Street bridge. He could see Adelphia, the Titans' stadium. The billboard had the dates of the exhibition games. Harry already had tickets for the one home exhibition.

Connor's place was in an industrial area. Harry parked in front.

"You were right," said Connor. "The part of the hard drive that was hidden had the good stuff. Some of it we may want to delete before we give it to the police. If we give it to the police."

"What do you mean? Why would we delete anything?"

"Look at this entry for August 12." Connor pointed at the screen.

> *A big guy, fat, came to the house today. He had a badge, flashed it at me, so I let him in. He didn't say his name clearly. I realize now he mumbled it on purpose. Because of what he was going to do to me. I should never have let him in. It was a big mistake. I was so nervous I didn't think.*
>
> *He talked to me about my website, said he could tell I didn't like Judge Merchant. I said it's a free country. He said it's not as free as you think, David, and then he hit me in the mouth. Then he hit me in the side of the head, and I fell down. I started crying, it hurt so much. He kicked me in my testicles. I screamed.*
>
> *He said, in a really low voice, down on his hands and knees, in my face, hateful, "David, if I ever hear about you again, you're a dead man." Then he got up, looked at me, and kicked me in the face. He had boots on.*
>
> *I went unconscious, I don't know for how long. When I awoke, there was a ring of roofing nails all around me, and one of those joke-shop plastic imitations of excrement on my chest.*
>
> *I can't tell R about this. Mustn't tell him. He'll be ashamed of me. I'm ashamed of me.*

"Huh," said Harry. "How about that?"

"Judith showed me the autopsy report," Connor said. "She got it from the medical examiner. You were right. No bullet wounds. Just some old bruises around the face, and in the groin."

"Huh. Bruises. Wonder how they got there? Must have fallen down some stairs, you know, landed on a fence at the bottom, straddled it," said Harry.

"Yeah, maybe."

"I really feel sorry for the cocksucker," said Harry. "My heart bleeds. I'm glad somebody beat the shit out of him."

Connor looked at him. "That's an idea. You're making me think. You said 'cocksucker.' That could lead us to 'R'."

"How? Who is 'R'?

"I don't know. Branstetter talks about 'R', and he talks about 'Rilke,' and he talks about 'my panther.' I don't know what any of it means."

He showed Harry the nude swimming passage.

"What I'm thinking," Connor said, "is let's try the angle that Branstetter really is gay. Where does that take us?"

"But you saw all the stuff on his website, about Treece and all. He hates homosexuality."

"I mean he's repressed, he never acted it out. He's in love with 'R' secretly. Hell, you tell me, you're the psychologist."

"OK."

"Then let's look for someone in Branstetter's circle who might be a love interest for him."

"I'll see what the cops have."

"Listen, Harry, who is Rilke? Is 'R' the same person? What is all this tiger and panther stuff? Is it a code for something else?"

"Beats me," said Harry.

"I did a person search on 'Rilke' in Tennessee. There are only two, and they live way out in Obion County. Reelfoot. To hell and gone."

"Maybe Rilke is an alias. Did you run it through Google?"

"Not yet. Let's see what we get." Connor typed it in. "A poet? A dead Austrian poet? Give me a break. I don't think so."

"Wait a minute," said Harry. "Look at the fifth entry. 'Rilke's Panther: A cry for freedom.'"

"Bingo," Connor said.

CHAPTER
SIXTY-FIVE

"So, the panther is the name of a poem? Or the poem's about a panther?"

"It's a poem," said Connor, "Rilke wrote it in 1907. Here it is. It's only twelve lines."

Sein Blick ist vom Vorübergehn der Stäbe
so müd geworden, dass er nichts mehr hält.
Ihm ist, als ob es tausend Stäbe gäbe
und hinter tausend Stäben keine Welt.

Der weiche Gang geschmeidig starker Schritte,
der sich im allerkleinsten Kreise dreht,
ist wie ein Tanz von Kraft um eine Mitte,
in der betäubt ein großer Wille steht.

Nur manchmal schiebt der Vorhang der Pupille
sich lautlos auf—. Dann geht ein Bild hinein,
geht durch der Glieder angespannte Stille—
und hört im Herzen auf zu sein.

"What's it say?" Harry asked. "I don't do languages. I don't even read Yiddish."

"It says the panther is trapped in a cage, in a zoo, I guess. He's walking back and forth. He's pacing mechanically to and fro. His eyes are dull and tired. From the bars passing back and forth in front of his eyes. It seems to him there must be a thousand bars, and no world on the other side of the bars."

"Your German must be pretty good."

"Yeah. Languages are easy for me."

"Not me. It's a left side, right side brain thing. We all have our talents."

"Chacun à son goût,"as the French say.

"Whatever. Is there anything else in the poem, anything useful?"

"Well, I don't know. It is a strong description of being trapped and hopeless. It says 'a great will stands benumbed, encircled.'"

"Huh," said Harry. "The diary is in English. Let me read the whole diary."

"I've printed it out," Connor said. "It's thirty-five pages long, and starts on January 1st. Makes me think there must be earlier years. Maybe on zip discs. Did you see any?"

"I don't know. I was moving pretty fast. And not thinking very well. I'm lucky I found the laptop. It was a pretty grim scene."

"Earlier years probably don't matter. He doesn't meet 'R' until January. He meets him 'at the U.'"

"Vanderbilt?"

"Maybe. You read it all and then let's talk. I'm going to make some phone calls."

Harry took the printout into Connor's conference room. Before he shut the door he asked, "OK if I mark this up?"

"Yes."

Harry closed the door, sat down, and read. From time to time he made notes in the margin, and wrote questions. He put brackets around seven passages:

*April 28. I must tell R about this. He really likes me.
I wish my German were better. He would like me
better then.*

*May 7. The judge is going to Canada. Must show
this to R.*

*July 28. I will do something for my tiger, something
very fine and noble.*

*July 31. My panther is trapped. His glance is dull. His
outlook is bleak. I must help him.*

*August 3. Food for my panther. I will not tell him.
My panther will never see this diary.*

*August 6. Long talk with R last night about my
problems. He loves me.*

*August 12. A big guy, fat, came to the house today.
He had a badge . . .*

Harry stood up, walked back into Connor's office. Connor was talking into the phone. He heard him say, "Ramp up the modalities." Harry snorted and went to the break room for a cup of coffee. When he got back, Connor was off the phone.

Harry said, "Connor, you were right. I think the guy was a repressed homosexual."

"He needed, perhaps, a forceful intervention?"

"He did. And I intervened, but not because he was a wanna-be. Hell, I don't have any problem with him being gay. Being straight doesn't win many prizes either. It's just majority behavior. 'Shack on some goo,' as your French say. What Branstetter needed, and what he got from me, was intense behavior modification. An ass-whipping. It's a psychological technique."

"Did it work?"

"It worked for me." Harry thumbed through the diary. "There are seven passages here. At least seven which help. Let's put the 'R' thing in the oven for a while. Keep thinking about it. I'm flying to Kenora tomorrow, then into Mektu."

"Your cell phone will work in Kenora. I don't know about Mektu."

"Doesn't matter. They have a radio phone. Or maybe it's a land line. I don't know where I'll be after Mektu."

CHAPTER
SIXTY-SIX

On August 21ˢᵗ, Judith was in her chambers preparing for the day's cases. It was 7:00 AM. The phone rang. It was Sheriff Bolden.

"Judge, glad you're there. I tried you at home."

"Problems?"

"No, but we've had another interesting development in your case. Nothing dangerous, of course, because Branstetter is dead. But I knew you'd want to know about this right away. It appears he killed a woman out in Belle Meade a couple of weeks back."

"Oh?"

"The weird thing is, the ballistics for Belle Meade match the Luger registered to him. The one he killed himself with."

Judith was thinking. "Belle Meade? A professor's wife?"

"That's right. I guess you saw it in the papers. Let's see, it was on August 3, to be exact."

"Chief, I think that's one of my cases, too. A divorce. Gloria Smith and professor husband Richard Smith. German professor at CTSU."

"Right. Small world, judge. I'm sorry it has taken us so long to get this match. Ballistics has been backed up, and the Branstetter suicide was a low priority." He paused. Judith said nothing. "Frankly, Judge, we had no reason to suspect a link."

"I understand, Chief. Thanks for the call. I'm going to have to think about this." Bloody hell, she thought. This is crazy. I'll talk to Connor and Harry tonight.

"Toby, this is Connor Graham."

"Hello, Mr. Graham. The judge is in the courtroom."

"Toby, I'm working on something for Judith. Just digging around at this point, trying to find who's behind all the troubles."

"Mr. Graham, I want you to know, anything you can do to help Judge Merchant, well . . . I say, just do it. I am really scared for her. Even worse things could happen at this point."

"Toby, I've got a lead. Please treat this very confidentially. I am looking for someone referred to as 'R.' Whoever 'R' is, he may be our bad guy. Or I may be just spinning my wheels."

"OK. Someone known as 'R'. How can I help?"

"I've looked at all Judith's cases that have had hearings in the last twelve months. I've found twenty-seven that have R as the first letter of the first name or of the family name of a party."

"You included both plaintiffs and defendants?"

"Yes."

"That's good. It could be either one."

"May I read you the names of these twenty-seven cases? To see if any of them strikes you as a case that might have a lot of tension?"

"Mr. Graham, they all have tension. This is a domestic relations docket."

"I mean, pressures, or behavior, out of the ordinary."

"I know. I had to say that. It's just that I'm mad. It's not fair to give a new judge this kind of docket. It's not fair to Judge Merchant."

"Judith loves her work. Even with this going on."

"She is a wonderful judge. I'll do anything I can."

"Listen to these case names. Stop me if one of them sounds like a hot one."

Connor read through the list of cases. Toby said 'yes' at *Robert*

D. Carbola v. Angelika Carbola, and again at *Gloria Jean Smith v. Richard T. Smith.*

"Tell me about *Carbola,*" Connor said.

"I'll have to get the file and call you back. And, Mr. Graham, I can only tell you what appears in the file. The public record, the information anyone could get by going to the Clerk's counter. If Judge Merchant wants to tell you more, that's up to her."

"I understand, Toby. Please get the *Smith* file too, because I'll have the same questions about it."

"I'll call you back in ten minutes."

Toby called back. "Mr. Graham, Robert Carbola is a welder. Thirty-five, remarried. He is under an order to pay child support to his ex-wife—they have three children—at the rate of $1193 per month. But he doesn't pay regularly, or on time, doesn't think he should pay, and Judge Merchant has had to put him in jail."

"Toby, how often does it happen that Judith puts someone in jail for not paying child support?"

"You mean, the same person?"

"No, no, I mean, in child support cases, how many times a month does she incarcerate?"

"Oh, three times a week, I'd say, for child support. At least that often. Sometimes more."

"So, it's not rare. Why do you think Robert Carbola might be 'R'?"

"Well, I don't know. He doesn't really feel right. But he's a very mad guy, that's why I picked up on his name. In his pleadings, he's representing himself, he talks about the court violating his first, fourth, fifth, and thirteenth amendment rights."

"What's that mean?"

"Mr. Graham, it means he's been poking around online and has come up with some fancy legal words. He doesn't begin to know what he means."

"Would he take a gun and go to Canada to shoot a judge?"

"I don't think so. He's not that organized."

"OK, we'll leave him aside for now. How about Richard T. Smith?"

"Well," Toby said, "this is a case which is past tense. We don't have the divorce any more, because the wife is dead. Somebody killed her a couple of weeks ago. So the case is over. But it was one which could have gotten very nasty."

"You think the husband could be 'R'?"

"It's possible. This guy is organized. Not like Carbola. For one thing, he had the sense to go get a great lawyer, William Bailey, after a bad first hearing. He had Thornton Tyler representing him at first. I really don't know much about Thornton Tyler, he doesn't come into Judge Merchant's court much, but Palermo ate his lunch that day. Smith stood up in court, started talking spontaneously from the counsel table. I mean, you don't do that. He was out of control, he looked out of control. Tyler had to make him sit down."

"A hothead?"

"That's not the feeling I had. It was more like he was above the whole proceeding, better than everyone else in the room. That it was inexcusable that his wife's case might be taken seriously, you know?"

"Yes."

"And when Judge Merchant started talking about the issues, equitable distribution and alimony, Mrs. Smith wanted permanent alimony, the professor just lost it. Stood up, waved his arms. I mean, it's just not done. He could be 'R'. Let's see, what else? They don't have any children. Married for ten years. He's a professor of German Literature at CTSU."

"Toby, can you fax me that file? I think I'd better take a look at it."

CHAPTER
SIXTY-SEVEN

Richard was at his office, thinking about the judge. I hope her arm is hurting her, he thought. Maybe I'll shoot her in the other arm, the superior bitch. He played it over in his mind, the scene in the water, the arm jerking, helpless, the paddle falling overboard. There was a knock on his door.

"Come in," he called. A student, he thought. Maybe it's Kelty. Onset of tumescence. The door opened. A man in a suit.

"Professor Smith?"

"Yes?"

"My name is John Carden, Detective John Carden. I'm from Metro Police."

"Do come in, Detective. Have a seat." Richard pointed to the chair opposite his desk. "It's about my wife?"

"Yes, it is. I'm sorry, I know this must be a hard time for you. I read your statement in the paper."

Richard saw that Carden was watching him closely. "Thank you, Detective. I know you have a job to do."

Carden opened a notebook and looked at it. He took out a ballpoint pen. He looked at Richard. "Have you ever known a David Branstetter?"

"Only slightly. He audited my German Literature in Translation course."

"Audited? What does that mean?"

"It means he just listened, took notes. He wasn't signed up for the course as a student."

"When did he do that?"

"Last semester. January to May. Why?"

"Did you know him socially?"

"No. That is, not really. We had a cup of coffee together once after one of my lectures."

"Did your wife know him?"

"I don't see how. I guess it's possible."

"You and Mrs. Smith separated in November?"

"Yes, the fifth. Right after she filed for divorce. She moved out, to a condominium. In Belle Meade. Where she was killed."

"So, from November 5th until she was killed, if she met Branstetter, you wouldn't know it?"

"Absolutely not. After we separated, Gloria and I were barely on speaking terms, to be quite honest. I think I told your colleagues that when they came to interview me."

"Yes, it's in the interview notes. You were hiking in the Smokies when she died?"

"That's right."

"So, her death was a surprise to you?"

"Absolutely. I read about it in the papers. Same as you."

"And where were you in the Smokies?"

"Gregory Bald to Clingman's Dome. Five nights. Detective, your colleagues have all this."

"Yes. So, while you were gone, David Branstetter could have gone to see your wife?"

"He could have gone to see the President, too. I mean, where is this going?"

"We think he killed your wife."

"You're kidding me."

266

"No, sir. The same gun that Branstetter used to kill himself killed your wife."

"Wait a minute," Richard said. "You're telling me Branstetter is dead?"

"Yes, sir. Killed himself. A week ago."

"I didn't know."

"It was in the news, in the papers. But it wasn't a big story."

"I've been pretty busy. And frankly, I'm a bit distracted."

"Of course. I understand. Why would Branstetter want to kill Mrs. Smith?"

"I haven't a clue," Richard said, thinking, why indeed? "I mean, the man was a kook, but he was highly intelligent. To murder a woman, to murder Gloria . . ."

"A kook?"

"A Nazi apologist. He admired Hitler. Loved all things German. That's why he attended my lectures. I'm a professor of German literature. In my line of work, Detective, you run into these people. They are an embarrassment, but they are part of the landscape. Intellectual skinheads."

"How well did you know him?"

"Hardly at all."

"But enough to call him a kook."

"As I said, we had a cup of coffee together. He gushed Teutonic nonsense all over me. The usual tripe. Hitler had bad advisors. Hitler was kind to dogs. What a great opportunity lost. That sort of thing."

"Yes. Well. He liked you?"

"I suppose."

"Did he know you were going through a divorce?"

"I don't know."

"You didn't tell him?"

"Of course not. Certainly not. Detective, I didn't like the man. My private life was none of his business."

"So, for example, I have to ask these questions, Professor, you understand, how would Branstetter get the idea to kill your wife?"

"I haven't the slightest."

"You didn't put him up to it?"

"Oh, this gets back to me, does it?"

"We have to look at all the possible angles. Rule things out."

"I suppose you do. Look, Branstetter was irrational. You have my wife's autopsy report. You know she was using drugs. Maybe Branstetter was too. Maybe they had the same drug dealer. I don't know."

"So, Branstetter wouldn't kill Mrs. Smith to please you?"

"I didn't know the man. He didn't know me. He heard me lecture. We spent fifteen minutes together at the university coffee shop. Why would he kill my wife?"

"Professor, we don't know." Carden stood up. "Thank you for your time."

Richard showed Carden to the door, shut it behind him. He went back and sat down at his desk. Maybe he did it, Richard thought. Maybe David did it. Oh, this is rich.

Harry took a cab from the Kenora airport to the float plane base of Remote Flying Services. Teddy, the pilot who had flown "Branstone" on July 10, wasn't there. The pilot from July 3 didn't recognize the Branstetter photo and couldn't describe "Branstone."

"We fly a lot of people to Mektu. Mostly use the Twin Beech, 'The Expediter.' Six passengers at a time. Ten trips to Mektu a week. I couldn't describe this Branstone for you if my life depended on it. And neither can Teddy, you can be sure of it."

"Thanks. I need to get to Mektu. Can someone take me?"

"I'll take you myself in the Beaver. Now?"

"Now."

It was late afternoon on the 21st.

"Mr. Mather," said the owner of Mektu Lodge, "this is the same photo the RCMP showed us. As far as we know Mr. Branstetter has never been our guest."

"I understand," said Harry, "but when I called yesterday, I had your desk clerk check the guest register for July, and she found a 'Branstone', staying with you from July 4 through 10."

"Yes?"

"Do you mind if I talk to your staff, see if they remember him, maybe can describe him to me? The name is so similar."

"Not at all. I was away from the lake for that period, or I would describe him to you myself. I take a personal interest in all our guests."

CHAPTER
SIXTY-EIGHT

Harry started with Ellen, a college girl from Winnipeg. She had been the maid for Branstone's cabin.

"Oh, no, that's not Mr. Branstone. He was much taller. Younger, too. A good tipper."

"Ellen, I'm a good tipper, if you can describe Branstone for me."

"Well, he was about six-one, like my boyfriend, but a lot thinner."

"How much does your boyfriend weigh?"

"Two hundred and forty pounds. He plays football."

"So, Branstone is one-ninety? One-eighty?"

"I'd say one-eighty, maybe a little more. Brown hair. Long, thin hands. Brown eyes, I think. I'm not sure about the eyes. Walked with a limp when he left here."

"A limp?"

"Yes. He fell down hiking his last full day here, and hurt his leg. Had to leave the next morning. He looked just awful. But part of his bad appearance was a hangover, I'm sure. He got really buzzo the night before he left. Drowning his pain, I guess."

"Did you see any blood? Any bandages?"

"No. His hands were scratched from the fall. He had on trousers and a long-sleeved shirt, so I couldn't see anything else."

"Hairline?"

"Full head of hair, cut fairly short with a part. Conservative. He looked like a lawyer."

"Attractive?"

"Yes, for his age."

"Which was?"

"About forty? Forty-five? I'm not good at ages."

"Scars? Pimples? Moles? Distinguishing marks of any kind?"

"No. He had a good complexion, and he didn't scratch his face falling down. No sunburn. He always wore a hat when he went out. He didn't have it on the last evening, though, or the next morning. Maybe he lost it when he fell. It must have been a bad fall, too, because he walked bent over that last morning, in addition to the limp."

"Ellen, anything else?"

"No. Sorry about the age.:

"You did very well." Harry got out his billfold. "Put this toward your college."

"Oh, Mr. Mather! A hundred American? Oh, my gosh. I mean, oh, my gosh!"

"Ellen, if you remember anything else, let me know. I'll be here tonight. And here is my card."

The dockmaster's name was Eddie. He didn't recognize Branstetter's photo, but he remembered "Branstone." His description was close to Ellen's.

"The guy who fell down, yeah. But that's not why I remember him."

"No?"

"Nah. See, my work, I get to look at a lot of customers, eh? Mostly they're pretty much the same, the men anyway. White, American, and overweight, like you. Maybe not so heavy as you. Fifty to sixty years old. Good fishermen for the most part. This guy comes in, slender, too young, got his own gear, big black rod tube. And doesn't know how to fish."

"Rod tube?" Harry was excited.

"Yeah, but that's not the point. About half the guests bring their own stuff. They all know what they're doing. The other half uses the guides' gear." Eddie was silent, looking out over the lake. "This guy comes in with a rod tube, comes to the boat the first morning with his rods. Doesn't want a guide. Has his own map of the lake. Doesn't ask for advice or nothing, eh? And his gear was all wrong."

"Too light? Too heavy?"

"Nah. His rods and reels were fine. But he had these orange Rattle Traps tied on. All he used the whole time, far as I could see. He'd do as good to throw rocks at the damn fish. Or spear them with a broom."

Harry laughed. He couldn't wait to tell Connor.

"Strange bird, too. Real quiet. I was glad to see him go. Got stinking drunk the last night, eh? They say he couldn't even eat dinner. Asshole, you ask me."

"Eddie, thanks. This helps a lot. Can I buy you some Rattletraps the right color for your trouble?"

"Nah, I got plenty. But you can buy me a beer at the bar in about an hour."

"You're on," Harry said. "And Eddie, I'm out of here tomorrow morning. What do I eat tonight?"

"You got just one night here at Mektu, the walleye, fried. A no-brainer. Don't order the green beans. They're canned."

Harry went to the Mektu office and used their landline to call Connor. He gave him "Branstone's" description, and told him about the injuries. Connor was jubilant.

"Harry, we may have our man. Professor Richard T. Smith. German professor at CTSU. That description fits a picture of him I'm looking at. I'm going to fax it to you. Smith had a bad case going on before Judith all this spring and summer. Just before Judith and I were at Manta. What's the fax number there?"

Harry gave it to him.

"Harry, it's getting deep now. I don't know what to make of this: The same Luger was used to kill Professor Smith's wife on August 3 and Branstetter on August 13."

"Oh, man," said Harry.

"Yeah."

"Do you think . . .?"

"I don't know what to think. Let's leave it in the oven for a while. Call me later?"

"Send the picture. Let me see what I can do on this end."

"Harry, how'd you do in the UT game, you know, freshman year, when the coach called your name?"

"Well, it was half way through the third quarter. I played the rest of the game. All my snaps were good. I've always had good hands. My blocking was OK. Best thing was, I recovered a fumble and took it in for a score."

"And you were a true freshman?"

"You bet. And it was my first time playing with the varsity."

"Harry, we need another touchdown today."

"I hear you, Coach."

The picture came through. Harry went to find Ellen. "Oh, yes," she said. "No question. Mr. Branstone, poor man. I doubt he'll ever come back."

Harry went to the dock. "Yep," said Eddie, "that's the asshole."

CHAPTER
SIXTY-NINE

Harry called Connor back. "It's Smith. I showed the photo around. He was here from July 4 to July 10."

"Bingo, my friend. Good work."

"Connor, I've got to prove the professor got shot up here."

"Why?"

"The Mektu people think he fell down hiking and hurt himself. He left here limping, bent over. They don't know anything about a gunshot wound. But it would be the absolute link. If he has a gunshot wound here in Canada, it practically establishes him at Manta, with a gun, in front of you on the cliff, in your gun sights. Connor, you reached out and touched someone on July 9th."

"Maybe."

"OK, maybe. I mean, look at it: Smith gets shot up here the same day you shoot at someone, whoever it was, on the cliff top across from your cabin. Smith has the motive to shoot Judith. He has the opportunity. He's on the neighboring lake. And he has the means, Branstetter's gun, which Branstetter loans him. If I find medical records in Kenora, a 'Branstone' with a gunshot wound, or whatever name he might use, and they recognize the prof's photo, we've got him."

"Harry, he was three hundred, four hundred yards away, maybe more. I absolutely did not see his face clearly. Remember that."

"Doesn't matter. You shot someone, whoever it was. But Professor Richard Smith, who had a red-hot divorce going in Judith's court, gets medical treatment for a gunshot wound here in Kenora. After being on the neighboring lake. And leaving the neighboring lake in bad physical condition. Is it the same guy who was shooting at Manta? Not definitely, but I'll take this to a jury any day. I like this one. Remember, I was a prosecutor for two years."

"I hope you're right."

"I am. But you know what fries my fat ass? Branstetter loans Smith his .222, and Smith returns the favor by using a Branstetter sounds-like name to set his buddy up for shooting the judge."

"Yeah, but Branstetter's no saint either. He shot up Judith's house."

"Maybe not. Maybe Smith did that, too. And the turd. And the nails. And the yellow star."

"Did Branstetter kill Gloria Smith?"

"Who knows? I sure don't. This professor is slick. He could have killed his wife and Branstetter too. He used Branstetter's .222 up here. Why not use Branstetter's Luger to kill his own wife?"

"Metro says Smith's alibi is tight on the wife. He was hiking in the Smokies when Gloria Smith died."

"Hey, I've seen a lot of tight alibis. I'll work on that when I get back."

"Good hunting tomorrow in Kenora. Keep me in the loop."

"I will. I'll fire up the cell phone." Harry paused, then said, "Hey, buddy?"

"Yes?"

"I've got to go now. It's time to buy a guy a beer, eh?"

"Connor, it's Judith."

"Hello, dear. How's the arm?"

"It's all right. I'm glad I called you at lunch, about the ballistics, I mean."

"Me too. I called Harry."

"What's he thinking?"

"We didn't push it. He's working on some other things up there."

"What do you think is going on with the ballistics match?"

"I don't know. I mean, I know some things I didn't know yesterday, but I haven't got the whole picture. Harry's working on an angle. Want to have supper?"

"That's why I called. Although I don't have any appetite. But I need to talk to you."

"Yes, and this isn't phone stuff, " Connor said.

"What do . . . OK."

"I'll pick you up at six."

CHAPTER
SEVENTY

They went to a restaurant near Harry's office, Mère Boules. Connor knew there would be enough noise that they could talk without being overheard.

"Judith, your phones may not be secure."

"I thought that's what you were telling me. Can we fix it?"

"Yes, but we don't want to. Not now. It might be useful to us. We can plant something, see if someone acts on it."

"Oh, Lord, I don't like living this way."

"No, I don't either. But, Jude, things are coming to a head. It won't be long until it's over." The server came. Connor ordered two glasses of the Coppola Merlot. "Here's more good news: Your computers are definitely not secure. I've been into them, poking around. There are Branstetter footprints everywhere. Your email . . ." Judith groaned.

"Your word processing, your judicial files, your calendaring. Everything. Even your home computer. Toby's PC, too. And new footprints pick up after Branstetter is dead."

"When were you at my office?"

"I wasn't. I did it from Connor Organizations."

"You can do that?"

"Oh, yes."

"Connor, sometimes you scare me. What else can you do I don't know about?"

"Love you forever."

"I know that already."

"That's the part that's important."

Connor told her about Professor Smith being at Mektu, about his injuries, about Harry checking out Kenora clinics tomorrow.

"My God," she said, "it sounds like he's the one."

"Yes, it does. Jude, would Smith dislike you enough to want you dead?"

"Oh, yes. It's the Greek thing. Kill the messenger. The messenger runs all day in the hot sun to bring the news that the battle is lost, and the king kills him. Connor, judges are just the messengers. We don't make the law, we just apply it to the facts. But in divorces, in custody cases, we say things people don't want to hear, so we get the blame."

The server came back and took their dinner order. Judith was quiet for a few minutes, sipping her wine. Then she said, "You know, this judgeship, this domestic relations docket, is like a stomach. Whatever the mouth eats, whatever gets filed at the clerk's counter, three thousand cases a year, it all goes through the stomach. And some of it is toxic."

"Like Richard Smith."

"Yes, like Smith. Or Branstetter. I can name four more, too, right now, without much thinking."

"Toby gave me *Carbola*."

"Yes, that's one. You've been talking to Toby?"

"I hope you don't mind. He wants to help you."

"He's a dear, and I don't mind. Do we tell him about his PC?"

"I don't think so. He only has your docket, and your opinions in progress, right?"

"That's right."

"Then let's play it close for now. The fewer people who know what we know the better. That's you, me, and Harry for now."

"Not even Sheriff Bolden?"

"Not yet. Tell me about Smith hating you."

"Well, he had a lot to lose. Palermo was going after his 401k, also his publishing royalties, and she was going to try hard for permanent alimony. Smith was just furious. He almost shouted at me. He was over the edge and falling fast. It was scary. Toby was horrified. The professor is just better than you and me, Connor. I had no right to be grading his papers."

Connor took Judith home and went back to his office. He pulled up the CTSU website, found Professor Smith's course offerings for the spring semester, then his reading lists. There it was, Rilke's "Panther." Then after six minutes' work he was in the CTSU class lists and grade reports. No Branstetter. He printed out the student names for all three of Smith's courses. Harry would need them.

Harry flew out of Mektu at 8:00 AM on the 22d. He had a list of all the medical clinics in Kenora and Fort Frances. There were none listed for the road west to Winnipeg. He rented a car in Kenora and started knocking on doors. By 1:00 pm he was in Nestor Falls.

"Connor, no hits so far. No Branstone, no Branstetter, no photo recognition. I had to lie a little bit, say I was FBI, working with the Mounties."

"What's next?"

"I'm going to try Fort Frances and International Falls, and then quit. I'll turn in the car and fly home. I can't get out until tomorrow morning."

"Maybe it's not Smith."

"It's Smith. But I can't check every damn walk-in clinic on every route from Kenora to Nashville."

"No, you can't."

"That's if he was driving. He might have flown back. I mean, he didn't have a gun, so flying home would be that much easier. All he'd need would be a fake photo ID. But hey, I found a great pastry shop in Nestor Falls. They had napoleons. Can you believe my luck? Oh, I'm staying at the Holiday Inn in International Falls tonight. I hear they have fried walleye."

"Shack on some goo."

"I intend to."

The next day, August 23, Harry was on the plane to Minneapolis, making notes in Judith's file.

> **What have we got? Two people dead, a shot judge.*

> **A litigant mad at the judge in generally the right place, at exactly the right time, to shoot the judge.*

> **A gun in Canada from Nashville, a gun which also shot up the judge's house.*

> ** Smith did it all. Poor Branstetter figured out he was being set up, so Smith killed him. Used the Luger on him, making it look like he had killed Mrs. Smith and then committed suicide. Metro likes the suicide. But Branstetter was afraid of his own shadow. He wouldn't kill the prof's wife, much less himself. Cowards don't kill themselves.*

> **Besides, why would Branstetter want to kill Gloria Smith? Did the prof hire him to do it? The prof, allegedly hiking in East Tennessee, two hundred miles away? Maybe. How much did Branstetter like the prof? A whole lot. Especially the furry panther crotch glory.*

> **Maybe Branstetter would do it, kill Gloria. Maybe Smith gives him the cue, the Becket thing, "Will no one*

rid me of this false priest?" Branstetter takes the cue, and solves Henry II's problem.

** No. It doesn't fly. "Timid computer geek kills professor's wife." I don't think so. Smith did it. Got to break his alibi.

CHAPTER
SEVENTY-ONE

Harry got to Nashville at 5:10 pm, August 23. He was tired. He visited two walk-in clinics before going to bed. No luck. He called Connor. "I'm hitting it again bright and early tomorrow. I'm done for tonight."

"Go to bed. No news here. Except I got the class lists for Smith's courses last semester. No Branstetter. But I thought you might want to talk to the students in the translation course. See if they recognize the Branstetter photo."

"I'll do it. Good idea. And good work. CTSU gives out its class lists?"

"Sort of."

At 8:00 am on the 24th Harry walked into the Nashville clinic nearest Professor Smith's house.

"Why, yes, Agent Mather. Very sick. Nail gun accident. Would you like to see the chart?"

"Yes, Dr. Patel, thank you." Harry flipped through the pages. "There's a lot to read here. Could you just make me a photocopy? The Bureau appreciates this very much."

"Connor, we've got him. At a clinic just off College Street, nearest his house, the dumb shit. And the doc has tissue samples. Sure wish you'd kept that turd."

"Harry, this is great news. Now we've got to decide what to do."

"Not yet. I'm going over to CTSU, see if I can find some students. Then we'll talk."

Central Tennessee State University was a big place north of the city. Harry started at the student center cafeteria. He found several English majors and some kids in Comp Lit. They hadn't taken Smith's course, but they knew Katherine Kelty. They knew she had taken the course, and they knew where she lived.

"Oh, yes, Mr. Mather," said Katherine, looking at Branstetter's picture. "He was there every day. The whole course. He sat in the same seat in the back, each lecture, taking notes. He must have been auditing, that's what we all thought, because he never came to the section meetings, only the lectures."

Connor was on the way to Harry's office. It was time, Harry said, for a council of war. "We've got the professor," he said on the phone from CTSU. "He can't get away. Now we have to decide what to do with him."

Connor wondered whether Harry was thinking what he was. At least considering the option. Had to be, Connor thought. I mean, he roughed up Branstetter and kept it a secret, even from me. And he took the laptop from a crime scene. I wonder how we'll ever explain that? If we have to. Maybe there's a plan that doesn't include the laptop. Connor knew one such plan. It involved a very private initiative by him and Harry.

Traffic was heavy. Connor turned on the radio. Football season was about to start. The radio was doing its best to think positively about the Commodores, as it did every pre-season. The new coach, no doubt about it, was going to bring Vandy a winning season. No longer would Vanderbilt be the doormat of the SEC. Disagreement.

286

Conference too tough, Vandy only in it for its share of the SEC gate. Mercenary self-immolation. Vandy should leave the SEC. Vandy should stay, suck it up, play with the big boys.

Then a caller told the adoption joke about Vanderbilt, and Connor laughed. The guy in the next car was laughing too. He would tell it to Harry. He turned onto Second Avenue, no parking spots. But he found one on First.

"So," Connor said, "the little boy tells the social worker, my daddy beats me. That's terrible, says the social worker, do you want to go live with your uncle? No, says the boy, my uncle beats me. How about your grandmother? says the social worker. No, my grandmother beats me. I want to be adopted, says the boy. You do? says the social worker. Yes, he says, I want Vanderbilt University to adopt me. You do? says the social worker. Why Vanderbilt University? Because, the boy says, Vanderbilt doesn't beat anybody."

"That joke," said Harry, "has moss. It is inconsiderate of you to repeat it. It is rude, and it is not based in fact. Vandy was two-and-seven last year. This year they will be five-and-four. At least. If you weren't my friend, I would be offended. But friends overlook flaws in each other. I am magnanimous."

"Thank you. You are large."

"Yes."

"Large of spirit, I mean."

"Of course."

"May I get you a cup of coffee?"

"Please."

CHAPTER
SEVENTY-TWO

When Connor got back with two mugs and the pot, he said, "Harry, what are we going to do about Smith?"

"Well, we can get him convicted, or we can just kill him."

Connor choked on his coffee, and put the mug down. "Well, I like the way you think."

"There's a joke with that as the punch line," said Harry. "It is better than the adoption joke."

"About the school teacher and the ice cream cone?"

"Yes. We are not having this conversation, of course."

"No. Right. No conversation. August 24, Second Avenue office of Harry Mather, P.I., 'Results now!', no conversation about killing Professor Richard Smith. We talked about Vanderbilt football."

"Because such a conversation about killing a slime ball would be conspiring to commit a felony. Which would embarrass Judith, our friend, if it came out," Harry said.

"Yes. And put our asses in jail."

"Yes," said Harry, "that too." He looked at Connor. "So, do we kill him?"

Connor reached for one of Harry's yellow legal pads. "Well," said Connor, "let's run it through drill. Let's first see if its even feasible. Then if it is, we can decide whether we have the stomach for it."

"My stomach is quite large," said Harry. "I trained it."

"First," said Connor, writing on the pad, "is the problem with Judith. Even if she would approve, which I doubt, she can't know about it. Not in her position."

"She might figure it out, that it was us," Harry said. "But you're right. She can't know. We can't tell her."

"If she asks us, we deny it."

"Yes," said Harry, "we have to deny it. I don't like that."

"Me either," said Connor. "OK, hold that thought for now." Connor wrote a "2" on the legal pad. "Change gears: How do we know what we know?"

"You mean, if we go to the police?"

"Yes."

"Well," said Harry, "first off, we deep-six the laptop. It helped us, but we could have gotten everything we have without it. Metro will never . . ." He stopped and thought for a minute. "I mean, the laptop doesn't cast a shadow for Metro to see. I wasn't at Branstetter's house. I didn't take Branstetter's laptop. You didn't work on it. There never was a laptop."

"And there's no other reference we know of about you beating up Branstetter."

"If there is," said Harry, "we deal with it when it turns up. When and if. But the laptop is a goner either way."

"I'll erase it, then melt it in the furnace back at the company."

"And destroy all the transcripts."

"There are only two. The one you marked up, and mine. They're locked in my safe. They go into the furnace with the laptop."

"We can tie Branstetter to the professor through the lectures. I found a student named Kelty who has Branstetter at all the lectures, taking notes faithfully."

"And Judith and Toby told us about his website," said Harry, "which we looked at."

"So, you just figured, being a P.I., that Branstetter might be interested in German lectures. So you poked around and found some at CTSU and Vandy. And talking to students, you found out Branstetter had attended Smith's lectures."

"So far, so good," said Harry, "and Judith told us Smith was one of her hot cases."

"So, when Branstetter's Luger killed Smith's wife, the two cases came together for us, and we started digging."

"It works for me," said Harry.

"I don't know," said Connor. "We're missing something."

"Maybe it will come to you," said Harry. "There's a third angle we have to consider, the whole question of who are the suspects if the professor has an 'untimely accident' that turns out to be murder."

"You mean," said Connor, "if we decide to take care of the professor ourselves, can we get away with it?"

"Yes. Let's say the prof gets killed. For example, he gets shot on a dark night with a gun that can be traced to no one, if it is ever found. No witnesses to the shooting. Clean. Who do the cops come to see?"

"Us?" asked Connor. "Why would they come to us?"

"Well, you know they'll come to Judith. If only because Smith was one of her cases. And they'll certainly want to talk to her because they think Branstetter killed Smith's wife, and Branstetter is a Judge Merchant case also. So, our friend Judith is in the middle of any investigation of the prof's murder."

"OK."

"So, the cops ask her, why does Branstetter shoot up your house, shoot you in Canada, and shoot Professor Smith's wife? And she says, I don't know, or the stress of litigation is horrible, or whatever she can say. And then the cops say, here you are, Judge, with two dangerous cases, and now both the dangerous guys are dead. Is someone protecting you? Who are your friends? And then they come to see us."

"I see," said Connor. "But we're clean."

"Are we?" asked Harry. "What if they start looking at the Canadian shooting again? Detective Blake at Metro has been helping me with RCMP information on fly-in services, and with border-crossing records. Why am I checking these things? Just curious, I say. But what if they keep going, and get to the Mektu people, me showing photographs to them? One of which is Smith? What about the walk-in medical clinics, particularly the ones here in Nashville, with me showing pictures of Professor Smith?"

"That would look bad, " Connor said.

"Very bad, " Harry said. "And you. You talked to Judith's clerk about 'R,' and he fingered Smith to you. We have to hope Metro doesn't talk to Toby."

"If they talk to Judith, they'll talk to Toby," said Connor.

"Yes," said Harry, "they will. Then the cops will work the courthouse rumor mill for whatever they can learn. And that will point right at us, me, the former law partner and you, her fiancé. We are going to be front and center in any investigation."

They were quiet for several minutes. Then Harry said, "Another thing. You got the picture of Professor Smith from somebody. Will that come out?"

"No," said Connor, "I pulled it from CTSU personnel records." Harry looked blank. "I did it online from Connor Organizations."

"Doesn't that leave traces of who made the request?"

"Not the way I do it. I also have his complete medical files for the last nine years."

"You can do that?" asked Harry, his eyes wide.

"Connor Organizations is very resourceful."

"You could be a P.I.," said Harry. "I could hire you from time to time. If you need the work."

CHAPTER
SEVENTY-THREE

To: dbranstetter@aol.com
From: cgillespie@esper.com
August 25, 6:01 PM
David—

I haven't heard from you in awhile, just thought I'd check in. Sure hope I didn't offend you about the Jewish stuff I wrote, how I hadn't had things happen to me like you have. I know things have been really bad for you. It's not ethnic stuff that's eating me up, its my ex.

Give me shout.

--Charlie

"So," said Connor, "what have we said so far? One, if we handle this ourselves, we have to lie to Judith, which we don't like. Two, if we go to the police, we may know too much, and they might just finger us for withholding evidence."

"Probably won't. And if they do, the downside is manageable," said Harry. "At least, I think it is."

"Three, if we handle it ourselves, do we get caught? We know we will get looked at hard."

"So," said Harry, "we go to the police?"

"Wait," said Connor, "there's more. Number four. Or maybe it's a part of three: Why would we even consider handling Smith on our own? The system is going to get him. We don't have to pull the sled. You said yourself that you like the prosecutor's case."

"Umm . . ." said Harry.

"He's got a wound in his side. Doctor Patel will testify it occurred so and so many days earlier, within a reasonable degree of medical certainty, which will take it back to July 9, or close to it. Smith was on site, well, one lake over, from where the judge was shot. He's using his buddy's rifle. They get him for Canada, and they'll get him for his wife, too."

"And maybe for Branstetter as well," said Harry. "I think he did Branstetter too."

"Right."

"OK," said Harry. "So, why would we even consider taking Smith out on our own? I'll tell you why: Certainty. If we do it, it gets done. If we leave it to the public officials, there's the chance they'll screw it up."

"Not this case. It's high profile."

"Even worse," said Harry. "Look at O.J. Simpson. He walked. I can't tell you how many 'sure thing' cases, high profile or not, I've seen go south. Look: Smith gets a slick defense attorney. The evidence gets tainted, some of it gets suppressed. The jury gets confused. Or, leaving all that aside, Smith jumps bond and leaves the country. Do I have confidence in the system? No, no, and no. I've been a part of it. I know how bad it is."

"So your vote is for self-help?" said Connor.

"I don't know, buddy, I just don't know," said Harry. "I guess what I'm saying is that all our options are bad. Taking justice into our own hands . . . means we are making our own laws. I said that I do some off-the-record stuff to help my friends. I'll deny that to anyone else. But that's where I am, Connor."

"Harry, this isn't new to me. I've been here before."

"I kind of thought so."

"I don't like taking justice into my own hands, either," said Connor.

"No."

"Sometimes you have to," said Connor, "and there you are."

"Yes," said Harry, "there you are." He looked at Connor. "So what do we do?"

To: dbranstetter@aol.com
From: cgillespie@esper.com
August 26, 5:42 PM

Hey, David, give me a shout. Or are you on vacation or something?

--Charlie

CHAPTER
SEVENTY-FOUR

Richard wasn't done with the Judge. Oh, no. Not by a long shot. Not by the hair on her chinny-chin-chin. Not by the hair on her chinny-chin cunt. She had embarrassed him. Sneered at him. Belittled him in a public venue. In front of Gloria, in front of the bailiff, the court reporter, two rows of spectators. That would not go unpunished. He had only begun.

It was too bad David was gone. He had harassed the Judge nicely. He had been useful. "Prosit," said Richard, hoisting his coffee cup to the dirty window which looked out onto Linden Street. He had rented a room off campus, a place he could get to without his car.

The Judge was back at work. It was business as usual inside her PC. Nothing unusual in the law clerk's PC either. He wouldn't go in except every ten days. And that quickly. David had taught him a lot, oh, yes. And Richard had been reading. The new guy, "Iowadad," in Iowa or wherever he really was, had taught him about masking. And the need for two PCs in this room—one clean, for snooping only, no email address, just the broadband connection. The other for email, files deleted after use each day. Both PCs with dedicated broadband, no phone lines. All cash transactions with the two broadband providers. Norton's Personal Firewall on each PC. One new email address for the one PC, freeoxen@earthlink.com.

Richard had done it all, setting it up at Linden Street. It was a poor part of town, but he could get here by bus, not park his car outside. He still had his university PC and his old on-line address at his office, rtsmith@ctsu.edu, and his PC at home on College Street, rsmith@aol.com. Those machines had academic work and personal finances. Private things to be sure, but no jeopardy. No jail time waiting in those files. But if these other skeins unraveled, if the Norns of Niflheim dropped their knitting . . .

"Iowadad" had taught him how to spoof the TCP/IP, as an extra measure, the transmission control protocol/Internet protocol. So the knitting would be really safe. And they were beautiful skeins, Richard thought. He did things right. He was on a roll.

He had killed David perfectly. The suicide was unquestioned. Richard had used the gun David had used on Gloria, that was a real stroke. It had kept the police off of him. Of course, he really was innocent, well, of Gloria, but manifestly so now. That made it easier.

And he had to say the events in Canada had really been quite successful, all in all. He was wrong to have been upset. He had made the judge hurt. He had shamed her boyfriend, the artsy boyfriend, shooting up his cabin, sinking his canoe, shooting out his window. Things really couldn't have gone better. The .222 falling into the water had proved to be pure serendipity. It meant he had to kill David, which was good, very good. The man had been a liability. He was gone now, and Richard had absorbed all David's skills. David had killed Gloria for him. David must really have loved me, he thought.

Yes, I'm on a roll. I do things very, very, well. I turn my reverses into gains, and my gains into bonanzas. I should go to Tunica and play craps, he thought. Bet on the come.

The judge is unfinished business. I have all the time in the world. Because there is no October 3 divorce trial. No depositions, no alimony, no Gloria, no problems. On October 3, I'm going to celebrate, have a great dinner, and drink expensive wine. I'll put a rose on Gloria's headstone that day out at Harpeth Hills Memory

Gardens. And then I'll piss all over her stone. That'll be a good memory for her in the Memory Gardens. Happy divorce, Gloria! Dickey-Boy is standing up here in the sunshine, waving the pony at you! Here's another memory: Remember riding the pony, Gloria? Good times, Gloria, all gone.

Now, the judge, on the other hand. The judge at this point is for entertainment. I don't have to kill her. She's off the case. There is no case. But I'm good at killing, and I do like the hunt. I'll wear camouflage and smear myself with deer urine and hold a knife in my teeth. Well, I really could do the Rambo thing, if I wanted. But instead the professor chooses dissimulation. A herringbone jacket and a button-down collar hide the gun. Academic publications cover the secret stories. I have a rich life, a life led on two planes. I do things well.

Judith had asked Bill Bailey, Richard Smith's second lawyer. to come to chambers when his case finished, a protective order, hotly contested, the last on her docket that day.

"Good job, Bill. You tried it beautifully. Hard facts. Not everyone could have won it."

"Judge, with respect, you'd have done it better. But thank you. I watched you try cases with Harry."

"Harry made me look good."

"He did that, but you really had a way with juries. I don't know, you smiled at them, whatever. They really liked you."

"Bill, do you still have an attorney-client relationship with Professor Smith?"

"Not ongoing, no. He paid his bill in full, and he's handling his wife's estate on his own."

"Good. I don't know how to ask this, and I will not take it amiss if you choose not to answer."

Bailey waited, looking at her.

"Bill, during your representation of him, I got shot. In Canada, as you know."

"Yes, Judge?"

"I've been thinking back to a hearing I had with Professor Smith before you represented him. Before the shooting. I feel now that if you had been his lawyer then, well, things might have been . . . " She stopped. This wasn't going the way she had planned. "Bill, did you ever have any sense that Professor Smith disliked me personally?"

"Judge, no. And I know where you're headed. I thought about your docket as soon as I heard about the shooting at your farmhouse, and then again after the thing in Canada. I wondered about Smith. I mean, I knew he had misbehaved at the April trial management conference. Back when Thornton Tyler represented him. In fact, your clerk talked to me about him, when he heard I was taking over the case."

"He did? That sounds like Toby. He never told me."

"So, I kept my ears and eyes open. Bottom line: Smith is bright, scarily bright. And smug. Arrogant. But I picked up no animus toward you. None. I would have been here before now if I had."

"Bill, thanks. Please continue keeping your ears and eyes open."

"I will."

"And I would really appreciate it if this conversation went no farther."

"Of course."

CHAPTER
SEVENTY-FIVE

To: iowadad@hotmail.com
From: freeoxen@earthlink.com
August 24, 3:32 PM
> Tnx. all done per your advice. e-mail here only.
> --rts

To: freeoxen@earthlink.com
From: iowadad@hotmail.com
August 24, 3:40 PM
<<<Delete this when read!<<<
> Good work. Good hunting. Write only from freeoxen PC. Go home, purge home PC all iowadad. Ditto office. I do not know you. You do not know me.
> <<<Delete this file now! Delete all cookies now!<<<

After Bailey left, Judith went to her desk to check her email. The state reminded her to register for the fall judicial conference. She hadn't signed up yet. The next email told her the Tennessee Bar Association was running a CLE trip to Cancun in February: sun, sand, and ten hours of continuing legal education. I wonder if Connor would go, she thought. We might be married by then. There was a message from Connor:

> To: mountkatahdin12345@hotmail.com
> From: cnr12345@hotmail.com
> August 26, 10:17 am
> Jude—The thing at the gallery starts at seven. Can you come? Done by eight-thirty. Supper after?

> To: cnr12345@hotmail.com
> From: mountkatahdin12345@hotmail.com
> August 26, 12:07 pm
> Perfect. Will work here until then. See you at seven. The only arty word I remember is pointillism. I will try to use it tonight.

> To: mountkatahdin12345@hotmail.com
> From: cnr12345@hotmail.com
> August 26, 12:10 pm
> Sparingly. Alternate it with "strong sense of line."
> Love you, Connor

When Richard read their emails, he got excited. He knew about the reception already. He scanned *The Tennessean* every day for anything on Merchant, Graham, Graham Gallery, or Connor Organizations. He had seen the write up, a new local artist named Bethune, female, someone who did watercolors. He went to his stack of newspapers. Yes, she had a series on the Hermitage, and flowers of the Cheekwood gardens. But Richard didn't care. He wasn't going for the art.

Connor and Nan Hodgkins had hung the Bethune show on Tuesday night. There were twenty-three pieces, four of them quite large. To make enough room, they had double-hung some of the gallery's many oils by David Richard Horowitz, part of the base holdings.

Connor remembered when Horowitz had begun painting, and had approached him for his first show. That had been fifteen years ago, when you could get a Horowitz for a hundred and fifty dollars. In two hours, over half the Horowitzes had had "sold" tags, and now the cheapest Horowitz in the gallery was three thousand dollars. And a good investment at that price, Connor thought.

Betty Bethune had called on Wednesday to ask to see her paintings, how they looked, before the Thursday reception.

"It's not a good idea. I'd rather you be surprised, Betty," Connor had said. "You'll see them with fresh eyes if you arrive just like a regular guest. And don't come early. Come at 7:30, when there are some people here."

"All right, then. This is going to be fun."

"Yes, and we're going to make you some money."

"Oh, Michael will like that," she laughed, "and I will too." Michael was Betty's husband, an economics professor at CTSU. "He'll be delighted if I make ten cents. He says art does not require marginal benefit."

"I think I'm going to like Michael."

Richard was in the foyer of the gallery. There he is, Graham, the snot, Richard thought. His oh-so-understated mock turtleneck and hound's-tooth jacket. Black tassel loafers. Just too much. Just too suave. I should have done him first, shot him first. Then the bitch. He owes me. He just doesn't know it.

I could buy a painting, and then ask for a discount. "Why?" he would ask. I could say, "Because you owe me." But, no, I wouldn't say that. Better, I'd say, "For unspecified reasons." What would he say then? That would get him. Or, I could say, "Because you enjoy your life." That would get him. But then he might get interested in me. Bad idea.

Richard looked around the entry foyer. The watercolor show was evidently in the next room. This space had mostly art supplies, some trendy greeting cards, a cash register, a couch with art books. "Bethune watercolors" said a placard with an arrow. There was wine here in the foyer, and finger food. Richard got a white wine and headed toward the Bethune show. He wanted to get close to Graham. Where was the judge?

He stepped into the next room. It was filled with bright paintings of flowers. He could see more in the next gallery straight ahead. In a third gallery to the left there were darker paintings. He looked in. No Graham. Two rooms opened off of the dark paintings. This was a big place. He walked through the first room of flowers and into the second one. There she was! The judge was talking to a woman, someone Richard knew, who was it? The guy in the Econ Department, his wife? Yes. Michael Bethune. Betty Bethune. Small world. He nodded at Michael. Professor Bethune excused himself and headed his way.

"Good of you to come, Richard."

"I wouldn't have missed it. You must be proud."

"This is Betty's first show. Yes, I am proud of her. She has worked hard."

"I hope she sells every single one."

"Oh lord, that would be wonderful," said Professor Bethune, "but I don't care. Just having the show has been such a boost for her. Graham Gallery is, well, I'll say it, the foremost gallery in the state."

"You don't mean it. I had no idea. Well, congratulations indeed." Richard said. He looked around the room. "So, is Mr. Graham here tonight?"

"Oh, yes. He's over by the big painting of the yellow roses. That's one of my favorites. Would you like me to introduce you?"

They walked over. Graham was looking at them, watching them approach. He doesn't know me, thought Richard. Good. He doesn't have a clue. I like this.

"Connor, I'd like you to meet a colleague of mine, Richard Smith, of the Modern Languages Department. Mr. Connor Graham."

"Professor Smith. Welcome to Graham Gallery."

"Thank you," said Richard.

"Are you a collector?"

"Oh, no. I know practically nothing about painting. But I wanted to see Betty's show."

"She will be pleased you came, I'm sure. She's talking to my fiancée just now, over there." Graham was looking at him calmly.

"Thank you," said Richard. "I'll speak to Betty after I have seen the paintings," Richard gestured with his wine glass to the room, and the rooms beyond. "Michael, Mr. Graham," he said, and walked away.

Enough of that, he thought. Well done. I'm at your place, drinking your wine, talking polite talk, and you don't even know who I am. He touched his side, fingering his scar. I hate you, Mr. Tassel Loafers Graham. You're next, after the judge. He looked around the room. Got to look at all these fucking flowers, and then look at the Hermitage stuff, then twelve words with Betty and out of here. No talking to the judge, that would be pushing it. Oh, I could. I could do it, I could get away with it. Evening, Judge Merchant. No, there won't be a trial on October 3, no. Downcast eyes, introverted, shaken by Gloria's death. Wouldn't be here tonight, were it not for Betty. Not ready for a social life yet.

CHAPTER
SEVENTY-SIX

Connor walked back into the foyer, nodding to newcomers, and went into his office, pushing the door closed behind him. From a green cardboard file box atop his work table he took out a stainless five-shot Smith .38, pushed it into a pancake holster, and clipped it into the small of his back. In thirty seconds he was back outside with the guests, scanning for Judith.

"Jude, don't look now. Just look at me. When I walk to the other side of this room, glance into the Hermitage space. Professor Richard Smith is in there."

"Oh, Connor. What should I do?"

"Nothing yet. Let's just see how it plays. Michael Bethune just introduced me to him. I acted as though I didn't know him, thanked him for coming. Very low key. Smith knows the Bethunes from CTSU."

"So everything is all right?"

"I don't know. But I will be with you until he leaves. You are safe, Jude. Trust me. There's no need for you to talk to Smith. Stay away from Betty for now. He intends to speak to her after he has seen the paintings. I think he'll leave after that."

"Unless he plans to kill us in front of witnesses."

"There is that," Connor smiled. "But it's not his style."

"I'm so glad Harry isn't here. He might do something."

Richard was outside, walking to his car. It was a beautiful evening. I live on two planes, yes. A man living in two realities. I can go anywhere, do anything, talk to anyone. Good evening, Betty. Oh, I am astounded, just swept away, particularly by the anemones. The quality of light.

I can march through the enemy's camp, and they see nothing but mist. I will have my way with them, when I choose, on my schedule.

It was August 27, the morning after the Bethune opening. Eleven of the paintings had sold last night. More would sell today, based on the *Tennessean* review Connor was reading. Judith and he were at Connor's, finishing breakfast. Harry called on Connor's cell.

"Where are you?"

"At my place. We're about to come in. Why?"

"She have a regular docket today?"

"Yes."

"Good. You need to give her a heads-up, and then you and I need to talk when she's not around."

"What's going on?"

"Blake called me from Metro. He wanted me to get a message to her, so she didn't get blind-sided."

"Blind-sided by what?"

"You won't believe this, buddy. Blake's on his way to arrest Professor Smith for felony murder of his wife. For procuring Branstetter."

"You don't mean it."

"I do mean it. Let's you and me talk after Judith is in court."

"Right. In person, at the company."

"Good. Tell her about it, and tell her the newspapers are likely to want a statement."

"What should she say?"

"She should say, 'The canons of judicial ethics prohibit me from making any comment.'"

"Got it, Connor said. "'The canons of judicial ethics prohibit me from making any comment.'" Judith looked at him, eyebrows raised.

"When are you coming out to the company?" Connor asked.

"In about an hour."

When Judith got to her chambers, her clerk said, "Judge, the phones have been ringing off the wall. Professor Smith has been arrested. Channel Five is sending a camera team for an interview. Both the papers want statements."

"Toby, get Maria to put this on my letterhead, ten copies, all originals: 'To whom it may concern. Re: Arrest of Professor Richard Smith. Text: On such and such date, the case of *Smith v. Smith*, use full names, docket number such and such, was filed in this court. On blank, the case was closed, due to the death of Mrs. Smith. Fill in the date. The canons of judicial ethics prohibit the undersigned from any comment about any ongoing litigation, as well as *Smith v. Smith*, even though it is closed. JJM.'"

"I'll get right on it, Judge."

"Hand it out to anyone who asks. I am in court and not to be interrupted."

"Yes, Judge. In fact, your docket today would choke a horse."

"Joy."

CHAPTER
SEVENTY-SEVEN

Harry's Lincoln Navigator was parked in a handicap slot when Connor arrived. Harry was still in his car, listening to the radio. Connor walked up to the driver's side. Harry rolled down the window, raising a finger. The Titans coach said, "He knows his routes, he knows our schemes, he's not going to have start-up problems." Then the interviewer said, "Coach, his whole background is the West Coast offense . . ."

"I'll be in the office," Connor said, and walked inside.

In five minutes, Harry was there. "You know, we could pull it off. We really could."

"What?"

"Win the AFC, go to the Super Bowl again. It could be like the 1999 season all over again. Remember the wild card game with Buffalo?"

"The Music City Miracle? Of course I do. I watched it on TV."

"I was there."

"I know."

"But you have to remember how it was. I'm talking about belief here. That's the important thing. Purpose. Because what we did then we can do again now. A minute and forty-eight left in the game, we kick a field goal, we're up 15-13. All is well. Then that fucker Rob

Johnson drives down the field, beautiful, eats up some clock, great drive, and the Bills kick a field goal. 16-15. But we have purpose, we believe in ourselves. We don't give up. They kick to us. Lorenzo Neal gets the squibber, gives the ball to Wycheck, who throws to Dyson, who goes 75 yards for the touchdown."

"And it really was a lateral. The replays proved it."

"Damn right. And the next week we beat the Colts in the divisional playoff, and then the Jags for the AFC championship, and we go to the Super Bowl. We can do it again this year."

"Now, would you please tell me about Professor Smith?"

"I practice neural pathway cleansing, diversionary neural pathway cleansing. If I can't figure something out, I think of something else. The Titans are not only my team, they are my mental broom."

"I thought Vanderbilt was your team."

"I don't want to think about Vanderbilt. Not today. Bad broom."

"So?" Connor asked. "What has the Titans broom accomplished?"

"I'm fucked," said Harry. "Broom didn't work. I can't get anywhere with it."

"Oh, great."

Harry walked around the office, hands behind his back. "This is either very good or very bad. I can't figure which. The facts are, Metro found a bunch of love letters, that's what Detective Blake called them, at Branstetter's place. Love letters from David Branstetter, computer wizard, to Professor Smith. He evidently never mailed them. Can't tell. Might have mailed the originals and these are the copies. They were tied up with ribbon. Blake says he calls Smith a panther. His panther. How about that?"

"OK, love letters. And they arrest Smith?"

"One of the letters says, 'Richard wants me to kill Gloria. Next week he will be out of town. He will have a solid alibi.'

"That's all?"

"Not quite. Smith had earlier denied knowing Branstetter, except for having a cup of coffee after one lecture. They've done fibers and particles at Branstetter's house. Smith is all over the place, wool from sport jackets, skin flakes in the carpet and sofa. It's Smith's DNA."

"He gave them DNA samples?"

"Not in today's case. In the old case, when they investigated his wife's death. And the prof was clear on that one, none of his hair, skin, or fibers at Belle Meade. And here's some other news: Metro has two backcountry reservations for Smith, July 1 to 12, and July 31 to August 4. His car was parked at the Cades Cove ranger station 7/31 to 8/5, according to Park records."

"What about July 1 to 12?"

"They had already deleted the log for July. So, he had a reservation for then, but there's no confirmation he used it."

"So he could have been in Canada."

"Oh, yes. One more thing, you'll like this, there was a DNA match at the Belle Meade condo to a West End drug dealer. But the guy has an unshakeable alibi for Gloria's time of death."

"So, Metro really thinks Branstetter killed Mrs. Smith?"

"They always have. And now they know why, they say. Branstetter was in love with Professor Smith. He killed his wife for him."

"Will it stick on Smith? Procuring a murder?"

"I don't think so. But I didn't say that to Blake. I said, 'Good work, Jay.'"

Harry stood up and went to the window, looking out at his Lincoln Navigator. "Connor, the last thing is, too bad to ruin your day, they are looking for a missing laptop. The love letters talk about it, the 'diary on the laptop.'"

"You know where this puts us, don't you?" Connor asked.

"Sure do," said Harry. We are in a world of hurt. Have you melted the laptop yet?"

"No. I was going to do it today."

"Don't. We can always do it. Put it and the transcripts in a manila envelope. Seal it, date it, sign the flap, open a safety deposit box downtown today, and lock it up. If we have to disclose it, we will.

But the damn thing can probably stay missing. Murder investigations always have unanswered questions."

"Harry, aren't we going to have to give them what we know?"

"Maybe, but not yet."

CHAPTER
SEVENTY-EIGHT

Prof Hires Geek Lover To Kill Wife

Nashville, August 28
Copyright © The Davidson Tribune

Metro Police yesterday arrested Professor Richard T. Smith, 38, of Central Tennessee State University, charging him with hiring the August 3 killing of his wife. The shooter, says Metro Detective J. Blake, was David Branstetter, a man engaged in a homosexual tryst with Professor Smith. David Branstetter, 42, committed suicide shortly after killing Mrs. Smith, the warrant alleges.

In an exclusive interview, The Tribune has learned that Branstetter, formerly Vice President of Omega Computing on Nolensville Road, was deeply distressed about the care of his son, Joey, 16. Branstetter's ex-wife, Jean Cummings Branstetter, has custody of the son. They reside in Clarksville. The Branstetters divorced three years ago.

"David was upset," said Candace Tribecca, a fellow employee at Omega Computing. "He opened up to me. He would talk to me at lunch about his son, his ex-wife, his new love. He just adored Professor Smith. He went to all his lectures at CTSU. I thought it was so sweet."

Professor Smith, 38, is an Associate Professor of Modern Languages at CTSU, where he has worked for twelve years. He and his wife, Gloria Jean, separated in November, shortly after she filed for divorce. Trial was set for October 3 before Judge Judith Merchant.

The August 3 killing was done, the warrant alleges, "at the instruction and direction of Professor Richard T. Smith, who purposefully and with intent to establish an alibi absented himself from Davidson County during the shooting."

The warrant additionally alleges that Smith killed Branstetter on or about August 13, to conceal his (Smith's) role in his wife's death, and to conceal a homosexual tryst between himself and Branstetter.

Professor Smith is being held without bond. Arraignment is scheduled for 9:00 a.m. August 28 in Davidson County Criminal Court, Division 2.

"Are you going to the arraignment?" Judith asked Connor.

"No, but Harry is. Smith doesn't know Harry."

"He barely knows you."

"Well, he's seen me through rifle sights, if he's really the shooter, and he saw me last night at the Bethune show."

"I think he's the shooter," said Judith. "He makes a lot more sense than a computer designer, or whatever Branstetter was."

"Yes."

"What about Canada?" she asked. "Do you want me to call Detective Blake for you, set up a meeting, so you can fill him in?"

"Not yet. Harry and I are working on something. We want to wait a bit. Can you live with that?"

"Yes," she said, "if there's a good reason. I mean, we're not withholding any physical evidence. What Harry found out at Mektu . . . I don't know, Connor."

"Jude, there's the whole publicity angle for you. 'Judge Shot in Canada' will be on the front page again if Smith gets charged with the Manta business. The way Harry figures it, let Smith go down for felony murder of his wife, and the murder of Branstetter. If Manta doesn't have to come out, so much the better for you."

"Well, that's true. Yes."

"So anyway, me being at the arraignment would raise questions we don't want raised. Harry will fill us in."

"Or the *Davidson Trib*, the bastion of accuracy," she said.

"Guys, you should have seen it," Harry said. "It was straight out of one of those TV shows. The shackled defendant, hair unkempt, being read his rights. Judge Palmer, I'm so glad it was a woman, says, 'Professor Smith, you are being charged with procuring David Branstetter at a time or times in advance of August 3, to kill your wife Gloria Jean Smith. You are also charged with killing David Branstetter on or about August 13 of this year, with intent to conceal a sexual relationship with said David Branstetter, and with intent to conceal your role in obtaining Branstetter to kill your wife. Do you understand the charges?'

"At this point, Smith tries to raise his arms, wants to wave them about in protest, I guess, but he can't, because they're shackled at his waist. So he is jerking at his chains, looking wild, and then he starts yelling, 'This is a travesty! Do you hear? This is ludicrous! I want a lawyer! I want a lawyer! I want a lawyer!' Two bailiffs grab him by the shoulders. Then he shouts, 'you are all buffoons, all of you. All fools, fools, fools, fools . . .' And then he gets quiet, and Judge Palmer starts telling him about his right to counsel, counsel of his choosing, and so on, and Smith listens for a little bit, and then he starts singing. I guess it was German, I couldn't understand it, but it was the tune of 'Mack the Knife,' I swear."

Connor sang, "Und der Haifisch, der hat Zähne . . . Was it like that?"

"Maybe," said Harry, "could be. But I'm sure of the tune. And he's got his chin tucked down against his chest, he's looking up over his glasses, over the top, at the judge, like he knows a secret about her, and he's singing it to himself."

"Nice man," said Judith. "What a scene."

"That's the part about the shark's teeth," said Connor, "how they are hidden and waiting."

"Oh, great," Judith said.

"I hope they put him under the jail," Harry said.

"What's the word on the street?" Judith asked.

"Too early to tell," Harry said. "But he's hired Ray Martinson."

Professor Smith, I'm glad you called," said Martinson as he entered the prisoner interview room.

"Can't we meet some place better than this?" Richard asked, looking around.

"I'm afraid not. Not now. Don't worry, Professor, I'll get you out of here. We need to talk now."

Richard said nothing. He looked around the room, at the smudged walls, at the coffee stains on the table. There was trash in the wastebasket. "I was meant for better than this," he said.

"Yes, well, Professor, that's why I'm here. Let me say, it is good to meet you in person, even under these circumstances." Richard said nothing. "I knew David Branstetter," Martinson went on. "He was my client, as you know." Martinson opened his briefcase.

Richard stood up, and started walking back and forth. Martinson looked at him. "Sit down, Professor."

"Walking helps me."

"All right then. Go ahead and walk."

"Mr. Martinson, excuse me, I'm not myself. Yes. Yes. I'll sit down." He did, but then he got up. "This is ludicrous! I am not a man to put in jail! I am Richard T. Smith! I am a professor, an author, a scholar! I am not some piece of Tennessee shit, some nobody to put into a jumpsuit and chains!"

"'I was meant for bigger things,'? Isn't that what Scuffy said?

"Scuffy?"

"Scuffy the Tugboat."

"What the hell are you talking about, Mr. Martinson? Just what the hell are you talking about? Are you here to help me, or to ridicule me. Have you gone crazy?"

"Professor, I am sorry. No. I was trying to inject some levity into this difficult moment. It was a poor attempt to get you to focus on the task at hand." He paused. Smith was walking back and forth in the small room, as fast as he could. "The task at hand," Martinson repeated.

"Yes."

"To get you a reasonable bond so you can get out of jail."

"I'll do anything for that," said Richard, "including sitting down." He sat. "Where do we start?"

CHAPTER
SEVENTY-NINE

It was August 29th. Summer is almost over, Judith thought. She looked at the draft she had written on her yellow legal pad:

> *The Hon. Judith Merchant*
> *and*
> *Mr. Connor Graham*
> *request the pleasure of your presence*
> *at their rites of marriage*
> *Saturday, the 12th of February*
> *half past four o'clock*
> *Christ Church Cathedral*

"I think it's lovely," said Judith.

"I think it's pompous," said Harry.

"I think it's high time," said Connor, "or the *Tribune* will write about a 'longstanding, unsanctified tryst'."

Harry picked up a second legal pad from Judith's desk, and wrote quickly:

> Connor and Judith want you to know
> the bluebird of happiness

sings aloud in Nashville.
Come share our joy as we pledge our love
at 4:30 pm
Centennial Park Lawn
Saturday, February 12.
Bring a dish to share
in case you want to eat anything.

"There," he said, "that's how I'd do it." He handed the pad to Judith. She read it.

"Harry, you're terrible," she said. "I almost think you don't want me to get married."

"No, no, I do. I really do. You guys are going to be very happy together. I'm in favor of it. But please, no pomp, no gut-wrenching 'I take thees'."

"There are things," Martinson said, "that I know about Mr. Branstetter which the state would like to know." Richard looked at him. Martinson tried again. "I was wondering if you would call me to represent you. It's very good that you did."

"Mr. Martinson . . ."

"Let me continue. There are certain advantages in my being your counsel, beyond my considerable expertise, I mean."

"Oh?"

"Yes. For example, I cannot be compelled to testify about Branstetter facts now, because I am your counsel. Those things now become privileged. Otherwise, they would be fair game, with him being deceased."

"I see."

"For example, that you paid most of my retainer for David Branstetter."

"He told you that?"

"He was proud of it."

"This will not come out now?"

"Absolutely not."

"That is good, very good. It would be misunderstood."

"Quite so," said Martinson. "Mr. Branstetter was a troubled man."

"He was a sick man."

"Strong words, Professor Smith."

"I am a strong man, Mr. Martinson. I am not a pansy."

"Let us leave aside character assassination, Professor. It will not help you. I take it you have a decided animus against homosexuality."

"I do."

"I am sorry. It is unnecessary for you to take a position on private behavior. However, it may be helpful for your case."

"It is also true."

"I have no doubt. Now, let us review: Branstetter loved you. Says the state, anyway. And this embarrassed you, and you covered it up by killing him."

"It embarrasses me to have it said, yes. But it is now, this moment, that I am talking about. It embarrasses me now. Back when David was alive, I had no clue he felt that way."

"You wouldn't have. Poor David, poor man. He must have felt quite hopeless."

"Evidently. He killed himself."

"Yes. And your wife too. Because he loved you."

"If in fact it was he who killed her. If he did, I wouldn't know why he did it. It's just so hard to believe. I keep going back to the fact that Gloria was with the wrong sort of people. Anyone could have killed her."

"Well, we know you didn't kill her, Professor. That much is established. The police have you two hundred miles away, when Mrs. Smith died, on the North Carolina-Tennessee state line."

"Yes."

"But the state says you hired Branstetter to do your dirty work while you were gone. That you hired the love-sick Branstetter, a man who would have walked over coals for you."

"Spare me."

"Well, it's true, isn't it? That he was devoted to you?"

"I don't know. I'm starting to be afraid that it may in fact have been true. That's why I need you, Mr. Martinson. It looks bad. My wife, the divorce plaintiff, a woman who wanted to take me for everything I had, she ends up dead. And this—this sick man—says he did it for me. Counselor, I am frightened."

"You should be. Professor Smith, the state will prove your presence in Branstetter's home. Or will try to, by fiber and particle analysis, and by DNA analysis. And they will introduce your statement to Detective Carden, that you only knew Branstetter casually. That you had 'a cup of coffee together once' after one of your lectures. That he knew you through your lectures, nothing more, and that you only knew him from the one coffee conversation. And didn't like him."

"Yes, I remember I told someone something like that."

"Detective John Carden. You told him that in an interview on . . .' Martinson looked at his notes, ". . . August 21st. You also said, 'We spent fifteen minutes together at the university coffee shop. Why would he kill my wife?'"

"That sounds about right."

"Whatever were you thinking, Professor, to say something like that?"

"Mr. Martinson," said Richard slowly, "I suppose some part of me knew that Branstetter's, that David's, feelings for me were not just shared interest in things German. I suppose I didn't want the detective, didn't want anyone, to think I would spend time with someone like that."

"But you did? Spend time with him?"

"Yes."

"Why?"

"Well, we did share a German interest. There was that. And we were both lonely. We drank some beer at times, listened to German music. He was very intelligent. I did read some poetry to him. I suppose some part of me was gratified by his admiration."

"That's quite natural. Quite natural. I believe I can take most of the sting out of your unfortunate statement to Detective Carden. I think I can make the jury understand your reluctance to be candid. I will do my utmost."

"Thank you."

"In fact, Professor, I want you to know that I will spare no effort, leave no stone unturned, in your defense. I will hammer off the very hinges of hell to defend you. I will challenge the state's fiber evidence, I will challenge their so-called DNA evidence. We will hire our own experts to analyze their alleged evidence. We will cast doubt upon their science. Perhaps some of their evidence will be lost before the trial begins. Who knows? Stranger things have happened. Time is on our side, Professor. Time is the defendant's friend. Father Time and I have a close working relationship. Wait until you see the motions I file, the delays I will bring about. They will tire of this case, Professor. Entire rain forests will be cut down to provide the paper for my . . ."

Richard interrupted. "Mr. Martinson, I do not want delays. I want this over. I am innocent."

CHAPTER
EIGHTY

It was August 30. The courtroom was full. Martinson was speaking to the level of bond.

"Your Honor," said Martinson, "my client has ties to this community which I do not need to recite. Not for those of us who live here and know the standing of Professor Richard T. Smith. But His Honor being from Memphis, let me urge to you that Richard T. Smith is a distinguished Associate Professor of many years' standing at Central Tennessee State University. One of our fine state institutions. He owns his own house, a Victorian mansion on College Street."

"Objection!" said Attorney General Jeffrey Taylor. "Your Honor, I would not interrupt Mr. Martinson's argument were it not for a serious, and I am sure unintentional, misstatement of fact. Mr. Smith rents his house on College Street."

"I speak under correction, Your Honor," said Martinson. "My client leases his beautiful home. I have been to his home. It is a serious tie to our beautiful city, whatever the legal title. It is lovingly furnished with art and memorabilia of Professor Smith's travels. There is a framed Dürer print, your Honor, over the fireplace which . . ."

Richard was glad he had told Martinson where the spare key was hidden. He had wanted to wear his best suit and French cuffs for this hearing. He hadn't expected Martinson to do a *House Beautiful* argument. The judge appeared to be listening intently.

". . . which alone would keep my client from leaving the jurisdiction, were he guilty. Which he is not. My client looks forward to his vindication. He invokes his right to a speedy trial, he insists upon it, the speediest possible trial, consistent with orderly justice. My client, as I have said, is not to be upbraided for the acts of a sick man, a deranged man who killed himself, a man who killed my client's wife, killed my client's wife!, in some twisted version of spontaneous gift giving.

David Branstetter is dead, Your Honor. He is not here to speak about Professor Smith's innocence. He is not here to tell us how he," Martinson looked around the courtroom, "a man we might call a crippled magpie, brought a blue stone to lay at his lover's feet. His imagined lover. To ask him to build a nest with him. He did not know that Richard Smith is an eagle, an eagle! A magnificent creature, a healthy soaring bird who does not notice the thoughts of magpies." The courtroom was silent.

"No, Your Honor, David Branstetter had his thoughts. But Richard Smith did not know them. He did not know David Branstetter's thoughts. David Branstetter lived a life of unrequited needs. He was lonely, he was hopeful, and he was desperate. Finally he did a desperate thing. He killed to please the eagle. But the eagle did not know. David Branstetter died with his secret, by his own hand, afraid to tell the man he loved."

Martinson looked around the courtroom again. He spoke now to the back row, in a booming voice, "And now this man, this good man, this educator of our children, this distinguished scholar, this pillar of our community . . . This fine man asks you to return him to his life's work, to the tending of the sacred flame of literature. Let him go to his quiet Victorian home on College Street, there to prepare his lectures for the coming semester." Martinson paused.

"I ask you, Your Honor, that bond be set upon my client's own recognizance." He sat down.

Harry wondered what this judge would do. He was old, late seventies it looked, brought in specially, because of the connections of the case to Judith. What book there was on him said he was defense-oriented. Just what we need, thought Harry, a playing field that slopes uphill.

"Mr. Martinson, General Taylor, I have listened carefully to the charges and to your arguments," the judge began. "The Court is impressed with the substantial ties the defendant has to the greater Nashville area, to this community of educators. The court is also impressed with the gravity of the acts alleged by the state." He paused, and then continued, "Bond will be set at twenty thousand dollars."

Conversations began in the rows of benches. Reporters left the room. Harry could see Martinson was jubilant as he turned to whisper to his client.

Harry's phone rang. It was September 5. The Titans were playing the Jaguars in the first real game of the season that night in Jacksonville.

"Harry, this is Jay."

"Detective Jake Blake. Greetings."

"Harry, don't call me 'Jake.' You owe me, remember? You call me when you need help."

"Sometimes."

"*Jake Blake*, for Christ's sake. What were my parents thinking? Makes me sound like some private investigator."

"A low life. A shamus."

"Yes."

"Like Philip Marlowe."

"Marlow would be OK. Harry, I need help."

"Jay, I'd be glad to help. What could I know that you don't already have? Nothing."

"Harry, cut it out. We know you were at Branstetter's house. The probate court had Branstetter's box drilled. Nothing in it but Boy Scout medals and diary printouts. The guy was anal. Year after year, back to high school. Including this year's diary through August 12. You're the fat guy."

"J-A-Y Blake, sir, my friend and colleague, let us have a very private meeting. At the place and time of your choosing."

CHAPTER
EIGHTY-ONE

"Ah, shit, Connor, I don't know how to play it. I think I can deal with Jay, but I don't know him that well. I could be in for a bad ride."

"Take a lawyer with you?"

"Hell, I can't do that. I thought about it: 'My client declines to answer, asserting his rights under the Fifth Amendment to the United States Constitution.' I might as well say, 'Guilty and not cooperating.' We want to cooperate, Connor. At least, I think we do."

"How about immunity?"

"I could get it, I think. I think Blake would go for it, if he wants to be very official. But he may want to keep my whole involvement quiet, in exchange for real help. That way, he looks good, and he cuts me a substantial favor. Then I really owe him."

"Does he know you were at Branstetter's a second time?"

"I don't think so. All he said on the phone was he had a diary printout through August 12, and I was the fat guy."

"So he doesn't know about the laptop."

"Except that the love letters talk about it, and now it's missing. He may figure me for it."

"What are you going to do if he asks about it?"

"Lie my ass off," Harry said.

Jay Blake sat down in Harry's client chair. He looked around. "Classy," he said, "understated. Probably no fifth of liquor in the lower desk drawer."

"No secretary with marcelled hair," said Harry.

"No snub-nose thirty-eight in a shoulder holster."

"No name on the door in gold letters," said Harry, grinning. This is going very well, Harry thought. Blake wants to deal.

"No satellite," said Blake.

"What?"

"The three reasons why there will never be a satellite around the earth. You know them?"

"No," said Harry.

"I do. Learned them in the fifth grade. *My Weekly Reader*. One, you could never get anything, a baseball, say, going seventeen thousand miles an hour for enough miles to get it out of the atmosphere. Two, if you did, if you did that amazing impossible thing, it would burn up, the friction with the air. Three, if you did get it going fast enough, long enough, and it didn't burn up, you could never hit the angle right. The baseball would fly off into outer space forever, or it would fall back to earth."

"I'm completely convinced."

"So was I. *My Weekly Reader*, I can still remember it. My point is, there's reality as people say it is, and then there's the real facts as they develop."

"You want to talk off the record," said Harry.

"Yes, I do. I don't care what we tell the world you did or did not do. You can write the press release, and I'll read it out. But I need to know everything you know. And everything Connor Graham knows. I'll protect you both."

"So," said Judith to Toby Malone, "Connor walks in and asks me, would I consider a honeymoon to Germany, and I say, 'What's not to like?' And he says, 'Well, the time of year.' He's thinking about February, he says. 'We'll leave right after the wedding,' he says, 'spend three nights in Paris, and then go to Germany.' 'Berlin?' I ask. 'Munich?' 'No,' he says, and then he names a whole lot of places no one's ever heard of."

"Oberniederdorf?" Toby asked.

She grinned. "That was one of the big places," Judith said. "But Toby, here's the best part: He's been thinking about this for a long time. He knows how much I love Jefferson. When we went to Monticello, he found out that Jefferson had made a wine tour while he was envoy to France. Through parts of France and all the wine areas of what is now Germany. He knows all the dates and places Jefferson went. We are going to duplicate Jefferson's footsteps, on the same dates he was there, the same towns, vineyards, everything."

"That's absolutely so romantic," said Toby.

"Isn't it?" said Judith.

CHAPTER
EIGHTY-TWO

"I think it stinks," said Harry that night. "You're going to freeze your ass off."

"You're just jealous," said Judith.

"Am not. What a stupid idea. A 'wine country' trip without warm weather, without Chardonnay, and without friendly people."

"Oh, Harry, read the book." She handed him *The Wines and Travels of Thomas Jefferson* by James Gabler. "Jefferson brought root stock back to Monticello."

"Yeah, and what happened? I took the tour at Monticello. All the damn vines died. Which suits me fine. I don't like your Mr. Jefferson. He's the guy who said the country needed a revolution every so often to keep it healthy, and needed the blood of tyrants to water the tree of liberty. Bunch of crap. If it weren't for John Adams and a lot of luck, we wouldn't be here."

"You're in a bad mood."

"Another thing: Jefferson had concubines."

"One concubine. Maybe."

"Maybe, hell."

"Solomon had concubines."

"Did not. That was David."

"Same thing."

"Not the same thing. You're being anti-Semitic, Judith."

"Hell, Harry, it's your religion."

"My almost religion," he said. "if I convert."

"When you convert."

"You're a know-it-all, Judith, that's what you are, a damn know-it all. A real pain."

It was September 20. Connor called Harry at his office.

"Mather Investigations. Harry Mather speaking."

"Mister Mather, hmmm," said Connor, in a deep stage voice, "I am needing a detective, hmmm . . ."

"I've seen *Slingblade*. You're not Billy Bob Thornton."

"OK, then. OK, then. What I was thinking, see," Connor said in a fast New York accent, "what I was thinking was, see, you and me, see, we could go, I mean if you wanna, we could go up to Manta, you know, the lake, Manta Lake, and you know, see, like close the cabin?"

"I'm not going anywhere with Joe Pesce."

"Pretty good, huh?"

"Better than *Slingblade*. Are you serious about the cabin?"

"Well, I'd like to go. I could get Davey to close it for me. Or maybe someone he knows. But I've never done it that way before. And I just want to go back up there for a few days."

"Me too. I'll go," said Harry.

"You mean I don't have to beg?"

"I've been thinking it's time for some spiritual recharging."

"Harry, this is great."

"We'll take some photographs, too, of the angles of fire. The view from and to the cliff. The RCMP did all that, but we'll have our own, just in case there are any evidence problems. I think Jay is going to want to hang Canada on the good professor."

Richard told Martinson how it started, about David's regular attendance at the lectures, about David writing him a note, about asking him to have coffee with him.

I won't ever tell him we talked about the judge. Oh, no, that is my little secret, that one, that's yet to play out. I'm free, my bond posted. A bagatelle, two thousand and twenty-five dollars. Ten percent, plus a twenty-five dollar processing fee. Nothing. Lovely job Martinson did. I am fortunate in my lawyers. Bailey, and now Martinson. I am a lucky person. Fortuna smiles on me. This prosecution is nothing, a mere hindrance. It will go away.

"He came to my lectures in the translation course. He was really the most appalling anti-Semite. That's why he shot the judge, I suppose. He thought she was Jewish."

Martinson looked at him carefully. "If Branstetter did in fact do that," he said slowly.

"What do you mean?" asked Richard. He watched Martinson closely.

"I don't believe he would ever have been convicted of that. I had an excellent feeling about that case."

"Why was that?" Richard was worried now.

"The man was too, what should I say?, too housebound, too stodgy, to slog miles through the woods with a rifle, shoot somebody from the top of a cliff, and slog back out. Oh, no. I would have had the jury laughing at the prospect. An acquittal for sure. A hung jury at worst."

CHAPTER
EIGHTY-THREE

Connor and Harry flew to Kenora on September 30. Davey Barton met them at the airport and drove them to the floatplane base. "How's Ms. Merchant, Connor?" he asked.

"Fine, Davey. Thanks for asking. She's a little sore, but she's going to make a complete recovery."

"That's great," Davey said.

"We're going to get married on February 12. Can you come to Nashville?"

"Congratulations, my friend. I'm happy for you. Yes. You can't keep me away."

"Terrific, you can stay at my house."

"No, he can't," said Harry. "He's staying with me. You're the bridegroom. You have to be in contemplation."

"Wow," said Davey, "competition."

They worked on the cabin, and on the pictures, for three days. They also played gin, drank some Molson Canadian, and sat for long hours in the evening by the fireplace talking. Harry also cut some more firewood.

"You know," he said, "I'm going to put this place in my will."

"Harry, the cabin doesn't belong to you. You can't put it in your will."

"I don't mean the cabin. I mean the woodlot."

"Oh."

"See, I'm going to be cremated and sprinkled. The way it stands now, my executor is directed to sprinkle my ashes, my 'cremains,' the funeral people call them, anyway, I'm supposed to be sprinkled inside any Cracker Barrel restaurant in the state of Tennessee. But I'm going to add the Manta woodlot as a second option. With your permission of course."

"Permission granted. Who's your executor?"

"You are."

It was October 3d. Richard was at the Faculty Club, half way through a second bottle of Puligny Montrachet. At the club's markup, it was $90 a bottle, but a fitting accompaniment, an appropriate bedfellow, a necessary companion, for this fine Dover sole, new potatoes, and arugula salad. I'm making a statement. A statement to Gloria, a statement to these my colleagues who shun me, a statement to the entire feckless world that I am Richard T. Smith, Professor of Germanic Languages and Literatures. I come here, I drink the most expensive wine on the menu, I eat an elegant meal, I smile at these half-formed creatures who pass for professors, I nod, elegant in my Cardin suit, my copy of the *Neue Zürcher Zeitung* folded on the chair beside me. Fuck you, colleagues. Fuck you, Faculty Club. Fuck you, Gloria. You always loved Dover sole.

Christmas was coming. It had already snowed twice in Nashville, once on the day of the Vandy-UT game, great flakes swirling through the stadium, making windrows against the rolled tarps, against the risers under the seats. Harry had gone to the game. Vanderbilt had lost, 28-10, an honorable score, Harry said, and Vandy had scored first. Most credible he said, a harbinger of next year. A solid foundation for inevitable improvement. Next year, 5 and 4, no doubt, maybe even better.

He told Connor that he had never, not in his entire four years on the varsity team, played a game in the snow. "The weather is weird this year," he said.

"Yes," Connor said. "This was the earliest ice-out at Manta I can remember."

"El niño," Harry said.

"Tu madre," said Connor.

"No, I mean it, the Pacific thing. Maybe it made it warm in Canada and cold in Nashville."

"Yeah, maybe."

> To: freeoxen@earthlink.com
> From: iowadad@hotmail.com
> December 23, 5:45 PM
> <<<Delete this when read!
> Beware target disinformation. Vigilance always.
> Verify collaterally.
> <<<Delete this file now! Delete all cookies now!

CHAPTER
EIGHTY-FOUR

Harry told Judith he wasn't going to have a Christmas tree, he was going to do Chanukah instead. "That way I get more presents. One each night. And on the eighth night we'll have dinner together, potato latkes, brisket, applesauce, and sour cream. You have to get me eight presents, Jude, one each night."

"Harry, you're impossible. You're not going to convert."

"This is kind of a dry run. Eight presents, Jude."

> To: iowadad@hotmail.com
> From: freeoxen@earthlink.com
> December 24, 10:02 AM
> Help flt res trav agt asta

> To: freeoxen@earthlink.com
> From: iowadad@hotmail.com
> December 24, 10:15 AM
> <<<Delete this when read!<<<
> Airlines too hard. Trav agt e-mail to firewall. Then, 6, 7b. When in, 11a. Srch name travlr. Use dates to narrow.
> <<<Delete this file now! Delete all cookies now!<<<

Richard was happy. Time had passed. The Modern Language Department officially and loudly stood behind his right to teach, his presumption of innocence. Some of the ACLU types made a point of greeting him now, shaking his hand, hoping he would "soon have it behind him." Katherine Kelty was "thinking of" majoring in German. Richard was thinking of minoring in Katherine. Minoring deeply into Katherine. The New Year had come and gone. His trial hadn't even been scheduled yet. Martinson was keeping the D.A. tied up with motions.

Richard was also planning his German trip. Easy to find the judge and Graham. I don't know when they are leaving, or where they are landing, but the travel agent has them for two nights at the Cologne Hilton, I'll find them there. If I miss them there, I'll follow them to all of the other places on their schedule.

And when I'm done with the honeymoon couple, Kelty and I will go to Munich, to the Theresienwiese. It will be her junior year abroad. It will be cold, but we will sit on the grass, on blankets. My oxen will graze around us. We will pull more blankets over us. I will put my hand up her skirt, to the top of her thigh, and slip my finger inside her panties. She will be wet. We will couple on the grass, the oxen browsing around us. Then we will lead them into Munich, my oxen, to the Marienplatz. We will have Weisswurst and sweet mustard, she and I, from the stand in front of the neues Rathaus, and the oxen will have grain. We will watch the Glockenspiel in the clock tower strike the hour, then we will all go down to the Hofbräuhaus and drink beer, she, the oxen, and I. We will get shitfaced. In honor of the four deceased: the dead Gloria, the dead pansy David, the dead Judge, and the dead boyfriend.

Judith and Connor were at Connor's house, looking through the Wyeth books they had gotten at the Cheekwood. Fields of snow around the Olson house. A sleigh.

"When I was little and it snowed, it was a great event," Connor said. We never got snow in California. I always wanted to be in Tennessee in the winter."

"Well, for us in Maine," said Judith, "snow wasn't a chance. You could count on it. I remember how my grandfather always wanted snow by Thanksgiving, so it would be easier to track deer."

Connor told Judith how the power line outside his fifth grade window had stacked up with snow, an ever-mounting knife-edge of snow, thin as the wire itself, one inch, then two, three, four inches, all balanced on the wire, while he and the other children had watched, wondering when the principal would close the school, talking of would they have to sleep there, sleep all night under their desks? They had seen the custodian come out of the furnace room underneath the classroom, look at the snow, go back in, taking his shovel with him.

They had watched the kickball field get deeper and deeper, the swing set eerie with snow on the ridgepole and seats. Not a breath of air, just flakes falling.

"There's a line by Wallace Stevens," Connor said, *'It was evening all afternoon. It was snowing, and it was going to snow.'*

"Exactly," said Judith, "an afternoon with gray light, the certainty of great adventure."

Connor said that when he had been eight and in the third grade in Knoxville, there was a big snowfall that Thanksgiving, eight inches, then a melting for a few hours, enough to make water run in the alley behind their rented house, then a hard freeze which lasted for days. Years, it seemed, he told Judith, every moment being a glorious eternity. The alley behind his house had frozen solid with gray wavelets trapped in time, hard as steel.

He told Judith that sitting down on his sled, the ice had felt six feet thick. I steered with my feet at first, he said, until I was brave enough to go belly down, my face skimming just inches above the gravel trapped under the ice. Sometimes the gravel poked up through the ice and rasped on the runners, he said. Down the alley he would go right, out onto Twentieth Street--no traffic, nobody

345

could drive--right across Twentieth and into the next alley. Then back up and do it again. I had my Massachusetts snowsuit on, Connor said, a bulky, one-piece front-zipper job. My mother made it on her black Singer portable. It was fantastic, like the Flexible Flyer, my sled, a wonder of northern technology, fast, the best sled in the neighborhood.

"A one-piece snowsuit," said Judith. "Like Randy in *A Christmas Story*? So bulky you couldn't move your arms, and if you fell down you couldn't get up?"

"Almost," he said.

She thought about how Connor had grown up in three different parts of the country. "But you must have had lots of snow in Boston."

"Yes, but I was a teenager then. The world had fewer wonders then." Still, he remembered the snows in Boston, the cold wind whipping through Scollay Square, the sharp smell of coffee roasting. Sudden warmth and intense smells in a Fanny Farmer shop, condensation on the insides of its window panes. Outside, steam issuing from manhole covers, whipped away by wind through the canyon streets. The light bright and cold. A teakettle sign, with steam coming from it.

In his neighborhood in Tennessee, he said, he had thrown snowballs at cars, a high daring illegality, smashers right onto the oncoming windshields, chains going brack-brack-brack inside fender walls, chains that would come off soon in a great clattery rush. Slush hissing away from tires. People would shake their fists at him, or didn't even notice. Sudden shots from behind bushes, splashing on hoods, passenger doors, explosions of white skidding up and over windows and roofs.

Once he had hit a car with three older boys in it, college students maybe, and they had chased him. He had run behind the line of houses, downhill into the woods, tripping and falling. He had lain still, hoping he wouldn't be found, but they had found him. He had pretended to be unconscious. They had shaken him. He had acted groggy and hurt, and the boys had relented and told him to be careful and not do that any more, shit, what did he think?

CHAPTER
EIGHTY-FIVE

It was January 20.

"Mr. Martinson," Richard said, "you are a man experienced in the ways of the world."

"I am. Sometimes too experienced, I fear."

"You come into contact, necessarily into contact, with persons who evade normal procedures. Some of your clients, I would imagine, might make false documents, or know how to get them."

"Where is this going, Professor?"

"Mr. Martinson, my very existence is in jeopardy. Extreme measures are required."

"Extreme measures? You intrigue me."

"Not to put too fine a point on it, my whole life is forfeit if I lose this case. I will be ruined. Utterly ruined. Many of my colleagues shun me as it is, and I am still an innocent man."

"If you are convicted, you will certainly not be able to teach in a public institution. I think of this every day, Professor, I assure you."

"Nor in a private one. I will be reduced to tutoring German to individual students in East Overshoe, British Columbia, if I can find any. All because of what David Branstetter wrote, all because I had the goodness to socialize with him a few times."

"He has indeed put you in an uncomfortable place."

"I can prove my innocence. I know I can. If I can get to Germany, I can talk personally with David's on-line contacts there. These people are hard-core anti-Semites, real brown shirts. They were helping David. He wouldn't tell me how much."

Martinson looked at Richard sharply. "Branstetter had a think tank? Co-conspirators?"

"Yes, Mr. Martinson. I need to talk to them. Face to face, in German, on their territory where they are comfortable. He must have told them he was acting alone, completely alone. He would have told them, don't you see? He would have wanted to tell them about the good thing he was going to do. He couldn't tell me. I couldn't know his plans, if he loved me."

"Yes, I see. But Professor, you cannot leave Tennessee, much less the United States. It would violate the terms of your bond.:

"I know. We are speaking hypothetically, of a time when my bond conditions have changed."

"Ah, hypothetically."

"But even with my bond conditions changed, it might be unwise to travel as Richard Smith. Richard Smith does not meet with unsavory characters, if it ever came out, I mean. False documents for travel would help. Of course, when I meet with David's contacts, I will be Richard Smith."

"Are you speaking of an American passport?"

"And driver's license, with photo."

"Professor, I understand from my clients, the persons among my clients who, as you say, evade normal procedures, that a passport can be had for around eight thousand dollars, and an Illinois photo driver's license for five hundred."

"Can you put me in touch with someone?"

"Professor, when, I say when, your bond conditions are relaxed, you might want to go to Chicago." He took a blank 3x5 card and a Holiday Inn ballpoint from his desk drawer. In block letters wrote KOZLOSKI, 358 SOUTHSIDE AVE. He handed the card to Richard.

"No telephone number?"

"No telephone number. He is always in. He never leaves his equipment." Martinson took one of his business cards from a crystal holder on the desktop. On the back in light pencil he wrote in script *rstu.* "Be sure to give this to Mr. K., if the court does allow you to travel."

"Thank you."

"Professor Smith, I must specifically advise and instruct you not to violate the conditions of your bond, not to violate your travel restrictions. It would be illegal, and if you should get caught, it would harm your case immeasurably. Do you understand me?"

"I believe I understand you very well."

"We will apply to the court to allow you to travel out of state, and out of this country. The latter will, however, be difficult. You will need to have scholarly research plans for a German library, research which requires you to view original manuscripts."

"I understand. Please do not file such a motion yet. I need to think about what that research might be."

Martinson made notes in Richard's file. "Very well." Martinson looked out the window for a moment and coughed. "Professor, if you decide to travel anyway, don't tell me about it. And if you should see Mr. K., it is most important that you give him my card. He needs to trust you."

The next day Richard drove to Chicago. Four days later, on January 25, a FedEx delivery man made him very happy with a small bulky package. The same day, January 25, a different FedEx man in a different part of town made Ray Martinson happy too. He had received a referral fee from Kozloski.

CHAPTER
EIGHTY-SIX

The wedding is in eighteen days, Richard thought. The honeymoon will be memorable. He would attend the wedding, oh, yes. It was set for February 12 at the Christ Church Cathedral. High Episcopal. He would shave his head, yes, that would do it. Or he could wear the new red wig, use the red eyebrow pencil and mascara. He would sit in the back and hear the familiar words, until death do us part. And it will, he thought. I am death's agent.

Not even Fat Boy will recognize me. Maybe I'll even go to the reception. Mix and mingle, nod to the meddling Pillsbury puffed-up doughboy. Martinson says Fat Boy has been helping the cops. What does Mather know? Only what Lover Boy tells him. Fat Boy and Lover Boy. I should kill them both. I can get Fat Boy later, if I want. The accident in Germany comes first. Lover Boy and the judge, "tragic accident on the honeymoon trip."

It was the last day of January. Detective Blake was excited.

"Harry, we've been doing our homework. Everything you gave us checks out, and we've got even more. He's as good as convicted, attempted murder of a judicial official, and attempt to subvert the judicial process. We will try that case first, and convict him. It's severable from the wife and Branstetter. We bring those cases later, after he's already a convicted felon."

"Will this new judge let the state bring the newer charges up first?

"Harry, you know how much discretion prosecutors have. You've done it. Martinson will bellow and prance, but the A.G. says he won't get anywhere. Oh, this is good. How did you get Dr. Patel to copy his chart for you?"

"J-A-Y, you don't want to know."

Judith and Connor were married at four-thirty on February 12. They flew to Frankfurt the next day. At the church, Harry gave the bride away. Some say he had tears in his eyes. Afterwards, he denied it whenever the topic arose.